**Three generations of women—
each woman wondering what
the future held in store for her.**

Ernestine: She opened her home to a troubled mother
and teenage daughter, wanting to help them, if she
could. Only, she had her own crises to deal with—
and a suspicion that time wasn't on her side....

Veronica: When she left her husband after more than
twenty years, she was following a dream—to settle in
one place, at last. Only, it wasn't turning out as she'd
expected....

Simpson: She was dragged into a strange new world on
Whisper Mountain, away from the coast she loved, to live
with an old woman with baffling ways, and a mother she
barely recognized at all anymore....

Ellyn Bache

Ellyn Bache began writing freelance newspaper articles when her four children were small. As they got older and gave her more time, she turned her hand to short stories. It took her six years to get her first one published. Then, for many years, her fiction appeared in a wide variety of women's magazines and literary journals and was published in a collection that won the Willa Cather Fiction Prize. Ellyn began her first novel, *Safe Passage*, the year her youngest son went to school full-time. That book was later made into a film starring Susan Sarandon, and Ellyn went on to write other novels for women, a novel for teens, a children's picture book and many more stories and articles. There's more on her Web site, www.ellynbache.com.

THE Next NOVEL™

ELLYN BACHE

Daughters *of* the sea

I must go down to the seas again,
    for the call of the running tide
Is a wild call and a clear call that may not
    be denied....

For Linda
My all-time favorite
daughter-of-the-sea, sister-in-law and
walking-on-the-beach buddy

CHAPTER 1

Sometimes, in early June, the twilight on Whisper Mountain fell so clear and blue that Ernestine Truheart, whose lungs were the mushy remains of a three-pack-a-day habit, could stand on the porch of her old farmhouse and watch shadows shift across what was left of her barn and drink in air so nourishing that she imagined her thirst for oxygen had been slaked.

At seventy, Ernie was suffering from emphysema, chronic bronchitis or lung cancer—and maybe all three. She'd stopped going to the doctor six months ago. Someone dying as slowly as she was didn't need it all spelled out. And in early June, especially toward evening, she could almost convince herself she was well.

Out back, her garden had perked up from a shower that had left the leaves of the squash and cucumbers fresh and springy. Here in front, a handful of cats lazed on the porch and a couple more sat between the house and the barn, any place that wasn't still damp. Fortified by the clear air, invigorated by the shadow of the blue-tinged mountain in the distance, Ernie forgot her health long enough to pluck a cigarette from her pocket and put it in her mouth—not intending to light it, only meaning to let it hang between her lips, where it could call up all the pleasures of her youth.

From below, at the bottom of the hill, she heard a car pull off the blacktop onto the gravel lane and ascend toward the fork that veered right toward Ernie's house and left toward Marshall Banner's. Most times she craved company, but not now. She would have enough company later. This was probably Marshall's son, Owen, going to check up on his father. But then she heard the vehicle bear to the right and, after a moment, watched it emerge from the trees, a massive brown SUV that ground to an angry, skidding stop not five feet from the porch where she stood. On the side of the vehicle, emblazoned in orange, were the words Sovereign County Animal Control.

The driver's door opened, and a short, heavy figure slid out. At first, Ernie thought it was a man, but it was a woman with a butch haircut and puffy arms jutting out from the short sleeves of her khaki-colored shirt. Ernie removed the cigarette from her mouth and coughed for the first time in an hour.

The woman stood on the gravel, clipboard in hand, surveying the scene. Encased in a tight, scratchy-looking uniform that stretched around her lumpy curves, she looked like a dwarfed, ill-dressed version of the Pillsbury Doughboy. The name tag on the blouse, pinned above her heart, read Netta Brabham, Animal Control Officer.

"If it isn't the dogcatcher," Ernie muttered.

"You *got* any dogs?"

"No."

"Those your cats?" The woman swept her hand to include the cats on the porch and another three or four cleaning themselves over by the barn.

"They spend time there, if that's what you mean."

"You feed them, don't you?"

Ernie set the cigarette between her lips again and let it hang there.

"Well?" the woman asked.

Taking a drag of her unlit cigarette, Ernie inhaled deeply. The clean air that poured into her was supremely unsatisfying.

"If you feed them, then by law you're the owner," the officer explained.

"You think so?" Ernie exhaled, coughed a little. "The way I see it, cats don't belong to anybody. They belong to themselves."

"Cats in Sovereign County are required by law to be vaccinated against rabies," the woman went on. Then, when Ernie did not reply, "How many of them are there? Ten? A dozen?" she asked.

"I couldn't say." There was certainly not a dozen. Ernie thrust her free hand into her pocket. "A farm always has cats hanging around."

The animal-control officer directed her gaze at the ruined barn and fallow fields beyond it. "Not really a farm anymore," she sniffed.

Holding her cigarette between thumb and index finger, in the way her late husband, Knox, used to do, Ernie flicked it as if to shed ash. Maybe it wasn't a farm, maybe the barn was falling down, maybe the house needed paint. Ernie was falling apart, too. The house and grounds suited her. She did what she could: tended her garden, washed her supper dishes, let Marshall Banner mow the acreage that led down to the lake. Inside her pocket, her fingers discovered a sprinkling of cracker crumbs and a pack of matches. Something occurred to her. "You're the animal-control folks who put down the Nelson dog."

"It was a pit bull. Pit bulls are illegal in Sovereign County. Too vicious to keep."

"I see. Guilty by virtue of breed."

"Beg your pardon?"

"Never mind." Ernie pulled the book of matches out of her pocket.

"Name?" Netta Brabham asked.

"What?"

"Your name. You're the dowser, aren't you? The one who spots wells?"

"What is it you want with me, exactly?"

"These animals of yours, they're required to be vaccinated and wear their rabies tags."

"They're not my animals. They couldn't wear rabies tags even if they were." Ernie wouldn't put a collar on a cat. A cat would scratch and drive itself crazy, trying to get out of a collar. She remembered something else. "What about those dogs that had to be put down twice?" she asked. "The ones left in the gas chamber three hours before anybody discovered they were only half-dead?" The story had been in the *Whisper Springs Mountaineer*. "You the one who was supposed to be watching that gas chamber?"

"That was a year ago. We don't use gas anymore." Netta Brabham's face remained impassive, a pale sphere punctuated by a small lump of nose, narrow mouth, tiny slits for eyes.

"What do you do then? Give them shots?" Injections were supposed to be more humane. "Or do you slit them open and pull out the vital organs one by one?"

Netta Brabham didn't flinch. "We have an air-extraction chamber." She readjusted the clipboard in her hand, propped it against her ample stomach. "It's Emmeline, isn't it? Emmeline Truheart?"

Ernestine opened her matchbook and read the cover: Earn

Big Money At Home. "When did you start going from house to house after hours? Bothering people eating supper? Don't you have enough to do, chasing animals that bite somebody?"

"Part of our function is to canvass the county for rabies-tag infractions," Netta Brabham said.

Until the ski resort was built ten years ago and brought tourists from D.C. and Baltimore, nobody had cared how many cats anybody had or whether they were vaccinated. Nobody had ever died of rabies, either. Now the resort was failing, but the rabies hunt went on...the government...death and taxes.

"Like I said, the cats aren't mine. Not anybody's. Nobody owns a cat." Ernie counted five of the animals preening on the porch or in the distance. A sixth had disappeared. One big, gray tabby was stretched out belly-to-ground in front of them, as if to call attention to itself. Ernie lit a match and watched it blow out in the breeze while the other woman scribbled on her clipboard.

"Six cats. Though I guess there's a lot more. You get five days to have them vaccinated." She thrust her clipboard toward Ernie's chest. "Sign at the bottom."

Ernie ignored the clipboard and stared absently at the matchbook in her hand. She lit another match. The breeze had died, the flame burned yellow. She put the cigarette in her mouth, match to the cigarette. She hadn't done that since February. When she breathed in, smoke went straight to her brain and made her dizzy.

"I'll have to ask you to get off my property," she said.

"Just sign this and I'll serve you the citations."

"Over my dead body." Not mentioning that her body would be dead sooner than the woman thought. When you were ailing, it was important to have a sense of humor—a philosophy

Ernie had developed years ago when she'd been jack-of-all-trades for the *County Crier* and had written enough obituaries to learn that any life, even a grand one, could be reduced to a paragraph.

"Suit yourself," Netta Brabham said. "They'll just send the paperwork in the mail."

The smoke in Ernie's head gave her a slight buzz. "Like I say, they're not my cats."

Netta Brabham fashioned her mouth into a sarcastic grin. "Whose are they, then?"

"Mine," a male voice boomed.

Netta jumped, but Ernie was used to this. Marshall Banner was forever appearing out of nowhere. Right now, he looked like he'd gone off on one of his famous walks and had just returned after hiking for days. He had graying, blondish hair, dirty and far too long, and stubble on his chin that looked white against his sun-darkened skin. His face was all angles—sharp, high cheekbones, prominent nose, deep lines around his mouth and eyes. He was forty-six but could have been sixty. He looked like a ravaged Viking.

"They're my cats," he said. "They like to come down and sit by the barn. I live up yonder." He pointed in the direction of his house.

"She hasn't established what right she has to be here," Ernie told him. "She hasn't given me her name."

The woman pointed to her nameplate. "Netta Brabham." Which of course Ernie knew.

"She doesn't have any right to be here. After hours. On private property."

"They're my cats," Marshall said again. "Six of them most times, sometimes seven."

"Seven?"

"Sometimes."

The animal control officer wrote on her clipboard. "And all without rabies tags," she noted.

Marshall's eyes went vacant. Ernie wondered if he was going into one of his spells. "They're not his cats," she said again. "Not anybody's. A cat doesn't belong to—"

"I'll have to cite you," the woman told Marshall. "Name?"

She wrote it down and handed him the papers. "See you get them vaccinated in the next five days. There's been rabies around."

"There's rabies around every year," Ernie said. "Usually in a bat or a coon. Never in a cat or a human."

"It's bats or coons that pass it to cats or dogs, who pass it to people," Netta Brabham said.

"When's the last time a person in Sovereign County got rabies?" Ernie asked.

"Ernie, it's not worth arguing." Awareness returned to Marshall's eyes like a light being kindled. He clutched the citations in his hand, looking suddenly raggedly elegant, despite the stubble and sunburn on his face and his hairy legs jutting out from beneath his tattered shorts.

"In 1954," Netta Brabham said. "A dog got rabies in 1954."

"But not a person."

"No."

"In 1954," Ernie repeated. "Over half a century ago."

Netta Brabham opened the door of her SUV and threw her clipboard onto the passenger seat. She got in and started the motor. Ernie and Marshall watched her drive away. When she disappeared beyond the tree line, Ernie said, "You didn't have to do that, Marshall." He was forever trying to pay her back for what she'd done for him. By now he'd paid her thirty or forty times over.

"The cats do come up to my place now and then," Marshall said.

"Never." Cats were afraid of him, maybe rightly so.

"Well, anyway," Marshall said. He took a step backward, turning to start up the hill toward his house.

"Thanks, Marshall," Ernie called. Her voice had gone croaky, but not just because she resented being beholden to him. She saw the lit cigarette still in her hand, threw it down and ground it out. It was almost dark. Humidity had come in with the night. She shivered. The dry warmth was gone and her lungs were an old balloon, air scraping all up and down inside them. The sourness of age and illness settled over her like indigestion. She coughed. Thick fluid roiled in her chest. In the east, a full moon began to rise, early-summer pale. She sat on the porch step, tired of standing, tired of everything. She ought to go in and rest, but she waited.

CHAPTER 2

By the time the moon rose high enough to brighten the darkness, Veronica Legacy had been driving nearly eleven hours and was so tense that the tips of her fingers had begun to go numb from clutching the wheel.

"I'll drive if you're tired, Mama," her daughter Simpson said for the twentieth time.

For the twentieth time, Veronica shook her head. She'd stopped only twice since they'd left the South Carolina coast this morning and didn't mean to slow down now. The only way to get where you were going, she reckoned, was to plow on.

Eleven hours before, Veronica had left her husband, Guy, for the third and final time. Her first major departure, more than eighteen years ago, was one she rarely allowed herself to think about, and her second, a year later, had lasted only a week. This would be different—permanent. The third time was the charm, she'd always believed.

"I hope you're not just mad because Dad wants to move again and get another job," Simpson had said this morning as they'd packed the car. "He stayed all winter in Beaufort like you asked him to. You knew it would be time for him to go."

Well, of course, Veronica wasn't "just mad." Looking for another job was something Guy had always done three or four times a year, even before Simpson was born. Nor was Veronica leaving because Guy's behavior was so irritating, or because they'd fought so much this past year. Veronica was going because she'd watched Simpson, in cap and gown, walk toward them after her high-school graduation last weekend, and she'd seen a grown woman standing before her, tall and slim with lips that seemed sensuous but not pouty, and a strong, pretty jaw that looked determined without being stubborn. Veronica was leaving because she'd realized that if her daughter was a woman, then she herself must be approaching forty (thirty-eight, to be exact), and what had she ever done with her life except follow an itinerant carpenter from town to town?

Not that she hadn't tried to make a stable home. Oh, she had. But she'd failed utterly. Last August, after twenty years of wandering, Veronica had finally taken a stand. She had insisted they remain in one place an entire school year, so their daughter could graduate in June from the same high school that she'd entered in the fall. Veronica had chosen the most scenic, charming setting she could find—Beaufort, South Carolina—and had rented a duplex for them only ten minutes from the beach. Guy was always nicer if he could see the ocean whenever he wanted. To tell the truth, so was Veronica. The place had big windows, nearly new furniture, and was so close to a Laundromat that the air was always sweet with the scent of soap.

You'd think, after all that, Guy would have managed to settle in. But no! Not two months had passed before he'd begun complaining so bitterly you'd have thought Veronica had sentenced him to prison. "Beaufort's small," he'd said. "There's better work in bigger places. Foreman's jobs, project managers."

"Guy, you promised."

"They're calling for a colder-than-normal winter. At the very least we'd be more comfortable down in Georgia."

"The weather in Georgia is the *same*. What do you think's going to be different in Savannah? Or Hilton Head? Or Daytona Beach?"

"I wouldn't go to Florida," he'd huffed, offended.

Veronica had taken a breath. She'd known he wouldn't live in Florida; it was one of the many poorly thought-out and senseless tenets of his life. "The point is," she'd hissed from between clenched teeth, "we agreed to let Simpson finish school." Guy couldn't seem to remember that from one moment to the next.

"I moved sixteen different times before my father retired from the military," he'd replied, stabbing the air with a finger.

"Yes, and that's why you left home at seventeen, never to speak to him again!"

"Simpson doesn't show any signs of running away. Besides, what if I'd joined the army myself? What would you have done then? Some military wife you would have made."

"Oh, *fuck* the military!" And that had shut him up.

By Christmas the atmosphere around them had been so thick with tension that they might have been walking through a maze of spiderwebs. Instead of leaving as he normally did when he got restless, to drive up and down the coast from Virginia to Georgia in search of better work, Guy had come home each night to grumble and pace the floor. The thickening cords of his dissatisfaction had tightened until they'd all felt shackled by invisible bonds. In February, a young carpenter had been promoted over Guy, and Guy had claimed he was too humiliated to stay. But he had stayed, complaining more bitterly with each passing week. Even after the azaleas had bloomed in March, even after the temperature had soared unexpectedly into the nineties and the tall pines had begun shedding needles in the clinging heat, Guy had spoken of moving in such a strangled, restless voice that happiness might have been in the next town, the next room.

None of this had swayed Veronica. She wasn't going anywhere until Simpson had her diploma in hand. The girl was already nineteen-going-on-twenty, having lost two years of school because of her father's wanderlust. At the beginning of May, with the building season strong and vigorous and Guy's position assured, Veronica had quit her job at Tammy's T-Shirts so they'd be entirely dependent on his single salary. It had been a drastic measure, but necessary. For all his faults, Guy was not a man who'd let his family starve.

So Guy had stayed—until exactly one day after Simpson's graduation, just long enough to take the girl out to a celebration dinner, get a good night's sleep and gas up his truck.

Watching him drive off in his Ford pickup, in search of some other coastal town with plenty of construction work, probably a few hundred miles north of Beaufort where the summers weren't so hot, Veronica had no choice but to face the truth she'd been avoiding for more than twenty years. Guy Legacy would never settle anywhere. He'd wander from town to town until he was an old man nobody wanted to hire, never keeping a job or a house even half a year. When Simpson went off to college or to work, she'd have to track her parents to one address at Christmas and another at Easter and a third by summer vacation. Veronica would settle into her role as an aging camp follower who'd never once plant a patch of daffodil bulbs in the fall and watch them bloom in the spring—a woman who couldn't provide a secure haven for her only child to come home to. Guy's truck had no sooner disappeared from sight than Veronica had decided it was now or never. She'd dragged her box of maps from the closet and committed to memory every major route between coastal South Carolina and western Maryland.

"We're leaving, honey," she'd said to Simpson. "We're going somewhere we can settle for good."

"What about Dad?"

"You can wait here for him if you want, but he'll just be off again somewhere and wanting to drag you with him. The sensible thing is to come with me."

"Where are you going?"

"To stay with Ernie Truheart," Veronica had said.

"The one who sends the Christmas cards?"

"Yes."

"But you hardly know her," Simpson protested. "A Christmas card is not a relationship. I don't know her at all."

"Yes, you do. You were there with me once, but you were too little to remember."

"What's going on, Mama? This isn't like you." Simpson had extended a hand as if to check Veronica's forehead for fever.

"I'm not sick, honey." Veronica had caught her daughter's fingers in her own and moved them away from her head. "I'm doing this to keep myself well. We can't live like nomads all our lives. I've spent all the time I'm going to working in every cheap T-shirt shop in every beach town on this coast."

"Kmart and Wal-Mart, too, Mama. You always liked Wal-Mart."

"It's not just the jobs. It's the constant moves. It's the—"

"You did it this long. You never minded before this past year."

"Oh, I always minded."

"And you knew after Dad stayed here in Beaufort the whole school year, he'd be ready for someplace different."

This was just like Simpson, sounding so logical. But Veronica had only shrugged, because she knew it was impossible to explain to a nineteen-year-old what it was like to reach the very middle of life—thirty-eight!—married to a person who insisted on wandering the countryside, never living a neat plait of life but always a wild and unruly tangle, a thousand strands blown in every direction by the slightest wind.

"All I can say, honey, is that my mind's made up and it would break my heart if you didn't come with me." Veronica had seen that Simpson thought she didn't have a choice.

So at dawn this morning they'd finally locked the trunk of the Mercedes on what suddenly looked like pathetically few possessions to show for twenty-one years of marriage, *pathetically* few. She hadn't even tried to settle up with the landlord after she'd closed her checking account and counted the dismal balance. When you waited until age thirty-eight to get on with your life, you couldn't let a detail like rent reduce you to poverty. She motioned Simpson to get into the car. She couldn't bring herself to speak for the entire first hour of the drive north.

By the time they crossed the Cooper River at Charleston, she'd begun to revive. She'd forgotten how much she enjoyed taking the Mercedes out on the road. Under her touch, it hummed its perfect cadence as it always did. Putting more than two-hundred-fifty-thousand miles on the odometer hadn't affected its performance a bit. It was a perfect car.

It was also the only valuable possession she now owned—and that by a fluke—she realized as they headed toward Myrtle Beach. Nine years ago, Guy had built some custom cabinets for a rich corporate lawyer who'd bought the car for his mistress. When the mistress had left, just as Guy had submitted his bill, the lawyer had been so distraught that he'd offered Guy either a check for his work or title to the car, which was worth five times the pay he was due. Guy had taken the Mercedes and put it in Veronica's name. It was the only extravagant thing he'd ever given her. A navy-blue 300-D turbo with bucket seats, a sunroof and a palomino interior—camel-colored, actually, but she loved the term *palomino*—creamy leather upholstery that molded itself to her body every time she sat down.

Gliding along on what was now an older, more rutted section of highway, Veronica noted, as always, how solid the car was and how easy to handle. For a moment she felt so grateful to Guy for giving it to her that she had to remind herself it was not a vehicle he would have chosen for her willingly, even if he'd had the money.

Every ten minutes or so, Simpson cast a furtive glance in Veronica's direction and then tried to camouflage her curiosity by raising her hand to brush a strand of hair back from her forehead. This was unlike Simpson, who rarely fidgeted, and who, in any case, had the kind of silky dark hair that looked combed even if it wasn't. Veronica was almost relieved when her daughter finally blurted out, "Tell me the truth, Mama. Daddy called you from somewhere, didn't he? He found a new job and we're meeting him. Tell me the truth."

"I *did* tell you the truth. We're going to see my friend Ernie. Well, not so much my friend as my mentor. My *patron*. She's been asking me to come for years. What makes you think we're meeting Dad?"

"This is exactly the way he would have come."

And damn if it wasn't! Veronica was following Guy's path not out of nostalgia—certainly not!—but by force of habit, having traveled this way so often. How pitiful.

"This is ridiculous," she said.

"Of course it is, Mama," replied Simpson in her nurse-in-an-insane-asylum tone. "We need to head back to Beaufort right now."

"Never," Veronica said. But it wasn't until they got stuck in traffic in Myrtle Beach that she found a good place to turn off the crowded beach road and head for the interstate so they could make some time. It always felt odd to her, heading west away from the ocean, even when a road veered that way for just a few miles. Well, better get used to it. She was on a mission.

Seventeen years ago, on her second furlough from her marriage, when Simpson had been a toddler, Veronica had followed this same route—although the roads had been worse then. She might never have gone back if Ernie's husband, Knox, hadn't made her feel so guilty for taking Guy's only child so far away from him. A father needed his child as much as a mother did, Knox had told her, even if the mother and father were having their differences. Most men didn't want to admit how attached they were to their families, he'd said, but it was true.

Knox's speech had left Veronica in tears. Ernie had urged her to rest and think about her situation while she made up her mind what to do, but Veronica had headed back to Guy before the end of the week. The only smart thing she'd done was refuse to tell Guy where she'd been, a secret she'd kept from him all these years. She was glad of that now. Knox was dead and Simpson was grown-up and Ernie would relish some company. Once they got where they were going, Guy would never find them in a million years.

Veronica switched on the cruise control for the first time all day, feeling confident at last that this trip would go exactly as she'd planned. She was finished forever with sleazy apartments and rental houses in beach towns they couldn't really afford. She was finished with T-shirt shops. She would work in Ernie's garden, maybe have a garden of her own. It was what she'd always wanted. She would put down some roots.

So why was it that, the farther west they drove, the more she kept hearing the lapping, surging, sometimes pounding of the surf in the recesses of her mind? Why did her hands feel drier and more chapped with every mile they traveled? Was it just because she was nervous? Or was it, as she suspected, because every bit of moisture was being sucked from her skin, little by little, the farther she got from the ocean?

Sitting beside her mother in the front seat, Simpson Legacy knew she had every reason to be alarmed. Her mother was driving with the waxy glaze of someone rushing headlong toward madness or destiny, and Simpson wasn't sure which. Even Veronica's perpetual tan, which she attributed to her one-eighth or one-sixteenth Cherokee blood—she never seemed to be sure—had faded over the course of the day to a dusky pallor.

As the only one in the Legacy family with a clear-eyed view of the world, Simpson knew she should be doing something to bring Veronica to her senses. But for the first hours of their trip, Simpson honestly believed the plan was to meet her father somewhere as a surprise. And by the time she realized that Veronica was really running away, they were on Interstate 95 heading God-knows-where, and Simpson was too shocked to think.

"C'mon, Mama, let me drive," she kept saying. "C'mon, Mama, you must be tired."

But it was clear her mother wasn't. Veronica seemed more wide-awake than she had in a month, driving the Mercedes so fast and with such white concentration that pretty soon they'd probably wreck and die. "Mama, you're doing eighty. At least slow down." Maybe they'd be pulled over. But hours passed and they weren't.

"We need to make a pit stop, Mama," Simpson kept saying. Once the car was in park, she would grab the keys, demand an explanation, get things under control. "I'm not kidding, Mama," she said when Veronica ignored her. "I'm about to pop."

"Soon. Just a little farther. Hand me another one of those mints."

Inside the glove compartment were half a dozen tins of Altoids, the sharp peppermints Veronica said lit up her mouth. She sucked them one after the other, so that by the time they reached North Carolina half the tins were empty, clanking on the floor beneath Simpson's feet.

"At least tell me exactly where Ernie lives so I can navigate," Simpson demanded as they whizzed past the exits to Lumberton, Fayetteville and Raleigh.

"Western Maryland."

"I mean *where* in western Maryland?"

But Veronica popped another Altoids into her mouth and sucked with such intensity that it would have been impossible for her to speak. She stepped harder on the gas and propelled them up the interstate at light speed or just a little under.

"How about some lunch? I'm starving." Simpson's stomach had begun to growl so loudly even Veronica couldn't ignore it. "Lunch and a bathroom."

Reluctantly, Veronica pulled off at the next rest stop, but not long enough to eat. She clutched the keys so tightly she might have known Simpson planned to take them. In the bathroom, she didn't look into the mirror the way she usually did, or poke at the nonexistent circles under her eyes, or sigh as if to resign herself to fate. She just washed her hands quickly and purposefully and shooed Simpson back to the car. A moment later, she barreled onto the highway so fast that an eighteen-wheeler bearing down on them had to lurch wildly into the left lane.

"Mama, be careful!"

"Maybe we do need to eat," Veronica said in lieu of an explanation. She gestured toward the back seat and a foam cooler that Simpson hadn't noticed before. Inside were neatly wrapped pimento-cheese sandwiches, chips, cut-up carrots, Oreo cookies and a couple of Diet Cokes, still cold. It was the most elaborate meal Veronica had prepared in a month.

"I didn't want to have to stop any more than we had to, finances being what they are," Veronica said. "We might have to make dinner out of this, too. We won't be there until tonight."

"I could help you more if I knew where 'there' was."

"Whisper Springs. A couple hours west of D.C."

Simpson reached for the map and studied it as they devoured their sandwiches.

"West of Hagerstown," Veronica instructed.

And there it was, a tiny dot. A village. Home of Veronica's so-called friend or mentor or patron. Simpson stuffed the remains of their lunch into the empty chip bag. She picked up the Altoids tins from the floor. She cleared her throat. "Did you call to make sure Ernie still lives there? To tell her we're coming?" It was possible Veronica hadn't thought of this. If most people lived in a narrow little band of behavior, like a point on the wavelengths of light, and if all normal behavior was green, then Veronica and Guy were more in the range of purple—not as eccentric as yellow or red, but far enough off center that Simpson had to be vigilant. For the past month, even before this sudden departure, her mother had seemed to be wandering into some hot, bright, unaccustomed hue.

Narrowing her slanted, almond-shaped eyes into a squint that made her look somehow Asian and inscrutable, Veronica said, "Of course Ernie's still there. She lives on a farm. People don't move off of farms so casually. Not every couple of months like your father."

"But they do move sometimes," Simpson said levelly. "Sometimes they can't pay taxes. Or they get old and go to apartments."

"Not Ernie," Veronica snorted. "She's old, but she still grows a few vegetables to sell and helps the well-drillers by working as a dowser. Where else could she do that?"

"A dowser!"

"People who find underground water with a stick."

"I know what it is, Mama. It's some weird mumbo jumbo."

"I should have stayed with her years ago, so you could have had some roots. Then you'd know what I'm talking about."

Roots, Simpson thought. She closed her eyes, fearing that if she herself hadn't wanted roots so badly, they might not be on this misguided journey at all. Last summer, when her mother had suggested a full school year in Beaufort, Simpson had been practically limp with relief. A whole year in one place had sounded like paradise. She'd ignored her father when he'd suggested, two months after they'd gotten there, that it was time to move. She'd ignored both her parents as the year had progressed and the tension had grown. In third grade and again in seventh, Guy had changed jobs twice during the school year, and instead of putting Simpson in her new school in the spring, Veronica had taken her to the beach every day. Simpson hadn't enjoyed it nearly as much as her mother had. Even then, she'd known that frolicking in the sun would only mean she'd have to repeat the grade. She was probably the oldest high-school student in the Carolinas. She'd wanted to graduate. Even more, she'd wanted to be *part* of the graduating class instead of a late-in-the-semester addition.

It hadn't quite worked out that way. Simpson knew that high-school seniors already had friends and didn't need new ones. She knew from long experience that the only companions available to a newcomer were the ones nobody else wanted. She was two years older than most of her classmates anyway. She'd thought she'd made peace with being part of a family that traveled from town to town, allowing her to fit into one triumvirate only: Guy, Veronica, Simpson. But no: in Beaufort she'd wanted to *belong*. To make friends. Go to the prom. Feel that someday she'd come back for high-school reunions.

A month into the new semester, she hadn't made progress on any of these scores. One sunny day, she was reading a book alone at lunchtime when her English teacher spotted her and said—meaning to be kind—"I know it's lonely, but there are great riches to be wrenched from solitude, aren't there?"

Simpson was so humiliated that she didn't read another book in public all year. Instead, she made what her father had once termed *instafriends*—as in, "Beware of instant friends"—although she refused the ecstasy and cocaine the two girls offered and smoked their pot only occasionally. She couldn't get stoned too often, she explained (and was surprised how easily they accepted this) because she had to take care of her mother, who had a chronic condition. At Christmas, one of the instafriends overdosed and lived, but didn't come back to school. In March, the second one dropped out. Simpson was left with no other achievable goal except to go to the prom.

She'd gone out a few times with a marine named Ricky Lee Sowers, who worked at the air station. She didn't like him much. He said he'd take her to the prom—it wasn't cheap, considering dinner and flowers and all—if she'd have sex with him afterward. She agreed, partly because it bothered her to be not only the oldest high-school student in the Carolinas, but probably the oldest virgin. The dance was nothing special. They went to a motel where Ricky Lee closed the door and began pulling down the spaghetti strap of her dress, making Simpson realize she was about to consummate a business deal that amounted to prostitution. She hadn't had anything to drink, but she knew if he didn't take his hand away, she was going to throw up.

"I can't do it." Her voice was a raspy whisper that singed her throat.

"Can't *do* it? We had an arrangement. Do you know how much I've spent on this?" Ricky Lee dropped the spaghetti strap and stepped back.

The distance between them calmed her. "I'll pay you back," she said. "Every penny, plus five percent interest. If you take me home right now."

She could see he was angry, but also that he had no choice. Unless he wanted to force her, which he didn't. The next day, Simpson took most of her savings to the post office, bought a money order and sent it to him by mail. She was too embarrassed to face Ricky Lee in person. Later, when he called to thank her, she was too embarrassed to talk to him. She was still annoyed at being the South's oldest living virgin.

In the weeks after the prom, the situation at home deteriorated rapidly. Guy made sure Simpson and Veronica both knew how miserable he was, even though the weather had turned hot. He was a finish carpenter who'd sometimes take low-paying framing work just to be out in the heat at this time of year. He'd come home tanned the color of chestnuts, with cheerful smile lines etched around his eyes by the southern sun, his arms glistening with sweat. It had happened so often that Simpson had grown up believing the smell of sweat on a man was a sure sign of happiness. But this year he was glum. He came home and showered, leaving his work clothes on the bathroom floor where Veronica ignored them and Simpson picked them up. He drank beer. He studied the want ads. He sulked.

After Veronica quit her job so Guy wouldn't quit his, she began sulking, too. She'd sleep half the day and spend the rest of it sitting on the tall barstool beside the kitchen counter, still in her shorty pajamas, dreamily thumbing through women's magazines and twisting her hair into such tight corkscrews that even brushing wouldn't smooth them out. For all her talk of wanting a garden, she didn't venture outdoors once to plant or weed. She didn't cook meals or eat the ones Simpson set before her. She hadn't woken up until after Simpson's graduation. And now, this.

They traveled north at such breakneck speed that it took Simpson a while to notice that the ever-present coastal pines had given way to tall branched trees, spreading and varied, and that the terrain had lost its flatness and was rolling away from them in small, verdant hills. Where she could see the soil between tufts of grass, it was not the pale beige of beach sand, but a piercing piedmont orange. For all her family's traveling, she had been off the coast only a few times in her life, once to Columbia, South Carolina, for a school trip to the zoo, and another time to Atlanta. Mostly she had seen the world through movies. This was better.

Veronica opened another tin of Altoids. "Just because Ernie is a dowser doesn't mean she's some crazy country bumpkin," she said. "She lived in town until she got married and worked for a little newspaper. She did everything—got ads and hired delivery people and even wrote some of the articles. She didn't get married until she was forty."

"What about her husband?"

"Dead." Veronica popped two of the Altoids into her mouth to signal the end of their discussion. By Fredericksburg, Virginia, the whole car was filled with the scent of Veronica's pepperminty breath. And hours later, after they'd made their way around the Washington beltway and up the I-270 corridor through the hot, congested D.C. suburbs and beyond, to where the pitch of the hills grew steeper and Hagerstown, Maryland, came into sight over the heart-stopping summit of a mountain, most of the Altoids were gone and the sun had slipped behind the hills to the west. Veronica noted the sunset and offered more packed sandwiches.

"We've got to eat real food, Mama, not more pimento cheese."

"Well, we will, next time we see a place."

Considering that they were driving over lush uninhabited mountains, this didn't seem likely. In any case, Simpson wasn't really hungry. The road rose and dipped at feverish angles. She was used to flatlands; she might have been on a roller coaster. The world had gone topsy-turvy. It was her father who left, her mother who stayed behind. Her father who could drive hours without stopping, her mother who (on the rare occasions they were all in the same vehicle), said, "Come on, Guy, it wouldn't kill us to enjoy the scenery a little. You'd think we were going to a fire." Simpson should have grabbed the keys hours ago, during their second and final pit stop. But by then the dramatic pitch and roll of the landscape had begun to consume her. This was exotic. This was like nothing she'd seen before. This was thrilling.

True darkness came slowly. The moon filled the dusky sky like a big, pale saucer. Veronica was still doing eighty. They crossed another mountain, descended toward a sprinkling of lights in the valley below. More mountains rose in the distance. Veronica tapped her fingers on the steering wheel. "Not much longer now." At the next exit, she pulled off the interstate and wound down a smaller road and then up a narrower one. She seemed to know exactly where she was going. They turned onto a gravel lane, pulled up in front of a two-story farmhouse and ground to a stop. An old woman was sitting on the porch. She waved as if she'd been expecting them.

Ernie Truheart looked nothing like the savvy career type her mother had described. Tiny to the point of skeletal, she wore dark polyester slacks and a white shirt that hung to her knees. She held out wiry arms to Veronica, who rushed over and engulfed her in a hug that looked like it might break bones. Simpson held her breath until they parted.

"Well," Veronica breathed, clutching Ernie's hand and bringing her closer. "This is my daughter. Simpson."

The old woman nodded. "Haven't seen you since you were a toddler."

"See, I told you we were here before," Veronica said. "Simpson, this is Ernie Truheart."

Simpson didn't want to hug her. To her credit, the old woman freed her hand from Veronica's and held it out, her grip stronger than Simpson expected.

"You must be exhausted, both of you," Ernie said, though under the glow of the porch light she herself was the weary-looking one, her face drawn, her cheeks cobwebbed with wrinkles.

Simpson got their overnight cases from the car. Walking behind Ernie into the house, she noticed that the old woman's hair, pulled back into a ponytail, was dyed a deep, chestnut red except for the two inches closest to the scalp, where the roots were a solid gray. It looked ridiculous.

Or maybe just interesting.

Simpson wasn't sure if this was going to be better, or worse, than she thought.

CHAPTER 3

Ernie led the two women upstairs—Simpson to a small front bedroom crammed with dark, old-fashioned furniture that took up every inch of wall space, and Veronica to a more spacious room at the back, dominated by a massive, carved headboard and an assortment of bureaus and wardrobes and dressing tables. Nothing seemed to go with anything else. There was just a lot of it. In such cluttered surroundings, Simpson expected to feel uncomfortable, but instead she collapsed onto her bed and didn't open her eyes for nine hours. The next morning she came awake to cool air and a view of a distant mountain, feeling refreshed and energetic. The windows were open. In South Carolina, they'd been blasting the air-conditioning for a month. The fresh air and lack of humidity and green vista would revive anyone.

But Veronica slept on. She napped all that first day and into the next. Lying under the covers with the old yellowed window shades drawn against the sun, she closed her eyes tighter and pulled the sheets more securely to her chin every time Simpson tried to coax her awake. "Time to get up, Mama. You're setting some kind of record."

"In a little while, honey. Just a few more minutes."

But the minutes grew into hours and then days. "Time to get up, Mama. At least come look at Ernie's garden. Exactly the kind of garden you always wanted. I'm pretty impressed with it myself."

"Soon, honey, I promise."

"C'mon, Mama. Squash, tomatoes, even corn. I know you're tempted."

Veronica curled into a fetal position and turned away. Except when she was picking at the meals that Ernie fixed and Simpson brought up on trays, Veronica didn't even sit up. When Simpson suggested she get dressed, Veronica stared at her blankly, as if she didn't quite understand what this meant.

At first, Simpson reasoned that the trip had simply drained her mother of whatever energy she'd stored while moping in their duplex in South Carolina. Or maybe it was true, as Veronica always claimed, that she was a moon-driven woman, more active when the moon was waxing; practically manic when it was full, as it had been the night they'd arrived. Now, with the moon waning, she was naturally lethargic. But Simpson didn't believe this. The only moon powers she believed in were its pull on the ocean and its ability to make women get their periods, phenomena she'd experienced with her own trustworthy senses. So when her mother was still in bed on the third morning, Simpson was genuinely alarmed.

"There must be something wrong with her," she told Ernie. "She never does this."

Unperturbed, Ernie scrambled eggs in the cluttered kitchen and dished them onto plates. "She's eating, isn't she? She doesn't have a fever." After breakfast, Ernie picked lettuce and radishes from the garden out back and let Simpson load them into an old white van that looked and sounded as if it belonged in the junkyard. "Off to the vegetable stand," Ernie said, and drove away without giving the least indication of where this stand might be. She came back for lunch and went maddeningly about her business until late afternoon, when she settled on the living-room couch and napped through the entire hour of *Oprah*. Then she coughed for a while, quite frighteningly. "Well, I better start supper," she managed to say finally, and she did.

By the fourth morning, Simpson was even more frantic. "I'm not kidding, Ernie. My mother needs help." She addressed the back of the old woman's head as Ernie leaned out of a second-story window to dump dirt into one of the planter boxes attached to the sill. "My mother needs help," she repeated.

"She doesn't need help," Ernie said, tamping down the soil with her bare fingers. "She's just tired, that's all."

"Tired! She's been sleeping for days. She's having a nervous breakdown."

Ernie brought her head back inside the window frame and studied Simpson with a puzzled expression. "You think she's having a breakdown? I don't. She's exhausted, yes. Having a breakdown, no. You underestimate her."

But what else could it be? Simpson would have acted, would at least have called her father, but she didn't know where Guy was. On their budget, cell phones were out of the question. They could barely afford the prepaid phone cards they used for long distance. Veronica and Simpson rarely found out where Guy's new job would take them until he came back to get them. Simpson tried to imagine her father returning to Beaufort with news of his latest employment up the coast somewhere and finding them gone. It didn't seem possible.

Ernie clunked a pot of pink geraniums against the sill and yanked the plant out of its container. "Listen," she said. "Not every kind of tiredness comes from driving too long, and not every kind gets cured by a night's sleep. Give her a week. If she's not up and around by then, we'll call a doctor."

"But Ernie—"

The old woman stopped her with a grimy outstretched finger. "And don't write me off as some vegetable-growing crone who doesn't know a nervous breakdown from an ingrown toenail. I know more about medicine and doctors than you think." She sighed. "Hear that? I sigh all the time. Can't help it. It's from air hunger." Her breath whistled across the cracks and gullies of her chest as if to attest to some unarguable medical intelligence Simpson would not have wanted to challenge even if she knew how.

For one of the few times in her life, Simpson felt helpless. Her parents being who they were, she was used to taking charge. She'd learned early how to deal with adults, even the most difficult ones. Landlords would let her put off rent payments; electric company clerks would turn on their power even when they didn't have money for the deposit; bank tellers would refund bad-check fees. Extricating her family from the pitfalls of their gypsy lifestyle was what Simpson *did*. But Ernie was outside her experience. When the old woman leaned out again over the window box, the gray roots of her hair against the red dye looked exactly like a headband. How did you deal with someone who'd go around looking like that? You didn't.

"Besides," Ernie said from outside the window, "we don't have time for a doctor today. I have a well to spot and I want you to drive me."

"Drive you? Why? You've been driving to the vegetable stand yourself."

"I get dizzy sometimes."

"Then you shouldn't be driving at all."

Ernie thrust a geranium into the planter box and buried its root-ball in soil. "Usually I can manage short distances, no problem. If the room really starts spinning, Lily comes to get me. She owns the stand and gets a cut from my produce, so I don't mind asking. But outside of business I don't like to bother her."

"If you're dizzy you should stay home. Besides, what about Mama? We can't just leave her here."

"Of course, we can. What do you think she's going to do? Fling herself out a second-story window?" Ernie maneuvered herself back into the room and clapped some of the dirt off her hands onto the floor. For a seventy-year-old woman with breathing problems, she was remarkably agile.

"Your mother will be all right. I'll talk to her before we leave." Ernie reached into the pocket of her jeans and dug out a cigarette. She held it for a moment and then stuck it into her mouth with soiled fingers. "Put the screen back in, will you?" She shuffled out of the room, leaving Simpson alone and bewildered in the cool dazzle of mountain sunlight.

Veronica heard Ernie knock on the door, but she didn't budge. She knew she'd been in bed far too long. She had to pee and needed a shower. Later. Right now she'd grab just a couple more minutes of sleep.

Four days ago, her first morning here, she'd woken up so disoriented that she'd thought she was in some motel where the air-conditioning was set too high. She'd reached across the bed to nudge Guy, but as usual he wasn't there, probably off looking for some new job. She'd wrapped her quilt around her bare shoulders, padded to the window and peeked out under the shade. Good Lord! Whisper Mountain rose so blue and cold in the distance that she'd begun to shiver, even though it was June and sunny. Then she'd realized that she was at Ernie's. She'd left Guy, and this was where she planned to stay.

Of all the places in the world, why *here?* Way back in that summer camp for foster children, she'd learned this basic fact of life: mountains aren't friendly. They keep secrets, hide snakes and bears, and produce too much shade and too many thorns. That first summer, Veronica had gotten lost on her first hike in the woods and had come back with poison ivy that had left her arms and legs raw and oozing and so itchy she couldn't sleep at night. The camp nurse dabbed her with calamine lotion, but couldn't send Veronica home because her foster family was unreachable, off on vacation. It was Ernie, on one of her daily trips to bring vegetables to the camp, who noticed Veronica huddling on the bench at a volleyball game, picking at skin that looked like it had been in a fight with a bobcat.

Within an hour, Ernie had permission to take Veronica back to the farm and nurse her until she felt better. She didn't "feel better" until it was time to go home. Each year after that, Ernie retrieved Veronica from the camp on the first day of the session, holding over the director both the unreported poison ivy and the questionable legality of having turned Veronica over to Ernie, who was not a relative, the year before. For the next two weeks, Ernie spent more time with Veronica and was more a mother to her than most of her foster mothers were. They gardened and swam and visited Ernie's friends. Veronica loved her. When it was time to leave, she would have begged to stay except that she continued to hate the mountains. Just looking at them filled her with dread. She wanted to be with Ernie, but not *here*. In making her decision to leave Guy and establish a real home for herself and Simpson, how had she forgotten that? Veronica had crawled back into bed and slept so hard she woke up with knuckle marks on her cheek from lying on her fist.

For the next three days, in between the naps that sucked her down into oblivion, she gave herself endless pep talks. It was certainly the right time to establish a real home for Simpson, her last possible chance. If she was lucky, Ernie and Simpson would like each other. Now and then, when their voices drifted up from the garden below her window, she decided they liked each other already.

But *mountains*. And for that matter, *Ernie,* whom she hadn't seen for years and who looked like a fish about to turn side-up and float to the surface. Simpson was right: despite the Christmas cards and occasional secret phone calls, she hardly knew the woman. But then the pang shot through her again— the actual, physical pang she'd felt first when she'd laid eyes on Ernie the other night and had seen how old and withered she'd become. She wasn't at all the vibrant person Veronica remembered. Now Veronica struggled against the weight of her own eyelids. Her hands were dry and itchy, and her insides seemed to have shrunk. She let sleep claim her again, pull her down into the sweet, warm darkness.

She was swimming in the ocean. It was what she liked best. She floated on the swells in the silvered night sea, under a sheltering dome of stars. She felt safe. Then the scene shifted to noon, and she was on the shore, watching a family splash in the breakers in the distance: a wiry, bronzed husband and slim-hipped wife; their sleek, black-haired child. The three of them held hands. Each time a wave broke, the parents jumped and laughed and pulled the giggling girl up with them. Drawn by their happiness, Veronica traced their path toward the water. But the sea eluded her. No matter how fast she walked, the ocean was always a stone's throw away. She was hot and out of breath and the water was no closer. When she drifted up toward consciousness, through the heaped mound of covers that was making her sweat and struggle, the thing she couldn't swim away from was sitting right at the top of her mind.

She was pining for water. When you left the sea after so long living next to it, the separation left you stunned. That was why she'd felt like she was shrinking inside and her hands were so chapped. Funny, how staying in water too long could shrivel up your fingers, but it took moving away from it to produce that same effect on your innards. She was in a state of shock. No wonder she'd needed all this sleep.

But knowing that didn't make her want to get up.

"Veronica, I know you hear me," Ernie rasped. She knocked again. "You can't be as dead asleep as you pretend to be after all this time, unless some stray tsetse fly made its way to Maryland and injected you with sleeping sickness, which I strongly doubt." Listening to the silence behind the closed door, Ernie almost would have preferred Veronica to be suffering from the moon madness Simpson had described or at least something simple like cramps or a virus. But anyone could see Veronica wasn't sick; she was enduring one of those life changes that produce odd symptoms and persist for weeks unless you take serious action. It was a positive sign, Ernie told herself, that Veronica was only sleeping and not out wandering the countryside like Marshall Banner always did. All the same, Ernie was concerned enough that when Veronica answered her knock with silence, she felt she had no choice but to march right in.

After so many days, the room was not only stuffy; it was beginning to smell. Ernie tugged on a window-shade pull, which made the shade fly all the way up and over its roller, and brought in a flood of white sunlight. Veronica cringed and yanked the bedsheets over her eyes. Not to be intimidated, Ernie opened the window as far as it would go.

"Time to get up," she said. "The more you sleep, the more you want to."

"I can't, Ernie."

"Oh, rot. You've been in that bed three days and four nights. Your legs are going to atrophy."

Veronica lowered the top sheet to chin level and opened a green, slanted eye. "My *legs* are going to atrophy?"

"Medical fact," Ernie told her.

"Not after just three days."

"Not to mention that you'll feel a hundred percent better if you bathe and get yourself dressed. And not to mention that you're scaring the bejesus out of Simpson."

Veronica opened the other eye and edged up on an elbow. "Simpson doesn't get upset. She's solid as concrete."

"She's nagging me to haul you off to the doctor. She thinks you're having a nervous breakdown."

"Really?"

Veronica looked so crestfallen that Ernie, who thought being seventy and sickly was no piece of cake, decided that actually *getting* old was nothing compared to being thirty-eight and coming to the realization that you would. "I know you don't mean to scare her. That's why you have to get up."

"I will. Soon."

"Now. Today. I'm taking Simpson with me to spot a well and then out to show her the lake, and when we get back you need to be up and around to reassure her."

"Maybe I *am* having a nervous breakdown," Veronica mewed. "I'm not even sure I can get out of bed."

"Don't be silly. You're not paralyzed. You're not even mentally ill."

"How do you know?"

"You left your husband. You're upset. Who wouldn't be? This is not unusual behavior."

Veronica looked disappointed.

"Listen. What happened made you tired. You slept. Now you're awake. You'll be fine." Veronica's suffering might be as real as emphysema or chronic bronchitis or lung cancer, but it was less lethal in the long run, and enough was enough. Under other circumstances, Ernie might let Veronica sleep it off, the way folks let Marshall wander until he felt better. She'd let Veronica lie there until she came back to her normal self, even if it took a month. Sooner or later Veronica would get too restless to stay put. But Simpson was a child of the computer generation, the instant-messaging crowd, and expected life to work on the fast track. Simpson needed her mother now.

Veronica closed her eyes, maybe dozing again, but Ernie felt compelled to say what was on her mind. She started talking even though Veronica didn't seem to hear her. She lectured for a full five minutes about how Veronica damned well better get herself together or she, Ernie, would kick her right out.

The truth was, she hadn't known until she opened the door to this room which one to protect, mother or daughter. She guessed she'd chosen the girl.

CHAPTER 4

Once they drove off the farm, Simpson wondered why she'd confined herself to the house for three full days when all the time her mother's Mercedes had been sitting idle on the gravel driveway. Simpson could have escaped anytime she wanted, could have found a doctor, could have had everything under control. Well, not really. Not with Veronica refusing to get up. But after three days surrounded by ten times the furniture she was used to, staring out at fields and mountains as exotic to her as orchids, Simpson had begun to feel they'd landed in a picture postcard that wouldn't be real until she could explore it firsthand.

"We'll take the van, don't want to get mud on the pretty Mercedes," Ernie said as she tossed Simpson the keys. The gravel driveway tested the sorry state of the shocks and the gears ground so noisily that Simpson was relieved to find the town of Whisper Springs only a mile down the road. Happily, it didn't look as much like Mayberry as she'd expected. It was more like historic Williamsburg, about which she'd written a report in eighth grade when they'd lived in Virginia Beach.

Although only three blocks long, the main street of the town was wide and shaded, lined with refurbished row houses, identical except for their fresh gray or gray-green paint, drab but historically accurate. For color there were trendy banners hanging like flags beside most of the doorways, appliquéd with flowers and birds. And though the entire stretch looked like it had been fashioned by a single designer, each building was customized to its own purpose: residence, grocer, hardware store, a couple of bed-and-breakfasts. But mostly antique shops.

"Yuppie-town," Ernie muttered. "They did it when the ski resort went in, and even after the ski resort had its day, folks from D.C. kept buying the houses and turning them from Civil War–era tumbledown to early-American chic. They wanted everybody to renovate, no matter if they could afford it. You wouldn't believe the laws they got passed. They wanted to make Whisper Springs the antiques capital of Maryland."

"It's pretty," Simpson said.

Ernie snorted. "If you like theme parks, it is."

In the second block, a wooden awning had been erected over the whole length of the sidewalk, making the buildings look as if they shared a communal front porch. The third and final block was marked by a break in the line of houses, over-arched by a slab of dark wood, into which was carved the words The Springs At Whisper Springs. Beneath the sign, a wooden arrow hung from a hook, pointing to a glass enclosure at the rear of the lot.

"The springs?" Simpson asked.

"It wasn't enough that they had to come with their archi-tectural rules and their historic district," Ernie said, burrow-ing into the passenger seat. "They also had to enclose the springs and call them a cure for the aches of modern living."

"Are they?"

"I've been drinking that water the whole thirty years I've been here." Ernie exhaled so forcefully the phlegm rattled around in her chest. "You couldn't prove it by me."

They passed a single traffic light. The row of old-fashioned houses abruptly ended and they were in the countryside again. An occasional farmhouse, flanked by barn and silo, sat in the midst of fields pocked by massive outcroppings of gray rock. Here and there, cattle grazed, or a patch of ground had been leveled and planted with corn. In the distance, on the lower slopes of the mountains, whole hillsides had been turned into apple orchards.

The road dipped precipitously and then began to rise. They rounded a curve. Ski Whisper Springs, a billboard proclaimed. Just beyond the sign, a landscaped entryway announced the turnoff into Whisper Springs Ski Resort. Condominiums spilled down a side road, angled gray boxes with chimneys jutting from steeply pitched roofs. Judging from the number of For Sale signs, every unit seemed to be on the market. In the distance, several ski runs threaded through the trees on the mountain, crisscrossed by a couple of ski lifts.

"Some doctor from Hagerstown developed it about ten years ago," Ernie said. "It took him an age to get the approvals, and two years after it opened, the cable on one of the lifts broke and a teenaged girl got injured. And that was the end of that."

"You mean it closed down?"

"It's open every winter, but it gets mainly day-trippers and a few weekenders. The condo builder went bankrupt. I think the only one who made out is the doc who developed it, who's probably still a millionaire." Ernie squinted into the sunlight, crow's-feet fanning out onto high cheekbones. "Come to think of it, he was probably a millionaire all the time. Doctors. What do they make a year? A quarter of a million? Half? Too much."

Simpson was tempted to probe the source of Ernie's bitterness toward doctors, but she shrugged off the impulse and concentrated on the road. Beyond the ski resort, it narrowed, and the landscape seemed more unkempt, wilder. Finally Ernie motioned Simpson to pull onto the shoulder beside a pickup truck printed with the words Weeks Well Drilling.

A stocky man with a mat of curly gray hair slid out of the truck as they approached and offered Simpson a rough hand to shake. "Buck Weeks," he said before turning to Ernie. "While I was waiting, I found you a branch." He pointed to what looked like the better part of a small tree lying on the ground.

"Who do you think I am, Paul Bunyan?" Ernie reached into the pocket of her bleached-out jeans for the same cigarette she'd been mouthing all morning, still smudged with potting soil.

"I can cut you a piece of it, however much you want. Like last time."

Ernie grasped the cigarette between thumb and index finger and pointed it at him. "This time I'll find my own."

She set about examining the trees at the edge of the scruffy field beside them, peering intently at the low, newly sprouted branches. After several long minutes, she motioned Buck to cut the one she wanted, such a frail forked limb that the extensive search seemed silly.

"Watch," she told Simpson. The branch had a short central section, then split into two. Buck trimmed off the leaves with a utility knife and handed it back to her. "Two things to remember," Ernie said. "First, it has to be strictly fresh. Second, it always has to have a fork." She jammed the cigarette into her mouth and gripped the forks of the branch with either hand, letting the straight section stick out in front of her like a horizontal antenna. The cigarette clung to her lower lip as if glued.

Without another word, Ernie began to walk into the field; straight for about twenty paces, then twenty to the right, another twenty back toward Simpson and Buck. Weeds and thick grass bristled at her ankles, which were bare between her sneakers and her too-short jeans, but she paid the underbrush no mind. Once, she almost stumbled, too preoccupied to let go of the branch long enough to get her balance.

After a time, she moved to a second spot and walked the same rectangle there, then to a third location and a fourth. The morning cool had given way to a balmy warmth. A few fluffy clouds edged across the sky, then drifted off, leaving the field bathed in sunlight. Sweat beaded on Ernie's nose as she walked, and her mouth dropped open with exertion, but the cigarette remained dangling from her lip. The outstretched branch began to look heavy in her arms. A few strands of hair escaped from her red ponytail. Rather than letting go of the stick to tend to them, she let the hair blow into her face.

"She looks like she's in a trance or something," Simpson said.

"Naw. Just concentrating," Buck replied.

Trance or deep concentration, Simpson didn't like it. She wasn't sure what she'd expected—Buck and Ernie studying the terrain, perhaps, putting their heads together to deduct a logical place for the water—not this random hocus-pocus with a stick.

Buck leaned back against his truck. "See them rocks over there?" He pointed to a cluster of the gray rock outcroppings that seemed to be everywhere. "This is limestone country. There's rocks like that under the ground. They got holes in them something like Swiss cheese. What you want to do when you drill is hit one of them holes because there's water in there. There's caves and caverns filled with water. Sometimes you can dig down two hundred feet and not find a thing, and you move over ten feet and hit all the water you could want."

In the middle of the field now, Ernie repeated her pattern for the ninth or tenth time, moving with a slow, eerie patience. The scene might have been out of a distant century except for Ernie's jeans that hung from her bony hips and the garish gleam of her gray-and-red striped hair.

All at once, the branch snapped down in front of her with a flick of her wrist.

"See?" Buck said.

"She's tired. She can't hold it anymore." Ernie seemed to be pulling up on the branch without being able to right it.

"She ain't as weak as you think," Buck said.

Simpson squinted against the sun. Was this some conjurer's trick? Still in her trancelike state, Ernie inched forward, apparently concentrating all her effort on keeping the branch from springing out of her hands and falling to the ground. It was a hell of an act.

A few paces farther along, the branch snapped back up as suddenly as it had dipped, so quickly that Ernie was thrown off her stride. Ernie stopped a moment, then stretched her arms out and held the branch as before, but with her shoulders and back relaxed now, as if a burden were lifted.

The branch didn't move again, stayed horizontal as Ernie continued across the field. After a few yards, she turned and retraced her steps. At the same place as before, the branch snapped toward the ground.

"That's the spot, then." Buck fetched a post-hole digger and a stake from his truck and started in Ernie's direction.

"How can you be sure?" Simpson asked, dogging his steps.

"You seen what happened. It always worked before."

"Yes, but why?"

Buck shrugged. "Beats me."

Simpson sniffed.

"Laugh if you want to, but it's so."

"I wasn't laughing."

Buck glared at her and quickened his pace. At the spot where the branch had dipped, Ernie dropped her stick and pulled the cigarette out of her mouth. "See?" She dug at the ground with the tip of her sneaker. "The water's right underneath here."

"You're putting a lot of faith in the behavior of a tree branch." Simpson looked from Buck to Ernie with what she hoped was righteous skepticism. "It's weird," she said.

"It is," Ernie agreed.

Buck thrust the post-hole digger into the soil and dug, marking the place Ernie had found. "I'll tell you what. I'd rather have Ernie spotting water with a tree branch than waste my day drilling two or three times and coming up with nothing." He finished digging and jammed the stake into the hole.

"But what *makes* the branch dip?" Despite the heat, goose bumps rose on Simpson's arms. She hated illogic.

"The water makes it dip," Ernie said. "What did you think?"

"I mean what principle?"

"Some magnetic force. The water pulls the stick down like a magnet."

"That sounds pretty unscientific."

"Why?" Ernie took another drag of her filthy, unlit cigarette. "Water runs underground and above ground, both. It goes from streams to rivers to bays to the sea. The water is all connected. Everybody knows that. And people are connected to it, too. As much water as we've got in us, you might say we're bodies of water ourselves. So why would you be surprised there's some kind of attraction?"

"You mean the water inside a person is trying to join its friends? And it uses a tree branch as its medium?" Simpson turned scornfully to Buck. "And this works every time?"

"Just about," Buck said.

Ernie frowned. "Unless I get distracted. Then it's only eighty, ninety percent."

"Let me try it, then, if it's such a sure thing." Simpson reached for the limb. Buck's thick hand stopped her.

"It don't work for everybody," he said. "Only for them as got the gift. And somebody's got to teach you. A man got to teach a woman or a woman teach a man. I ain't got the gift, so I can't teach you. And Ernie can't because she's a woman."

"Now I've heard it all."

"Maybe you don't believe it, but that's how it is." He flicked a fly off his forearm.

"I'm not so sure about a man teaching a woman and a woman a man," Ernie said. "Some people say nobody taught them at all, but I learned from my husband, Knox. It came down through the Truheart family from his mother. Knox could do it but his brother couldn't." She dropped the cigarette and ground it out on the soil as if it had been lit. "I know it sounds crazy. Thirty years ago I wouldn't have believed it any more than you do. You'll find out same as I did. Not everything makes sense like a straight line."

"That's why it's called witching," Buck said. "Because you either got the gift or you ain't. You're either a water witch or you ain't. That simple." He turned and headed back toward his truck.

A thin film of perspiration glazed Ernie's face; she wiped it with the back of her hand. Her forehead shone in the sunshine and her eyes gleamed with what had to be an unholy light. *Witch*, Simpson thought. Exactly.

"Don't get any ideas," Ernie said, as if she were reading Simpson's mind. "Having the gift has nothing to do with why it's called witching. I don't like to correct Buck to his face, but he gets it wrong. They call it witching because the early American settlers used witch-hazel branches."

"Oh. Witching as in horticulture, not as in broomsticks."

"You're a quick study, girl."

Veronica spent almost twenty minutes in the shower. Her hair was a tangled mess of dust from the road and sweat from her long sleep, the curls so tight she had to apply conditioner twice before she could run a comb through it. Never in her life had she gone this long without shaving her legs. She was still soapy when the water suddenly ran cold, warm one second and icy the next. She rinsed off as fast as she could, grabbed a towel, fled the bathtub. Ernie had promised she'd feel better after she showered, but she was freezing and her hands were so chapped they were cracking. When she opened the medicine cabinet to look for lotion, one of the hinges broke off with a bang, leaving the mirrored door dangling. Veronica jumped back. She wanted coffee.

At the bottom of the stairs, she heard rustling in the kitchen. Ernie back so soon? Then a huge dog bounded into the hall. Or—no!—not a dog. A wolf! Gray with black mottling on its fur, some wild creature down from those horrid mountains. It screeched to a stop in front of her, its nails skidding on the old wooden floor. She bunched her robe to her chest and froze. Her heart slammed against her chest. The beast stared at her in confused silence.

"Don't mind her, it's just Rita," a woman's voice declared.

"Rita?" The name sounded tropical.

"Mostly dog, partly wolf," the voice asserted. "A wolfdog." A dumpy woman emerged from the kitchen. She was about the same age and height as Ernie, but much rounder, her girth hidden by a voluminous green shirt and baggy black pants. "Sit down, Rita," she commanded. The dog did.

The woman looked distinctly undangerous, maybe even vaguely familiar. Tentatively, Veronica descended the final step into the hallway. "Your dog about scared me to death."

"She's harmless. Not even a good watchdog. Refuses to bark." The woman put her hands on her wide hips and studied Veronica. "I hear you left your husband."

"You did?"

"Don't remember me, do you?" The woman grinned, revealing a gold-capped eyetooth. "Lily Foster. Live on the farm over yonder." She waved amorphously. "I brung you a strawberry pie back when you was little, and I brung you one now. I just set it in the kitchen."

Then Veronica did remember. This was Ernie's friend with the vegetable stand. Lily had brought Veronica her first strawberry pie back when her lips were so swollen from poison ivy that the soft home-baked filling was one of the few things she could eat. The following year, when Ernie had rescued Veronica from camp, she'd taken her to Lily's farm to help candle eggs in a refrigerated shed so cold they'd had to wear sweatshirts on the hottest day of the summer. "Sure I remember. Do you still have chickens?"

"Still keep chickens. Still grow my garden. Still run the produce stand. Like to kill me, at my age." She cackled merrily. Rita flopped down on the floor with a grunt that sounded like contentment. "Where's Ernie?"

"Spotting a well. She took Simpson. My daughter."

"I know who Simpson is. Saw her that time she was a baby." Veronica had forgotten that.

"Well, I got errands to run. Just dropped in to bring the pie. Have you some while it's still warm."

"Thanks."

Lily snapped her fingers. Rita sprang up and followed her out the door.

In the kitchen, an ancient percolator sat in the corner of a sagging Formica counter. Next to the percolator was a can of Maxwell House, a ring of measuring spoons, and a juice glass filled with packets of Sweet 'n Low and Equal. Veronica brewed the coffee and stared at the pie. She nibbled a bit of the filling from her fingers. It was delicious, big chunks of fresh strawberries in a syrupy glaze, held together by a buttery home-made crust. It tasted exactly the same as it had when she was eleven—sweet, like being rescued and set free. She sliced a piece and put it on a plate. She drank two cups of coffee. She ate another piece of pie. She felt much better. Ernie had been right: showering helped, ditto for caffeine and sugar. She was here to establish roots, and now she was ready. She'd get used to the mountains. They were just scenery. She didn't have to go hiking in them. And if she missed being near water—she'd always made it a point to look at the ocean every day or two, even in the middle of the winter—well, there was water here.

Right here on the farm. She rinsed her breakfast dishes, put on a bathing suit and headed toward the mowed path she remembered from nearly thirty years ago, to meet Simpson and Ernie at the lake.

A fine, dappled sunlight filtered through the trees along the path. Then the trees gave way to open field and the kind of clear, sharp heat that always made her long to swim. In her mind's eye, Veronica saw the lake as she'd seen it as a girl: trees thick on the far side, grass growing all the way down to a graceful stand of reeds, with the water blue and silky, set off by the ripeness of green foliage. She told herself that the moment she saw the water—and even better, when she stepped into it—her shrunken innards and chapped hands would probably plump right out.

"I'll drive back," Ernie said after Buck Weeks roared off in his truck. She opened the door of the van and slid into the driver's seat before Simpson could protest.

"I thought you got dizzy."

"Only sometimes. I'll be okay now. The sun burns it out of me."

"Burns out the dizziness?"

"Yes. Sure."

"I never heard of such a thing."

"There's a whole lot you haven't heard of."

Simpson got into the passenger side, buckled her seat belt, tugged at the strap until it cut into her belly. "Do you actually get dizzy, or not?"

"Sometimes."

"Maybe the reason you said you were dizzy was to get me out of the house so I'd forget about getting help for my mother.

Maybe you thought she'd make a spontaneous recovery while we were gone."

"You never know." Ernie revved the engine, pulled out onto the road. "When Knox used to dowse, he could tell how deep the water was in any pocket he found, and sometimes how far down they'd have to drill."

Simpson looked out the window to express her disinterest.

Ernie concentrated on the road, hummed a tuneless song for a few beats. "Sometimes I'd like to trade this van for one of those little Nissans. If I had the money, maybe I would. Trouble is, little cars aren't big enough to haul vegetables to Lily's. Especially the Silver Queen corn in August. It's bulky, corn."

"Then why haul it? Why not sell it at your own place?"

"No traffic. Besides, I've helped Lily going on twelve years. Everybody sells at Lily's. Sally Richmond, Lou Burke—he's the one with the orchard—everybody."

"Why are you telling me this?"

"If you're going to live here, you need to know." They flew over the crest of a hill and bumped hard at the bottom. They had reached a stretch of road built before the days of grading standards and not repaired much since.

"This isn't the way we came," Simpson said.

"It's the back way. I want to show you the lake."

"What lake?"

"There's one on the property. At the far corner."

"What about my mother?"

"This won't take long."

They turned onto an unpaved lane flanked by an over-grown field, bumping over ruts and potholes toward the rise of a hill. To their right, cows grazed in a fenced-off pasture. This must be the land Ernie had pointed to from her garden, the parcel she'd sold off a couple of years ago. Simpson tried to situate herself in relation to the house, but found she had no sense of direction. At the top of the incline, Ernie stopped. "There."

Below them, a handsome lake spread across several acres, blue-green and peaceful, with slim finger bays reaching out in various directions. Along the near bank, weeping willows bent toward the water, their long green strands floating in the shallows. Clusters of reeds marked the shore far to their left, and closer to them was a cleared area, more soil than sand, that served as a beach. Immediately below them, at the bottom of the hill, a gray, weathered dock stretched for about fifty feet into the water.

"Knox found the springs that feed this," Ernie said as she got out of the van. "This was such a big low spot, he decided to dig a lake instead of just a pond."

She motioned Simpson to follow her as she picked her way down the incline, through high green grass. Although Ernie sighed occasionally and strained for air, she didn't slow down. At the bottom, the ground grew marshy. Cattails rose from the mud. A shed to the right of the dock seemed to be sinking into the ooze.

"I always hate getting my feet in this stuff, but there's no choice," Ernie said as she marched through the muck to the dock. Although some of the planks were rotten, Ernie strode onto it boldly, seeming to know where to step. "Knox stocked the lake with fish the first couple of years." She sighed again. "He used to catch quite a bit. I forget of what."

Tiny waves lapped at the supports of the pier beneath them like a gentle inland sea. Abruptly, Ernie stopped walking and turned a suspicious eye on Simpson. "You know how to swim?"

"Of course."

"Then get a bathing suit and come in for a minute. There's some suits in that shed." She pointed to the weathered structure sinking into the mud.

"A swim! What about my mother?"

"She'll be all right." Ernie was unzipping her jeans. A moment later, she stripped them off to reveal an old-fashioned skirted swimsuit beneath. She dipped a toe into the water. "Go on. Change your clothes."

"No. You go ahead."

"Fine." Without warning, Ernie jumped off the end of the dock. Simpson was accustomed to old women sunbathing on the beach, at best wading up to their ankles in the ocean. Ernie's splash rose and soaked Simpson's legs, a cold surprise. The old woman's head disappeared, then bobbed up, hair plastered to her skull. She began to breaststroke out toward the middle of the lake, her breath loud and raspy from exertion. Even from this distance, her lips looked blue.

Sprinting to the shed, Simpson found several bathing suits hanging on a hook, including a black one-piece exactly her size, placed there as if planned. She changed in a rush while trying to remember the details of a TV show she'd seen about the dangers of hypothermia. Seconds later, she dived off the dock, into the bright shock of cold. When she looked again, Ernie had rolled onto her back and was floating. Out of breath? Simpson moved her chilled limbs as fast as she could.

"The house is beyond that cornfield," Ernie called, lifting a hand to point.

If Ernie was going to drown, would she be making conversation?

"Look," Ernie called again. Simpson was so distracted by

the old woman's condition—or lack of a condition—that it took her some time to turn around and become aware of the slender silhouette emerging from the cornfield in the distance. It took her even longer to realize that the figure was Veronica, making her way to the water. She was wearing the same sturdy bathing suit she kept for jumping the breakers in the ocean, a favorite pastime. Considering how long she'd been in bed, she looked pretty good. Even her hair was combed.

"Mama?" Simpson called. "Are you okay?"

"Of course I am," Veronica said. "I'll be even better after a little swim."

But even as Veronica said that, she knew it wasn't true. Emerging from the cornfield for her first view of the lake, she looked down and saw not the oasis she'd imagined, but a little ordinary spit of water, surrounded by hills. It was flat and silent, closed in by landscape features instead of stretching out and out, and worst of all, hardly moving.

Veronica had lived on the coast so long that she knew what only coastal people do: that the ocean is breathing. The sea waters are the lungs of the earth, keeping the world alive breath by tidal breath. When the sea inhaled, water fell away from the shore, and when it exhaled it came careening back in its never-ending affirmation of life. Veronica didn't know why this wasn't evident to everyone. She realized now that even the bracing cool air coming down from the mountains hadn't kept her from feeling smothered the last few nights, so far away from the rhythmic breathing of the sea. No wonder she'd had trouble waking up.

She remembered Guy saying to her once, years ago, that if you followed it long enough, every road led to water. "I thought that was Rome," she'd replied. But he'd said, "No, water," and he was right. There were bodies of water everywhere, just like this one. She'd been wrong to think, even under the sugary spell of strawberry pie, that one kind of water was as good as the other. It simply wasn't true. What Guy had been referring to was the sea.

Seeing her mother wade into the water, slowly because of the chill, Simpson relaxed for the first time in days. Even a three-day nap hadn't rendered Veronica unfit for swimming. That meant she was truly okay.

With the first shock of cold behind her, Simpson's muscles warmed, and the water parted and bent to the motion of her limbs. She did a long, strong crawl into the middle of the lake.

"You *do* swim," Ernie said, stroking up beside her.

"I said I did. Why didn't you believe me?"

"Water people sometimes don't. Fishermen. Boaters."

"Who told you that?"

"I saw it on *Oprah*."

They were both treading water now. Ernie was breathing hard, but her lips were not as blue as before. "I'm surprised they don't do dowsers on *Oprah*," Simpson said. "It's probably a good living, dowsing."

"I wouldn't take money for it."

"Why not?" Simpson watched her mother, in up to her knees, take one tentative step at a time. By June, the water in South Carolina was toasty.

"Because it's a gift, like Buck said. I don't think it's right to take money for something that's a gift. Some do. But not me."

"You sound like a voodoo woman."

"Voodoo woman. Right. That's me. Living on Social Security and the sale of raw vegetables."

But from the looks of the house—the peeling paint, the old wallpaper, the barn falling down—pensions and vegetables didn't allow Ernie to live too well. Simpson frowned, then noticed that Veronica had finally propelled her body into the water and was swimming toward them with the same old-fashioned sidestroke she used in the ocean, once she got out beyond the breakers.

"Whatever you said to her, it not only got her out of bed, it got her moving again," Simpson said to Ernie.

"I told her the truth. I said I knew she felt bad inside, so bad she didn't think she could stay awake. I told her sometimes what matters is not how you feel inside, but how you act on the outside."

"You took her on a guilt trip."

"Always very effective," Ernie agreed.

For a time, the three women swam, each in her own circle. The water had become the same temperature as Simpson's skin, no longer a source of pain. In the distance, the light on the mountain picked out such clear outlines of trees that she imagined she could see individual leaves. Now that her mother had recovered, they could head back to South Carolina to wait for her father, even if they had to stay in some cheap motel. She just hoped they hadn't missed him. For the moment, Simpson folded away that possibility and surrendered to the chilly water. On every side of them the hills rose blue in the sunlight, sheltering her like a cradle of arms.

CHAPTER 5

Owen Banner had lived for twenty-three years with the stigma of being Marshall Banner's son, and for this reason he felt he had not come into the world the way normal, carefree people do, but rather had been flung into it by some capricious spirit who laughed and said: All right, now, have at it. Make order!

He never had, quite. His father was one of those people to whom something spectacular and tragic happens once, when they are young, and who ever after muddle along, too damaged to do much else. Their survival is like a constant clutching at an edge. And because they do not think clearly—at least not all the time—it becomes everyone else's responsibility to look after them, whether they want to or not.

Owen had known this since boyhood. Dutifully, he'd done what he could to parent his father and create a sense of normalcy. This is hard for a child. At thirteen, when his mother died and his father asked Owen to help bury her in their garden, Owen was too young to realize they ought to get a death certificate first. The sheriff arrived and nearly arrested Marshall for murder. Marshall explained about the persistent infection that had kept Rose in bed nearly a month and how she'd taken her medicine, but refused to go to the hospital. The police were not impressed. Although the family doctor vouched for Marshall's story, Rose's body was exhumed and an autopsy was performed. The investigation took weeks. When it was over, Owen and Marshall had held a second, private burial. Rose still rested a few yards from the house, beneath a trellis of climbing red roses to honor her name. The grave was unmarked in any other way.

During high school, Owen had looked forward to moving away from his father as soon as he could. But even the University of Maryland offered no real escape. Several times a month, Owen anxiously drove the two hours back to Sovereign County to check on things at home. If Marshall was off on one of his walks, Owen stayed until he returned, sometimes three or four days. By the time Owen had received his business degree, he'd put a hundred thousand miles on his car. And even now, living half an hour away in Hagerstown, where he managed Computers Plus, he would drop everything if Marshall asked him to, even when the request was as impractical as it was today, so ridiculous that if Owen hadn't trained himself to act by rote, he would have refused flat out.

"Take a long lunch," Marshall commanded on the phone, though he certainly knew the drive from the store to the farm and back was lunch break and more. "Come out here and round up seven of Ernie's cats and take them to Potter's Veterinary Clinic for rabies shots."

"Rabies shots?"

"Right. Got to do it before the end of the week. Come up to my place first and I'll give you the money."

"You could take them yourself, Dad."

"No," Marshall grunted. He did not say, "No, I got fields to mow," or, "No, an upholstery job just came in," or, even,

"No, I don't mess with cats." He just said, "No." Owen took an early lunch.

As usual, his father had not shaved for several days. He had lost weight and needed a haircut. But he had showered and wore fresh clothes.

"Seven cats," he reminded his son.

"Why seven? Why not all of them? Which seven am I supposed to 'round up'?"

"Any seven. Can't tell one from the other," Marshall declared. A weighty patch of silence filled the air. Owen could feel the flicker of attention sparking and gutting in his father's brain. Then Marshall dug a wad of bills out of the desk drawer and said with perfect clarity, "Pay the vet with cash. Get a receipt."

It took less than two minutes to drive the short distance down the hill to Ernie's. Marshall's house was only a paltry brick ranch, which he'd rented from Ernie until Knox had died, when out of kindness or pity (Owen was never sure), Ernie deeded it to Marshall outright. But Ernie's house and grounds had been tidy and picturesque during Owen's growing-up years, the quintessential farmstead with all the components: red barn, two-story frame house swathed in white paint, rolling fields set against a blue mountain backdrop. No longer. The green June fields and lush mountains threw the buildings into sharp relief, making each one look as if it were suffering a lingering disease. One half of the barn was still intact, but the other half had been reduced to a scrap heap, with planks of wood falling in on the stalls and so many roof timbers torn loose that the dirt floor was open to the sky. At Ernie's house, the paint was chipped and worn gray; most of the porch posts were rotting through; the planter boxes on the second floor were falling off their hinges, weighted down by a burden of newly planted pink geraniums blooming in bright celebration among the decay.

Owen noted as he turned onto the drive that at least he wasn't going to have to make small talk. Ernie's van was gone and the only car in the driveway was the Mercedes that Marshall said had arrived earlier in the week. Curious as Owen was about a luxury car with out-of-state tags, he was too anxious to be back to work to speculate about visitors who might have arrived. He concentrated on the cats.

In the heat of the day, most of them had disappeared into pockets of shade. Preening under the bushes or lounging beneath the trees, they looked so placid that a stranger would never suspect they were actually half-wild, given to scratching and then bolting off. Owen pulled on the pair of sturdy leather gloves his father had pressed into his hand along with the money. On the porch, two of the cats were napping beneath a porch swing suspended from a chain, so rusty that it seemed likely to fall and decapitate them at any moment. Owen grabbed both creatures in a single brazen swoop and flung them into his car before they could dig their claws into the thin fabric of his shirt. It took him twenty minutes to capture another five, each one meowing maniacally and shedding fur. By the time he'd driven into town and secured vaccinations at Potter's Clinic, his extended lunch hour was long over.

"Nine apiece for the shots," a gum-chewing desk clerk told him. "That's sixty-three dollars." She counted out a pile of tags while Owen counted out bills.

"What name you want them registered in?"

"Pardon?"

"You have to register them in somebody's name." The clerk nodded and cracked her gum. "Required by law."

"Put them in the name of Marshall Banner." This seemed only fair since Marshall was footing the bill. Owen pocketed the large remaining wad of his father's money. At this time of year, most people paid Marshall in cash for mowing or plowing. He often stuffed it into his desk rather than going to the bank. Owen made a note to speak to him about protecting his assets.

On the drive home, the cats were less frantic than they had been earlier, but Owen closed the windows just in case. If one of them got the notion of jumping out, the others might follow. No point losing them after all this trouble to make them legal. The car grew hot, stuffy and full of cat dander. Owen was not particularly allergic, but his eyes began to water from the sheer enclosed mayhem of hair. On the last stretch, he began to sneeze.

He rounded the bend in the farm lane, turned right toward Ernie's, and through blurred eyes saw that the van had just returned, along with Ernie herself and two guests, one of them driving. His head was so stopped-up he wasn't sure he'd be able to make conversation.

When he opened his car door, seven frightened, matted cats bounded out in what seemed a single, panicked leap, raising a cloud of dust in the yard. At the same moment, a girl in a black bathing suit emerged from the driver's seat of Ernie's van. Owen's sinuses cleared. The girl's hair was dark and shiny, her figure at once rangy and full, her skin as golden as varnished pine. She gazed at the retreating cats with unruffled calm. In the midst of the bright, chaotic scene, she was the single point of peace. Owen realized then that if he'd been flung into the world to soothe and order it, then this girl—whose name he had not yet learned—was certainly part of the plan.

Ernie had known she was in trouble from the minute she'd stepped out of the lake. It was lunacy to swim in that water this early in the season. She was too weak; she hadn't been swimming for a year. When she'd put on her bathing suit she'd only meant to wade in and check the water. She'd done it because she felt challenged by Simpson—by the girl's skepticism about dowsing and even more by her way of staring openly at Ernie and making her feel every second of her seventy years. Ernie had been so wrought up about this that when she'd plunged into the lake she hadn't even felt the cold. She'd stroked away from the dock with a fierce, angry strength that had stayed with her the whole time she was in the water. It wasn't until she'd waded out and walked to the shed to strip off her wet bathing suit that she'd turned into a mass of gooseflesh, shaking so hard that both Simpson and Veronica had had to help her dress. They'd insisted on driving her home at once, planning to change out of their own suits later.

Simpson drove while Veronica settled Ernie into the back. Before Ernie knew it, Veronica had gathered up the old towels Ernie kept in the car to protect the upholstery from vegetable stains and draped every one of them over Ernie's shoulders. She was too weak to protest. Her chest felt frozen; her fingers were ice. When she started coughing, her usual hacking and rolling degenerated into a labored effort that brought up wads of sour yellow phlegm. Between spasms, she had trouble catching her breath. It seemed hours before they reached the gravel lane. And though the house was only a few yards away, Ernie knew the minute she stepped from the van onto the driveway that she wasn't going to make it.

Lack of oxygen occupied nearly all her attention. Her lungs simply weren't filling with air. But oddly enough, Ernie noted with perfect clarity how Owen Banner stood in the driveway, his shirt and khaki slacks coated with cat fur, staring at Simpson as if the sight of her had riveted him to the gravel. And she registered how Simpson, with her slim curves held tight in the grip of her bathing suit, was enjoying it. Ernie struggled for air and thought how unfair this was: that she was choking up her lungs while these children were so spoiled by youth that they thought every kind of pleasure—even this flirtation, even now—was their due.

The next thing Ernie knew, she was inside the house, lying on the couch. Three faces bobbed above her, grim with concern: Veronica's, Simpson's and Owen's. Her mind must have blanked out for a moment. Then she remembered Owen and Simpson looking at each other. "No!" she wanted to shout. "This will never do! Stop! Be cautious! Look closer." Couldn't the girl see how light Owen's hair was and how dark his skin, a combination reserved for changelings and gypsies? Like father, like son. Or so she feared. Simpson didn't need to mess with any relative of Marshall's.

But the girl seemed oblivious. And even if Ernie summoned the strength to speak, what would she say? You couldn't preach sense to someone whose life was just beginning when yours was very nearly ending. There was a whole world between you—more. All Ernie had to do was look at her friend Lily's spoiled grandkids running riot in her house to see that the younger generation found their elders so superfluous they could hardly be considered human. No: every generation was an entity unto itself. Simpson wouldn't listen to a word Ernie said.

"You okay, Ernie?" Veronica asked.

"Of course I am," she lied. As cold as she'd been back in the van, now she was covered with sweat. A slimy worm of weakness threaded its way through her belly. Seven years since Knox died with no one to tend to, and now that she finally had Simpson and Veronica to care for, just what she'd been needing, here she was, gasping for air. Perspiration pooled in the hollow of her throat; she started to cough. She held her breath, willed it to stop. She wasn't about to do a sickbed scene. She damned well wouldn't.

Please, she thought.

Whenever she was in trouble and needed help, all she ever had to do was think hard: *Please, God*, or just *Please*. Right then, that second, she always felt as if a thin membrane had been pierced and she was on the other side of whatever separated her from the help she needed, and she got the help at once. She'd learned about this more than a quarter of a century ago when she was losing her baby, when she'd uttered the first quick *Please* and knew, before an instant of time had passed between the prayer and its answer, that she must hold her breath and push. At once the dead infant with a hole in his spine had come slurshing out and the pain was gone. She'd prayed in this way a few other times since then. She trusted that some immutable law of nature was at work. It was that simple.

Please, she thought.

The coughing should have stopped, but it didn't.

Standing, watching the old woman, Simpson forgot she was in her bathing suit being studied by the best-looking, politest-sounding male she'd seen in quite a while. "I'm Owen Banner," he'd said while they were carrying Ernie inside. "My dad's a neighbor. I'll call Dr. Wilson." He left and came back, and even with Ernie coughing what sounded like a death rattle, Simpson couldn't help turning around to look in his eyes.

She was surprised that she recognized him at once, as someone she'd known all her life—a thought that struck her as so bizarre she quickly dismissed it. If she recognized Owen, then she must have met him before. They might easily have run into each other in one of the forty or fifty towns she'd lived in, growing up. Or maybe she'd met someone who looked like him. His blond hair and olive skin were common in the Carolinas. But what seemed most familiar were his eyes. They were a clear and unyielding gray, exactly the color of sorrow.

Then Veronica said, "Boil some water. Maybe some steam would help."

"Lotus-root tea," Ernie gasped.

This brought Simpson to her senses. Lotus-root tea! Magnets attracted to water! Strangers she recognized on sight! Simpson fled to the kitchen, put on the kettle and ran upstairs to put on her clothes. By the time she came down, a male nurse had arrived—in his car, not an ambulance—wearing a white smock and explaining that Dr. Wilson had sent him over from the office. He gave Ernie a shot and bent toward her with his stethoscope, going about his business, even as Ernie tried to wave him away. Before long, her coughing slowed enough to allow her to sip tea between spasms. Gradually, her breathing calmed.

Owen left his phone number and departed, saying if they needed anything give him a call. Ernie fell into a snoring, sniffling sleep. Simpson felt once again as if she were trapped in another dimension, a picture postcard, as attractive as it was strange. They were in a place where medical personnel, if not the doctors themselves, still made house calls. A place where wells were dug based on the behavior of tree branches and strangers seemed eerily familiar. Nonsense! Now that the old woman had settled down, it was time to begin thinking clearly.

"Thank goodness we're here, Mama," Simpson said too loudly and too brightly. "We can help Ernie get someone to take care of her."

Veronica looked up with interest. To Simpson, this seemed a sure sign that the medical crisis, if not the swim, had brought her mother back to her senses. "Right now Ernie belongs in a hospital," Simpson continued. "I'm surprised that nurse didn't suggest it."

"Ernie would never go to a hospital," Veronica said. "Her husband died in a hospital when a heart procedure went wrong. She hates all that."

"Then someone needs to come in. This is no time for us to be here for a visit. We need to get her taken care of and then get out of her way."

Veronica fixed Simpson with a cool, appraising gaze. "We couldn't leave now," she said.

"I mean as soon as the crisis is resolved."

Veronica shook her head. "We couldn't."

"Why not?"

Veronica's eyes were the same blue-green as the lake and perfectly lucid. "Because she's dying," she said. "Do you want us to leave her to die alone?"

Ernie heard that—and could have told them she wasn't dying at all, not yet, what kind of invalid did they think she was? This was just a temporary setback.

But she didn't quite have the strength to open her eyes.

A lapse of time passed then. She must have been sleeping

because she awakened to a snuffling buzzing in her ear, which turned out to be the sound of her own snoring.

She gave herself over to a brief personal inventory. Chest: better. Breathing: easier. The wretched cough: gone. Except for her weariness, her mind was clear. She raised her right eyelid to take in the room.

The TV was on. Oprah was interviewing a pregnant prisoner who wanted to keep her baby. Veronica was not in sight. Simpson was curled into the armchair next to the couch, watching Ernie and not the TV. The expression on the girl's face was softer than it had been earlier. None of this morning's horror at finding Ernie's features marked by age and her behavior marked by witching. Ernie was so relieved that she managed to prop herself up on an elbow.

"Feeling better?" Simpson asked.

"Much."

"Should we call anyone? You might be laid up for a while. We should let the family know."

"There's no family. Call Lily, maybe."

"No family?"

"Knox's brother is dead. Never liked the man anyway." Ernie wrinkled her nose.

"You don't have children?"

"I lost a baby once. Knox had a son from his first marriage." Ernie trailed off, losing her focus.

"Don't you keep in touch with him?" Simpson asked. "Knox's son?"

"He was killed in a crash when he was eleven. Less than a year after Knox and I got married." Her elbow collapsed beneath her and she stretched out flat on the couch, finding the effort of holding up her head too arduous.

"I'm sorry," Simpson said. "It must have been terrible."

"Yes." It was, but not for the reasons the girl imagined. Sometimes Ernie still believed she'd caused Kevin Truheart's death by wishing so fervently to have him out of the way. It was an unkind thing to do to anyone, much less an eleven-year-old whose mother had died. But the boy had resented Ernie, and she him. He had been a thorn in the early months of her marriage, Lord forgive her, but it was true. And who was to say that wanting him gone hard enough hadn't made it happen?

"In every generation a few get into car wrecks and don't survive," Ernie said. "There's always a certain percentage."

"That's different from having it happen to you personally."

"I suppose," Ernie whispered, and turned her gaze to the ceiling because otherwise she might have said it never happens just to you but to everything it touches, a tidal wave flooding everything in its wake. She might have blurted out that the person responsible was another youngster, only fifteen years old, too young for a burden that size. She might have said that ever since that car flipped, thirty years ago and a generation away, the world had never been quite the same color and there had never been enough light.

Then Veronica's voice came at her, slicing away the mist of that memory and saving her from confession. "Don't worry about anything, Ernie," she said, appearing at the back of the room. "We'll stay here till you're back on your feet. Simpson and I are here to help you out."

"Help *me*?" Didn't Veronica see that it was she, not Ernie, who needed help? "I won't be down long."

"Well, there's one thing I want to do when you're feeling better."

"What's that?"

Veronica held up a small box imprinted with a photo of a young woman's face. Ernie squinted and couldn't make it out at first, then recognized a package she kept in her medicine chest. Miss Clairol. "Touch up your roots," Veronica said.

"I'm growing it out." She'd hated the chestnut color from the day she'd put it on—a permanent dye, too, not one of those temporaries.

"Then we'll bleach out the red and put some toner on so it's all the same shade."

Veronica's own hair was the same natural brown it had been when she was a girl, and just as unstyled and unruly, so Ernie wasn't sure how she knew about hair dyes. She put her fingers to her scalp. No wonder Veronica thought Ernie was the one who needed attention. It had nothing to do with the cough. Even without benefit of a mirror, Ernie realized her hair must look even more outrageous than she thought.

It was then, standing beside the couch with the bottle of dye in her hand, that Veronica got her first real sense of what they were in for. There was Simpson—ever-practical, ever-capable Simpson—huddled in an armchair, looking so troubled Veronica wouldn't have been surprised to see her biting her nails or scratching the skin off her arms. There was Ernie, trying to feign health even though her complexion was still as pale as an egg. Veronica was the only one steady on her feet.

Somehow, astonishingly, Veronica was in charge. She'd thought about leaving Guy a thousand other times, but until now the moment had never seemed right. Amazingly, she'd waited to flee until the exact time when Ernie needed her, during a full moon that gave her the energy to do it. And having arrived here, she'd somehow been given a chance to take a three-day nap before the crisis. This was no accident.

On the couch, Ernie's eyes closed. A moment later she had dozed off, still touching her hair where the roots had grown in gray.

"I think she'll be okay now," whispered Simpson. "She seems a lot better."

"Maybe so," Veronica said. But she knew otherwise. Despite the peaceful expression on Ernie's face, despite the normal rise and fall of her chest, Veronica felt the presence of the old woman's death as surely as if it had touched her with cold fingers. She'd experienced such moments all her life, foretellings of joy as well as sorrow. Until now she'd never been wrong—except, she supposed, when she'd first looked at Guy and decided she would be with him forever.

Setting the package of hair dye on the coffee table, she went into the kitchen to begin her work. For three days, Ernie had cooked for her. Now she would return the favor. The sagging counters were piled with cookbooks, dish towels, salt shakers, tins of spices, items she hadn't noticed this morning when her whole mind had been set on coffee. Every object looked as if it had been gathering dust and grease for years. Even the refrigerator was yellowed with age, its door splattered with bits of caked-on food. But inside, it was newly stocked. Fresh milk in glass bottles such as Veronica had seen only on TV, brought by sitcom milkmen, with a layer of cream on top that made her cringe until she realized it could easily be skimmed off. Half a dozen jars of homemade jelly and relish. A hunk of cheese wrapped in cloth. A bowl of strawberries. Except for the plastic squeeze bottles of mustard and ketchup, there was almost nothing from the supermarket. Oddest of all, on a china tray, securely wrapped in plastic, was a whole chicken. It was newly plucked, obviously right out of a henhouse rather than a grocery store, its skin specked with blood where the feathers had not come out easily. Veronica shuddered. Lily must have brought it this morning, along with the pie. Unappetizing as it looked, she would cook it for Ernie. This was what she was here for. This was what she would do.

She prepared the chicken for the oven, then let herself out the screen door to the back. Between the house and the nearest cornfield was the plowed rectangle of Ernie's garden, shaded now as the sun slanted low to the west. It was every bit as big and lush as Simpson had said, exactly the kind of plot Veronica had always wanted. Guy had never understood, but it was so. In the hot sand of the southeastern shore, during their abortive stays in rented duplexes with tiny untended yards, the seeds she'd planted sprouted but never thrived, only shriveled up in the sterile dryness. She had always longed for more.

Now she was looking at it. Early peas tumbled over a chicken-wire trellis, onions jutted finger-high from the compost-rich soil; pale lettuce began to head; heat-loving tomatoes and green beans had begun to reach for the sun. The only thing missing was collards, which Veronica liked very much. She would put in a few seedlings. In the meantime, she gathered snow peas, lettuce and carrots for their dinner, while the late-afternoon light on the mountain turned the trees from green to blue, and the freshened air slid into the valley and cooled her arms.

But the joy she might have taken in the sweet green vista was muted by this: that the polished light and rich bounty made almost a mockery of Ernie's condition. That Ernie's illness was more than Veronica had bargained for. After years of idle travel, coming and going at will, she was tied to a place she couldn't, shouldn't, leave—but for a heavier reason than she'd expected. It made her feel responsible in a way she'd never known. It scared her. She was on her own.

CHAPTER 6

When Guy Legacy left Beaufort, South Carolina, after nine months of being sequestered there, he was so annoyed that he drove only as far as the northern outskirts of Charleston. He intended to get good and drunk and stay that way as long as he felt like it. Usually these job-hunting trips took less than a week, scoping out a new town, securing a new position, driving back to gather the family. But this time he planned to be gone a good long stretch. He'd make his way up the coast at his leisure. He wouldn't call Veronica until he damned well felt like it. Maybe he'd stop to see if his old buddy Witherspoon still worked in that bar at Carolina Beach, up the coast in North Carolina. He would take his sweet time.

It was 6:00 p.m. when he checked into his motel and went looking for a bar. He was not usually a big drinker, just enjoyed a couple of beers after work. In Charleston, it took nothing less than Jack Daniel's to make him forget the censure in Veronica's eyes when he'd left. After all, what had she expected? He'd stuck it out through Simpson's whole senior year. He'd gone to her graduation. He'd done what he said he would.

He drank his whiskey with water at first, then straight. He didn't leave until closing.

The next day, he woke up with his mouth parched and

puckered, his head pounding, his stomach in a storm. It was after checkout time. He might as well spend another day. Nearly a week later, he'd been drunk so long and felt so miserable that he made himself get moving. He still planned to look up Witherspoon in Carolina Beach. After that, he'd head north to the Outer Banks or southeastern Virginia. Virginia Beach. Portsmouth. Norfolk. His father had been stationed in Norfolk when Guy was a kid, and Guy had avoided the place ever since their fiery final fight. He wouldn't mind going back now. It was always interesting to see how a place had changed.

He never traveled north of Virginia anymore. Veronica said that just went to show that even a drifter—a term he hated—could get set in his ways. Maybe so. But the one time he'd taken work in Ocean City, Maryland, the seawater had been so cold, he couldn't swim in it until after the Fourth of July. Part of the pleasure of any summer, he believed, was swimming. They hadn't been to Maryland since.

Guy drove up Route 17 past Myrtle Beach, across the border into North Carolina, and north another hour to Wilmington. Carolina Beach and Wrightsville Beach were the two barrier islands east of the town. He hadn't been there for years. At Carolina Beach, there was an actual boardwalk, which he didn't remember. Even the bars seemed to have been upscaled some. Guy ordered a beer in each place he stopped, sipping slowly while checking for any sign of Witherspoon. After the third bar, he switched to bourbon. Witherspoon must have moved on.

It was just after ten when he left. Considering how low he was on cash, he knew the motels on the beach, even the grungy ones, would be too expensive. He'd go back into Wilmington, find something cheap. In the morning, he'd get an early start up the coast. No more liquor. No more stops.

The last thing he remembered was the road rising at the northern tip of Carolina Beach, lifting him onto the Snow's Cut bridge. Maybe he was too drunk, or maybe just too distracted, to see a lone biker pedaling along the roadway.

Parker Dean was a sophomore at the University of North Carolina at Wilmington, who rode his bike almost every night. It was Parker's misfortune that Guy could never drive near the water without turning to look at it. It was both of their misfortune that Guy was so drunk that his truck swerved when he craned to catch a glimpse of the Intracoastal Waterway, just where it diverted part of the Cape Fear River toward the sea.

Guy woke up in New Hanover Regional Medical Center with his right shoulder bandaged and a headache as big as both the Carolinas creeping into the fuzzy, drugged murk of his thoughts. A nurse's voice drifted down to him. It had a light, airy, floating quality, which told him he wasn't quite awake. "Is there anyone you want us to call, Mr. Legacy?"

Well, of course, there was. His address was on his license; anybody else would have called Veronica already. Even considering the conditions under which he'd left, she'd certainly come to get him, to nurse him back to health.

"Is this right, Mr. Legacy? This Georgia address?"

Guy was conscious enough to recall that he'd renewed his license last in Jekyll Island, Georgia, where he'd worked two winters ago. He mumbled his Beaufort phone number and closed his eyes again. When he opened them a few minutes or a few hours later, he saw not the nurse before him but a rangy black policewoman.

"Your number has been disconnected," she said in a crisp, unsympathetic tone.

"Try again. Must be some mistake." Veronica wouldn't have forgotten to pay the bill. She loved having a phone.

"We tried several times. The phone's been disconnected."

Guy opened his mouth to argue, but his head and shoulder throbbed with pain. The next thing he knew, someone was giving him a shot. The policewoman kept talking, but he only half registered what she was saying, and it affected him no more than if she had been telling him a bedtime story. He drifted off again and woke up to the sight of a candy striper wheeling in a lunch tray.

He must not be badly hurt, he thought, or they would be feeding him through tubes. A gray, creamy soup sat before him, mottled with chunks of what might have been insect parts. A square of red Jell-O shivered on a white plate. He realized he could eat if he wanted to; despite the bandage on his shoulder, he could move his fingers.

But only his fingers. Not his arm.

His right arm. His hammer arm. His livelihood.

A bilious anger shot through him—at himself, he supposed, for getting into this situation. In the days before Veronica had started describing Guy as an itinerant or a drifter (reserving the term *nomad* for herself), and hitting him with a barrage of terms like *maturity*, *settle down* and *middle age*, his health had seemed somehow charmed. Now, a month into his fortieth year, he'd pulled a stunt worthy of a teenager. Before this, he had never in his life—never—spent a whole week drinking. He might not be able to negotiate a construction site for months.

A single knock came on his door, followed by an official-looking woman in a business suit, who was brandishing a file folder. Her nails were long and polished an aggressive red. "Guy Legacy?"

"Right here," he said, although the other bed was empty.

"I'm your care manager from Social Services. You came in as an emergency. Apparently they weren't able to find your medical-insurance card while you were in the emergency room."

"There isn't any medical insurance," he said.

"I beg your pardon?"

"I'm a carpenter. I travel. I don't have health insurance."

"Medicaid?"

"No."

"I see." She took a breath. "Then maybe we should explore—I could help you do the paperwork for temporary Medicaid. If the hospital bill exceeds a certain percentage of your annual income, you'll be eligible."

He shook his head. He wanted her to go away.

"Then, let me understand you. You're saying you can afford to deal with the hospital charges yourself?"

Guy grunted. Of course he couldn't. To avoid further conversation, he leaned over his tray and spooned some of the soup into his mouth. Cream of mushroom. The bug parts turned out to be mushrooms. He dropped the spoon into the bowl and poked at the Jell-O with his fork. The woman pulled a straight-backed chair to the foot of his bed and sat down. "I see you're from Georgia. Any family there?"

"No."

"No family." She made a notation in his file.

"No, I'm not from Georgia."

"Then where—?"

He speared some Jell-O and lifted it to his mouth, didn't chew, just let it slide down his throat. "What is it you want, exactly?" he asked.

"To help you decide how to pay for the medical services you've received. To find out if anyone's coming to help you. It's our responsibility to make sure you'll be taken care of."

"My wife may come after me." Though how he would get in touch with her, if the phone had really been disconnected, he didn't know. "Otherwise I'll probably take the bus and go home."

"Not under the circumstances, Mr. Legacy."

"What circumstances?"

"Wasn't Officer McKoy in here earlier?"

"The black woman?"

The social worker nodded. That was when Guy remembered Officer McKoy had told him not a bedtime story, but the details of his accident. He had totaled his truck. Most of his tools had been destroyed. "You gave permission for your blood alcohol to be tested," she'd told him, not gently. "Then you passed out." He did not remember the rest.

"You'll be getting a check from your auto-insurance company," the social worker said.

"I suppose."

She leafed through her folder and extracted a document, making room for it beside his lunch tray. "If you sign this, then the check will automatically be applied to your hospital bill. You won't have to worry."

Wouldn't have to worry? The pain was ratcheting up. His head swam. He wanted the social worker to go away. He took the pen she handed him and signed. She thanked him and motioned someone else into the room. It was Officer McKoy.

"Do you remember what I told you?" the black woman asked. "Do you remember what the charges are?"

"I beg your pardon?"

"You've been charged with driving while impaired," she said. "The boy you hit, the biker, Parker Dean, is in intensive care." Her expression grew stony and her voice mechanical. She might have been reciting memorized lines. "He's unconscious. He has a broken pelvis and three fractured ribs. Your bail has been set at twenty thousand dollars." She thrust a document at him, much as the social worker had done. It was the warrant for him to appear in court. "Your license has been suspended for ten days, which is the minimum under North Carolina law for this charge. Don't plan on going anywhere. There's a guard posted outside your door to see that you don't."

Guy closed his eyes. There was no way he could post bail, now that he'd signed away his auto insurance to the hospital. When they released him, he was going to jail.

Intensive care units are, above all, flooded with light. Guy had not known this until he went to see for himself. Half an hour before, he'd been discharged from the hospital in the company of his guard, a beefy man named O'Neal. Guy had had a brief discussion with the cashier, who presented him with the part of his bill that his insurance check wouldn't cover.

"Before we go, can I see him? The kid I hit?" he asked O'Neal.

"Why?"

"I feel like I need to see him."

Guy's shoulder had become a steady, throbbing source of pain. He had injured his rotator cuff, he'd been told, something he thought happened only to baseball pitchers. He might heal quickly or he might not. He had to give it some time.

"I can't figure guys like you," the guard said. "Wanting to check out the damage you done."

Guy hadn't been able to get in touch with Veronica. He had no license, no tools. According to Officer McKoy, he'd been lucky to be stopped by the concrete guardrail that kept vehicles from plummeting off the bridge. Parker Dean had not been thrown into the water, either, another fortunate turn of events.

The guard yanked Guy roughly toward the elevator. "If you want to see him, why not? Give you something to dream about at night."

The intensive-care nurse asked Guy if he was the boy's relative. Her tone indicated he'd better be.

"This is the guy who hit him," O'Neal said.

"Wait here." The nurse strode out of the bright center of the complex into the dimly lit, glassed-in cubicle where the patient lay and returned with a middle-aged woman who'd been standing by the bed. Her skirt was badly wrinkled. Guy did not register another detail about her, could not have said whether her hair was blond or brunette, her eyes brown or blue, though he knew at once she was the boy's mother.

"I don't understand your coming here," she said. "He can't talk to you. He can't do anything."

"I wanted to—I'm so—" He meant to apologize.

"You're so what?"

"I'm so sorry." For whatever good that would do.

"Sorry doesn't begin to cover it." For a long moment she glared at him. Guy thought she would order him away. "Go on in," she said. "See for yourself."

Inside, the cubicle was not even a room, just a bed and stacks of monitors, where the boy lay, attached to sensors and tubes that blinked in the faint light. His ribs were wrapped, but his broken pelvis was covered only by a sheet. Parker Dean was not really a boy. More a young man, tanned and slender.

Good-looking. He did not look "unconscious." He looked like he was asleep. He was the same age as Simpson.

On television and in films, hospital scenes were odorless. Here the smell of antiseptic was, not overpowering, just ever present, a whiff in every breath. Guy's stomach roiled and lurched. He thought he was going to throw up. Gulping air, he grasped the railing at the end of the boy's bed. *This could have been Simpson*, he thought.

Beside him, O'Neal scrutinized him, probably unsure whether to be alarmed. The guard grasped his arm. Guy stood motionless until the churning in his stomach stopped and his heart rate slowed. He turned slowly and walked out of the cubicle to the bright center of the complex, where nurses at a circular monitoring station watched numbers and graphs on a myriad of screens. Parker Dean's mother stood where Guy had left her.

"It's so dark in there," he said, though this was not what he'd meant to say, not at all.

"They keep the lights low in cases of traumatic brain injury," she said flatly. "He was on a respirator when they first brought him in. Now he's breathing on his own. Lucky for you."

"For him, too," Guy said.

"I hope so. They say he's gradually waking up. They don't know how much brain damage there might be."

It could have been Simpson, Guy thought.

"You were drunk," the woman said.

"Yes."

And Guy realized—even more than he had nineteen years ago when he first saw the red squalling body of his newborn daughter—that he was entirely responsible. For the first time in years, in some inescapable, unmitigated way, he was entirely responsible for everything.

CHAPTER 7

Each morning, Simpson walked by the calendar Ernie had hung in the downstairs hallway. Each morning, she could hardly believe how much time had passed. They had arrived in early June and now it was the end of July. Six weeks! Gone! And though their lives had changed completely, neither she nor her mother acknowledged it. Even practical, analytical Simpson found herself acting as if their new routine was familiar and accustomed.

One day, soon after they settled in, Veronica had spent a whole day dyeing Ernie's hair. What did Veronica, whose own mane was the same dark brown she'd been born with, and usually a tangled mess because of the chopped-off haircuts she gave herself at home, know about coloring hair? Nothing! Yet with more patience than Simpson thought possible, she stripped all the red from Ernie's thin long strands and spent hours applying toner and color until—miracle of miracles—she produced a becoming shade of gray. Simpson was agape. In return, Ernie showed both of them how to put up beans and stewed tomatoes in wide-mouthed canning jars, a task that was so exotic it made Simpson feel as if they'd traveled back to another century.

She felt that way about their surroundings, too. She and her mother had always lived in town, practically on top of their neighbors. Now, they were out in the country where they couldn't see another house. And they were pretending to be farmers. Each morning, Ernie instructed Veronica and Simpson to pick the produce she planned to sell that day—tomatoes, string beans, squash, the first ears of Silver Queen corn. Simpson loaded the harvest into Ernie's tumbledown van and drove the old woman to Lily's, while Veronica stayed behind to finish the garden chores on Ernie's list. Then she'd go inside and do the cleaning—although Veronica had never been much of a housekeeper—and prepare the meals.

At the vegetable stand, Ernie would help Lily candle her eggs, while Simpson unloaded the produce at the crossroads bordering Lily's farm. Half an hour later, the two old women would settle themselves under a hickory tree, their wares displayed on folding tables from Office Max, while Lily's wolfdog, Rita, lounged beside them, so fierce-looking she could have driven the customers away, except she was too timid to bark.

It was all very bizarre.

Once the stand was under control, Simpson could do whatever she liked for the rest of the morning. Without planning to, she usually drove to the lake for a swim. She loved her first view of the water, sparkling against the backdrop of mountain. Between the parking area at the top of the hill and the far shore in the distance, there was never another person in sight. Even at the ocean, even out of season, Simpson had never had a private beach before.

Except for that first day, her mother had not gone swimming again. "I'm an ocean lover," Veronica said. "Lakes give me the creeps. Too still. Too cold. And that yucky soft bottom." But Simpson enjoyed it. After her tussles with the fierce ocean undertow, the tranquil lake soothed her, even compensating for the feel of mud between her toes when she waded back to shore. The weather was warmer than when they'd first arrived. When Simpson dived in from the end of the dock, the chilly water jolted her only for a second now, then seemed to moderate. Gliding across the glassy surface without the inquiring presence of her mother or Ernie, she felt as she did nowhere else, that she could think openly about everything, even her father. For six weeks, Veronica had not uttered a single word about Guy. It was as if she'd banished him from her thoughts. Anytime Simpson asked about him, Veronica put up a hand to stop her, not angrily or desperately, as Simpson might have expected, but so languidly that the motion of her fingers was almost hypnotic. "I told you we were leaving him, honey," she'd say. "That's in the past, so what's the point?" And though Simpson meant to protest that a person's father was never in the past, even if he died, Veronica looked so genuinely vacant that Simpson wondered if her mother even remembered the two decades she'd spent with the man.

Stroking across the lake, switching from breaststroke to crawl to backstroke, Simpson let her concern flow through her mind until it settled finally on this: that her parents had not been unhappy. Not really. Not until Beaufort. They were eccentric, yes. In need of guidance, yes—and she'd provided it, hadn't she? But beyond that, they'd been satisfied with each other. A team. Not miserable at all. No matter where they lived, the two of them always checked out the seafood restaurants and rated the local chowders on a scale of one to ten, as if this were a sacred duty. On the Outer Banks, they always climbed the enormous sand dune called Jockey's Ridge. In Charleston, they took the sightseeing boat to Fort Sumter even though they'd seen it a dozen times before. In Myrtle

Beach, they spent a few hours at the old Pavilion and went on all the rides. Simpson had liked the rides well enough as a child, but it was her parents who never outgrew them. Her parents who went on the roller coaster, while Simpson stayed on the ground and watched. Her parents who chased each other around the track in those silly miniature race cars and then walked away laughing, with their arms around each other, no matter who won.

And even in Beaufort—even in Beaufort!—everything wasn't all bad. When Veronica insisted on buying an annual sticker for the state park on Hunting Island, just to show she meant to use the beach for the whole year, Guy said, "Well, we'll see if we actually stay," and griped about her spending the money. But Veronica had gone so often that Guy had finally started joining her, and as far as Simpson could tell, they had had fun.

And now—where *was* her father? When he'd returned to Beaufort and discovered his family gone, what had he done? Did he know Veronica had left on purpose? Did he suspect foul play and call the police? Had he gone looking for them? What was he doing now? Sometimes it took three or four times across the lake to worry these thoughts to a dull nub inside her head.

Then the tension in her muscles began to ease. Her head cleared. For all Simpson knew, Guy might be glad for this little reprieve, after his long confinement in Beaufort. Maybe Veronica needed a vacation, too. Besides, what could Simpson do? Once her mother rested, they would figure something out. Emerging from the water, she wrapped herself in a towel and drove back to the farmhouse, thinking that if not for the absence of Guy, things would seem as normal as they'd ever been. Maybe more.

At Ernie's, Simpson sneaked inside so her mother, still hoeing and weeding in the garden, wouldn't know she was there. The house fascinated her. It was larger than any place she'd ever lived, cluttered and haphazard with disarray. She could wander its rooms for hours. The Legacys had never had any furniture. Ernie had more than she needed, sofas jammed against end tables, chairs crowded against couches, bureaus and knickknack shelves hugging the walls, a table of claw-footed oak in the kitchen and another of dark mahogany in the dining room. At the far end of the dining room, a massive breakfront had been pushed beside a big china closet. In the living room, a cherry writing desk shared a wall with an old secretary filled with rusty paper clips and ancient ten-cent stamps. A mirrored bedroom vanity had ended up in the downstairs hallway because there was no room upstairs; an umbrella stand decorated with carved elephant heads stood by the door. An old wooden coatrack was piled with more winter coats than one old woman could possibly wear.

The clutter was not just furniture, but papers, too—piles of receipts and tax returns from as long as twenty years ago; a full year's worth of the *Whisper Springs Mountaineer*; months of the *Hagerstown Morning Herald* and the *Washington Post*, none of them recent. Ernie seemed not to be able to afford a newspaper anymore, or much of anything else. There was no computer. No magazines came in the mail, or even very many catalogs or offers for credit cards. There was just this jumble of old stuff. Though Veronica did most of the cleaning—such cleaning as Veronica ever did—Simpson knew she herself was the one who would have to organize the mess.

It became her project, that last hour before she picked up Ernie at noon, to work on this. Ernie was skeptical at first about the neatly labeled files and stacks of what would be trash as soon as she approved, but she got used to it. When finally the glut of paperwork had been tamed, Simpson squirted lemon Pledge onto each table and desk, rubbed it clean with rags, then ran her fingers across the grain of old oaks and polished mahoganies. Most of the furniture was so dark it absorbed what little light came into the house past heavy curtains, but Simpson didn't care. There was nothing she liked better than creating order.

Her only other job, twice a day, was to feed the cats out in the barn. One evening as she bent over the barrel of food, she heard footsteps on the hard clay outside and recognized the sound as if she'd listened for it every day of her life.

"So this is where she keeps the cat food," Owen Banner said, ducking under a fallen doorway support, wearing his short-sleeved, button-down dress shirt and crisply creased khakis from work.

Simpson rerolled the top of the big sack of dry food and put it back in the barrel where Ernie kept it. In the dimness, Simpson couldn't see the sorrow-gray of Owen's eyes, but she was sure she felt the heat radiating from his skin. "Ernie keeps the food here so the cats won't hang around the house all the time," she said. "She says on bad days she feels like some fat old feline is sitting on her chest, and she damned well doesn't want the real ones coming in and getting ideas."

"And how many feline-on-the-chest days is she having? A lot?"

Simpson was certain she could feel Owen's heart slamming against his chest in rhythm with her own. She couldn't look at him, and he seemed to be having the same problem. They both pretended to be absorbed in watching a handful of cats hiss and claw in each other's direction before settling down to eat from the long plastic planter that served as a trough.

"Ernie sighs a lot. She says she can't help it," Simpson said. "The cat-on-the-chest thing is just sometimes. But my mother says she's dying." Simpson fit the cover snugly on top of the barrel so neither the cats nor the mice could get to the food. She didn't look up. "I'm not sure about the dying part. Ernie's never too sick to go to Lily's. Or spot a well."

"Dying, but not right away." There was no irony in this.

"My mother says we have to stay until it's over. However long that is. I think we were going to stay anyway."

Owen seemed relieved. Simpson recognized the warmth in his gaze as something that had reached out to her in the past, though she couldn't have said when or where. He had lived all his life in Maryland. She'd never lived north of Virginia, except for one summer in Ocean City she'd been too young to remember. She couldn't have met him before. The idea was so illogical that it would have driven her crazy, if she hadn't wanted so badly to touch him.

After that, Owen drove out from Hagerstown two or three times a week to check on his father, and then came down to the barn. "Before you got here," Ernie grumbled, "he looked in on Marshall maybe once a month."

"If you don't like him, why don't you just say so?"

"I didn't say I didn't like him," Ernie said.

On each visit, Owen and Simpson shared their concern about the old woman's health, stringing the conversation out as long as they could. Owen looked at Simpson as if he'd never seen anyone so desirable. He stayed an hour, sometimes more. He didn't try to touch her. He didn't ask her out. It drove her crazy. In her confusion, she babbled answers to every question he asked.

"Where's my father? Wish I knew." She laughed because it was so easy to say. "He moves too much. He's not overly responsible. My mother, either." Her tongue loose and free. "I don't mean this in a bad way. They're just unusual."

"You should meet *my* father."

"I have." Twice she'd run into Marshall Banner while getting Ernie's mail from the box at the bottom of the lane. Tall and scarily unkempt, Marshall had collected his own mail and introduced himself in a surprisingly gentle voice as "the one who sees to the fields and has an upholstery shop up at my house. If you ever know anyone who needs work done, let me know." The second time he introduced himself again, in exactly the same words, as if he'd never laid eyes on Simpson before. A cold shiver ran through her at the memory.

"My father is beyond unusual." Owen seemed to know precisely what she was thinking. "Welcome to the club."

He took Simpson's hand in his own. She recognized everything about it: its warmth, its texture somewhere between leather and butter; the sweet, thick strength of the fingertips, the imprint of the palm. She could not draw air. She made herself let go.

They were "friends." They didn't dare stop talking. "My father says he's sampled the local seafood chowder in more than fifty towns along the coast and plans to keep moving until he tastes them all," she said.

"My father doesn't relocate," Owen replied. "For all the walking he does, he might as well have."

"Walking?"

"He disappears for three or four days at a time. Doesn't tell anyone he's going, or where. Then he comes back, and he's fine."

Simpson understood Owen: a grown child monitoring an errant parent, worrying more than he should. It was her own reflection in a different mirror, or skewed by the ripples of the lake. Together they moved out of the barn into the twilit yard. He was so close behind her that she could smell detergent wafting from his shirt. "Once, the year I went to college, he had a woman friend named Carol," he said. "She didn't get him to stop walking. She got tired of his forgetting to call. After it was over, he never seemed to miss her."

"If it had worked out, she could have looked after him. You wouldn't have had to."

Owen frowned. This was harder. It seemed to Simpson that each of them had been so preoccupied with parenting parents that neither had quite jelled. Their own emotions were sketchy and unfinished; they could not allow them, much less put them into words. They grew so weary they could hardly make a sound. What they really wanted was to fling themselves into each other's arms. The barn and the fields where they strolled grew dark except for starlight, silent except for crickets. They could have done anything they wanted.

But they didn't. For all Simpson knew, moving around so much, with so few close friends and shared confidences, she'd missed out on some essential fact of life. Maybe everyone felt this fearful and momentous recognition around certain members of the opposite sex. Maybe this would have happened sooner or later in any case.

She had never wanted to touch anyone so badly before, or felt it would be so dangerous. She might have been thirteen. Or maybe it was just that they were cautious people. They'd always had to be. In spite of the fire that drew them, it was wise to be tentative. When you recognized someone you'd never met before, you had to be careful indeed.

She would give it time. There was no hurry. This was the kind of place where a person could live forever.

Veronica could not have agreed less. She was glad to be with Ernie, who seemed to grow weaker every day, but being away from the ocean meant that her hands stayed flaky and dry even when she took extra vitamin E, and her nails split and broke as if they were made of glass.

"Your skin is parched because it's less humid here," Ernie said when she saw Veronica slathering herself with Vaseline Intensive Care. "And your nails would look better if you were more careful about wearing your gardening gloves. It has nothing to do with the ocean."

But Veronica didn't believe it. Every night, tired from the garden, she slipped into her pleasant dream about swimming under the stars. Then, just before morning, the scene shifted as always to noon. The sun was bright. The sand under her feet was hot. In the distance, the happy young family was playing in the surf, the dark-haired daughter splashing her parents, the parents lifting the girl by either hand to jump a breaking wave, the three of them squealing so joyfully that the sight made Veronica laugh. She moved toward them, drawn by their happiness and the cool, moving ocean. It was a place she could never reach. She woke up exhausted from effort, as far from the sea as she'd ever lived in her life. Later in the day, Simpson would say to her, "Come on, Mama, take a swim. It'll cool you off," and every day Veronica would refuse. She couldn't understand how Simpson could pretend there was no difference between enjoying the surf in the Atlantic Ocean and swimming in that little pisshole of a lake.

The truth was, Simpson was so unfazed that she might have lived in these mountains forever. The first time Veronica bought fish in the local grocery, she'd been horrified to find that what passed as fresh in Whisper Springs was actually brought up from Baltimore three or four days before, and now was less fit for the table than the garbage bin. Simpson, who'd spent all her life in towns where fish came straight from the boat, didn't even seem to notice. And when Veronica complained that the store carried oatmeal and cream of wheat but not a single box of grits, Simpson looked up and said, "Oh, they don't?" as if it had never occurred to her that she hadn't eaten grits for a month.

Mired in this train of thought, Veronica sometimes shuffled restlessly from kitchen to dining room while she drank her coffee, unable to ignore how dim the rooms seemed, even with the sunlight gleaming outside. On her previous visits, the house had struck her as sheltering and cozy. Now, she saw how dull and dowdy it was, how sepia-toned and static, with furniture so old all the upholstery had faded to a uniform shade of brown. Even with the windows open, the place smelled musty. Veronica yearned for the wide white swath of sunlight that hugged the southern shore, the need to race indoors to elude the fierce hot eye of summer. Here, the only brightness was the garden.

She dumped the coffee and rushed out back. But even the sight of the flourishing half acre before her didn't cheer her up. She'd always wanted flowers and vegetables like these, but considering all the grungy hard labor they required, she was no longer so sure. At any rate, the garden wasn't hers. Ernie had planted most of it before Veronica arrived, and now Ernie supervised it like an overprotective mother, telling Veronica how much to fertilize and where to weed and what to pick. In the past month, the vegetation had grown so lush that every inch of ground would have been covered if Veronica hadn't been so diligent about staking the beans and tomatoes and training the squash and cucumber and pumpkin vines into neat rows. The only things that weren't thriving were the collards Veronica had planted herself.

"The soil's wrong for them," Ernie had warned. "Not acid enough. And the climate's either too hot or too cold most every month of the year." But Veronica hated the only greens at the grocery, nasty bunches of kale that made her feel as bitter as they tasted. Finding no collard plants at the local farm supply store, she ordered some by mail, tiny seedlings that arrived in soil-filled plastic cups. Her tender care hadn't fazed them at all. They needed different fertilizer, she thought. Or more of whatever it was that acidified the soil. They needed— well, she wasn't sure what they needed. She damn well wasn't sure.

Wiping her forehead with the back of her hand, Veronica found herself searching for a barren patch of sand among the tomatoes, the kind of place where collards might throw open their outer leaves to the sun. She found herself longing for the sight of a cheerful crape myrtle festooned with magenta blooms, or a stately live oak hung with Spanish moss. She was sick of vigorous maple trees and the rampant growth of zinnias and marigolds and twenty kinds of vegetables. She wanted to be grateful, but she wasn't; her eyes saw the unfamiliar plants as strangers. Even the fields of undulating green made her dizzy. Just once she would have liked to spot a cluster of those wild red-eyed gaillardias that graced even the scabbiest beach in the Carolinas, and to look beyond them to a soothing blue swath of ocean.

Stop whining, she told herself. Bending to tie a tomato vine
to its stake, Veronica stared into the foliage to soothe herself,
only to come eye-to-eye with the ugliest, most prehistoric-
looking worm she'd ever encountered. She jumped back, her
heart clattering wildly in her throat. Good Lord! Then she saw
it was just a big tomato hornworm, thick as her thumb, chew-
ing away on the underside of a leaf, dropping its ratty, dark
green poop on the leaves below. She felt like a fool. The creepy
things were so close to the green color of the plant that spotting them always took her by surprise—though after all this
time, she ought to be over that. When she could swallow
again and breathe normally, she plucked the disgusting thing
off the leaf and crushed it with gloved fingers. There. She
pulled off her gloves and wiped her hands on her shorts.

A line of sweat trickled down her chest as she dropped to
her knees to do the last of the weeding. At least there was no
risk of fire ants this far north. The last time she'd tangled with
them had been back in Morehead City, when she'd stepped
into an anthill by accident and been swarmed from bare toes
to ankles by ants so tiny they looked like they couldn't do a
bit of damage. But they bit! They stung! She'd brushed them
off as fast as she could but still ended up with a dozen painful
bites that swelled into hard, red, itchy pimples that didn't go
away for weeks.

She couldn't believe her eyes were getting misty, thinking,
of all things, about fire ants! Even to herself, she sounded home-
sick. Which was ridiculous, because how could you be home-
sick when never in over twenty years had you ever lived
anywhere you could call home? How could you get on with your
life if you insisted on getting nostalgic for stinging insects?

You must not see the obstacles in your way, she had read

somewhere. You must concentrate on the straight line to your goal. She wiped her face, smearing it with dirt and not caring, and went into the house.

She wasn't sure exactly what to do next. Half-hungry, she decided she might slice some tomatoes to fry for lunch in a little while, not green tomatoes but nice red ripe ones. She'd fry them in oil and serve them on squooshy nutrient-free white bread the way Guy used to like them. Guy! What was she thinking? She was about to prepare an unhealthy, greasy dish her husband would have liked and feed it to a woman who was suffering from pulmonary distress! And all because of that *man*.

For six weeks, she hadn't mentioned his name. She hadn't exactly thought about him. But he must have been with her all that time like a sore beginning to fester. An unresolved moral issue. That was why she felt she couldn't get on with her life: Guy. She'd been wrong not to have it out with him face-to-face.

He'd been the most unfaithful man alive in terms of wanderlust, true. But as far as she knew he'd never gone after another woman, and certainly he'd never laid a hand on her or Simpson by way of abuse. She owed it to him to have been more straightforward. To have waited till he came back to Beaufort with a new job lined up, and issued her ultimatum then: settle down or split up. She shouldn't have left so stealthily or been so clever that he couldn't trace her.

But it was not too late. For all his moving, there was certainly a pattern to their migrations. They usually stayed in Georgia or South Carolina in the winter, North Carolina or Virginia in summer. If she had to bet, she'd say after nearly a year in Beaufort, Guy would go at least as far north as the Outer

Banks, or maybe into Virginia. He'd find a job and then get
an apartment and a phone. That was their routine. The least
she could do was call and have it out with him. Veronica
snatched the receiver off the kitchen wall and dialed North
Carolina information.

"What city, please?"

"Manteo."

Manteo had no number listed for a Guy Legacy.

Neither did any other town on the Outer Banks. She
started on Virginia. Guy wouldn't be in Norfolk or Virginia
Beach or Chesapeake because that was where he and his father had had their final falling-out, and Guy never wanted to
go back. But anywhere else was a possibility.

Moving north now: Eastville, Accomac, Chincoteague.
One summer they had camped at the beach at Chincoteague—or was it Assateague?—while they looked for an apartment. Veronica felt a little panicky; suddenly the names of the
towns ran together in her mind. All she remembered was that
Simpson was very small then, she couldn't remember how old,
and the three of them had slept in a tent for over a week. Each
morning before breakfast, they'd inspected each other for ticks,
which would crawl into the bedding from the sand during the
night and attach themselves to their skin. This wasn't nearly
as creepy as it sounded. It had just been part of the adventure.
It never occurred to them to worry about Lyme disease. They
hadn't been afraid of the wild ponies that roamed the marsh-
land, either. Once, when they'd left a bag of groceries on the
picnic table outside their tent, a big stallion had come running into their campsite, nostrils flaring, to inspect the food.
Another time they'd stood on the beach at twilight showing
Simpson a shell they'd pulled from the surf, when two ponies

thundered down the beach at breakneck speed, almost grazing them as they raced by, so that they would have been run down if they had moved so much as an inch. It sounded dangerous, but actually they had been thrilled. They had been glad to be spared, to be on the cooling beach at sunset, on that thin lip of sand at the edge of the water, laughing and alive.

"Who're you calling, Mama?" a voice said.

Veronica slammed down the phone. "You about scared me to death!" She put her hand to her throat, to a hot pounding pulse. "I thought you'd gone to get Ernie."

"I did. She's in the living room. I told her to lie down until lunch. You all right?"

"I'm fine. You scared me, that's all."

"Look at the phone. It's all muddy. Don't you want to wash your hands?"

Veronica looked down at herself. Her bare knees were crusted with dirt, her shorts streaked black with soil.

"Who were you calling in such a hurry?" Simpson asked.

"Farmer's Supply," Veronica said.

"It must have been some emergency, having to call Farmer's Supply before you even washed up."

"Hornworms," Veronica muttered.

Simpson gave her a look of disbelief, then dropped her voice and gentled it, the way you would with a child. "You ought to take a shower, Mama."

A rush of anger filled her. What a fool she must look like! She'd always believed each woman was the heroine of her own life—but obviously this wasn't true in her own case, since she seemed to have this urgent need to explain herself to Guy. She stomped up the stairs and ran the shower hard, but even the rushing water didn't help.

She heard Ernie coughing while she was getting dressed. Not just the hack, the persistent rumbling. She'd gotten to know the variations well. Barefoot, she ran down the stairs into the living room. "Here, let me fix your pillows." She plumped them behind Ernie's back and turned on the TV. "Wait here," she said, as if Ernie would get up, in any case. She brewed a pot of lotus-root tea. Under Veronica's ministering hands, Ernie relaxed so visibly that Veronica could almost feel the phlegm loosen in the old woman's chest. For the first time all day, Veronica remembered she was here to see Ernie through her illness.

She meant to carry out her plan. She meant to be strong.

CHAPTER 8

In the middle of August, in the middle of a heat wave, Marshall Banner received a summons to appear in small claims court for harboring seven unvaccinated cats. He had spent the morning mowing the shoulders of the road that bordered Ernie's land. On any other day he would have spent the afternoon outdoors, too. Despite the heat, he sensed the coming of autumn in the shortened days, the occasional shriveled leaf, the wildflowers blooming and dying in succession. He wanted all the summer he could get. But Owen kept nagging him to finish a chair he was reupholstering for one of the antique shops that gave him regular work.

"I'm in no hurry for the money," he explained when Owen pressed. "This time of year, I earn all I need baling hay or harvesting corn."

"I know that, Dad. But you'll run short by winter if you don't have upholstering lined up," Owen argued. "You want to finish the chair so people will know they can count on you."

Marshall considered that. He enjoyed reupholstering furniture in the middle of winter, when it provided welcome days of sweaty physical work he could do indoors. He liked tearing old frames apart and rebuilding them, especially when they were elaborate and frail and had been pronounced unfixable.

He understood the structure of chairs and sofas and tables the way he understood the workings of heavy equipment. He could not explain this, exactly. He didn't want to risk losing his clients.

So he gave Owen his word he would finish the job. That was how he happened to be home after lunch, cutting new fabric for the cushion of a Queen Anne dining-room chair that he'd promised weeks before.

Over the years, Marshall had grown skillful at working with fabrics, something he hadn't cared for in the beginning. He had learned to piece together the most difficult and intricate patterns, to cut so smartly and sparingly that he could make even the most woeful short cuts fit. His clients valued this in him.

He was dealing with such a case now, making less than a yard of cloth do the work of two. Upholstery materials were not always smooth and soft, but this burgundy-and-green velvet was—difficult to manage, but paradise for the fingers. He snipped with concentration, reflecting, as he sometimes did, that since Rose had died, fabric like this was the only soft thing he had to touch. The thought embarrassed him.

He did not hear the process server knock.

The knock came again. Marshall looked up. At the front door, he discovered a jowly middle-aged man, sweating profusely, holding a briefcase in one hand and a sheaf of papers in the other. Marshall had not seen a door-to-door salesman for years.

Curious, he motioned the man inside. The stranger glanced warily at Marshall's cutoff jeans and University of Maryland tank top. He frowned at the disheveled state of his workshop, in what had once been a living room. Instead of advancing into the house, the man stepped back a little before thrusting a document in Marshall's direction.

"Unvaccinated cats?" It took Marshall a moment to remember. "You mean the cats down at Ernie's? I got them rabies shots months ago."

"The way I understand it, you still have to pay." The man took a handkerchief from his pocket and commenced mopping his neck.

"I did pay," Marshall said. The vet had taken money for the vaccinations. Owen had given Marshall the receipt. Motioning his visitor to wait, Marshall disappeared down the hallway and in a moment returned holding a handful of metal tags. "They gave me these. It shows they're up to date."

"Yes, but—"

"It was my son who took them to the vet. Why would they care who takes them to the vet?"

The man stuffed the handkerchief back into his pocket. "What I mean is, if you can't show they're already vaccinated when the animal control officer comes, you still have to pay the fines even if you get them the shots later."

Marshall was confused. He was accustomed to having his mind come unhinged, a letting-go like slipping on ice, to which he submitted because he had no choice. But this was different. There was some piece of information here that he couldn't quite latch onto.

"They don't send the summons out until sixty days after they cite you," the process server explained. "They give you plenty of time to pay the fine."

Marshall remained mute.

"You can still pay up before you have to go to court." The man pointed to the summons. "Your court date isn't till October."

Now there was the beginning of a buzz behind Marshall's

eyes. He searched his memory for the scene in front of Ernie's house that early-summer evening. "The lady said they give you five days to get the shots," he remembered. "That's what she told me."

"I think they give you five days before they arrest you."

"Arrest you for keeping a cat?"

The man shrugged. "I don't know. I just deliver the summons."

The process server returned to his car and drove away. Marshall felt called to walk. His truck was parked in front of the house, but it did not occur to him to drive. He shoved the summons into the pocket of his shorts. He had not been to animal control for years, since after he'd buried Rose and decided to put aside his vow not to keep a dog. Owen would be lonely without his mother. A dog would help. On that visit to animal control, Marshall had gone by himself to check things out, intending to let his son choose his own pet, later. The place hadn't looked like a shelter. It had looked mean. The redness had come behind his eyes. A dog would not replace Rose. He'd fought the redness back. He'd gone home empty-handed. That was ten years ago. He still dreamed about it now and then.

Marshall wouldn't keep a dog. Hadn't kept a dog the whole time Owen was little and wouldn't have thought of it after Rose had died except he felt so bad for his son. He hadn't kept a dog since he was twelve and had lived for a few months with his uncle Roy. Roy's live-in girlfriend had a retriever puppy, honey-tempered and golden and pretty. Then Roy fought with the girlfriend and she left, but Roy kept the dog for spite. During the day, Roy worked and Marshall went to school. The dog was locked in the house. Roy would beat it if he came home and found dog crap on the floor. He'd beat it if it ate before

Roy gave it permission. He'd beat it any time he was in a bad mood. He'd say, "Damn thing makes too much noise. Damn thing don't need to sit on the couch." Though the puppy cringed and whimpered from the blows, still at first it ran to Roy whenever he entered the room and followed him everywhere, too stupid to be afraid or run away. Then one time, Roy hit the puppy too hard and the whimpering didn't stop. Roy snorted with disgust and went to take a shower. The puppy tried to get up. It dragged its hind legs for a few steps. Then it collapsed into a clump and moaned.

Marshall saw red then for the first time. He'd heard people talk about "seeing red" but didn't know it happened for real. It was an overlay in front of his vision, a lump in his throat, a physical ache in his heart.

He would have to kill the dog. Otherwise Roy would come out of the bathroom and kick it to make it shut up. Roy would let it lie there for however long it took to die. Once Roy came out of that bathroom, he wouldn't let Marshall touch it.

The dog gave a weak imitation of a yelp when Marshall picked it up. Gently as he could, he carried it outside so he wouldn't get blood on the floor. He laid it on the grass. The red behind his eyes got darker, a black-red, and in his ears there was a buzzing. With the sharpest knife he could find in the kitchen, he slit the puppy's throat, swift and deep so it died with only the briefest second's look of shocked surprise. He buried it in the field behind the house.

"Musta gone out to lick its wounds," Roy said later, though he knew the puppy couldn't get out of the house on its own. "If it don't come back, good riddance."

Marshall had not killed any living creature before. He'd killed since, but not before. He'd learned that day that when a thing is suffering and there is no help for it, you must kill it. Put it out of its misery. Once you do that the red retreats from behind your eyes and the buzzing stops. That is what he'd learned. But he did not like it, and he would not keep a dog.

The day was hotter than usual. Marshall walked along the road for a ways and then cross-country, through cornfields with stalks as tall as he was. The sweat on his chest and under his arms felt productive, as if he were doing important work. He came to a series of fallow fields lush with grasses and ragweed and Queen Anne's lace. On these outings, he often heard snakes slithering away from him into the undergrowth, and occasionally, he caught sight of a black snake or a copperhead, but he'd never been bitten. He did not see any snakes today.

Up a final rise, he spotted the animal shelter on the same three acres it had always occupied, tucked against a hill just north of town. It looked the same as it had ten years ago. One wing of a gray cinderblock building served as the office and the other wing housed the animals. Narrow runs extended outdoors, each one enclosed by chain link on the sides and top to cut off the possibility of escape. A half-dozen dogs, maybe more, shared each run. On the other side of the animal wing, there was a communal cage for the cats. As Marshall came closer he heard the din of barking and smelled the stench of shit. In the distance the mountain stretched so green and empty beneath the August sky that the crowded cages amid this bordering wildness seemed lunacy even to Marshall, who knew his own hold on sanity was tenuous.

When you lived in the country, people were always dropping off litters of puppies and kittens. They figured you had room. Mostly they didn't drop them at Marshall's because they'd have to drive up the hill to get there. When he discovered them at the bottom of the farm lane where it met the blacktop, he found them homes. He wouldn't bring them to the shelter. You had to be crazy. He wouldn't keep a dog, himself. A dog was loyal to the point of stupidity, but when something happened to it you felt guilty all the same. The farmers he worked for, mowing and plowing and baling hay, would take a puppy or kitten if you asked. So would newcomers like Celeste who owned the antique store he did so much work for. When people like Celeste moved out from D.C. or Baltimore, they could finally afford to live where there was enough room for a pet, and were lonely without one. Over time, he'd talked Celeste into three cats and a dog. Two of the cats lived in her store. In return, Celeste once gave Marshall a bumper sticker that said, "An Animal Should Be Able To Run If It Has Legs, Fly If It Has Wings, Swim If It Has Fins." He believed that. He'd always meant to put the sticker on his truck.

Inside the animal control office, he showed his summons to the receptionist. She stared at him so long that he looked down at himself to see what was wrong. In the center of his University of Maryland tank top was a circle of sweat that pretty much covered the image of the terrapin. His shorts were littered with scraps of jewel-toned upholstery fabric. "You'll have to see Mr. Murray," the receptionist said.

"Who?"

"The director."

"The dogcatcher?"

"He's with someone right now. You could wait for him over there."

The girl pointed to a row of molded plastic chairs in a bright, neon-green. Behind the chairs, the cinderblock wall was covered with notices about spay clinics and rabies vaccinations, which Marshall did not read. He looked at the posters featuring kittens and puppies. He blinked at the bluish fluorescent light. After his long walk through the hot day, the air-conditioning was too cold. He should have brought a shirt.

He sat down in the chair. Gradually he became aware of a half-opened door in a hallway to his left. A sign on the door said Don Murray, Animal Control Director. He couldn't see inside, but he could make out two voices, one male, one female.

"The reason we lend out the traps," the man was saying in a calm way, "is because you'd be surprised the damage cats do. People call to say they've scratched up their cars or clawed through the cover to their swimming pools."

"Swimming pools!" the woman piped.

"There are more here in the county than you think."

"I can't believe you lent them a trap to catch a harmless six-pound cat!" The woman's voice edged higher.

"People think of dogs as the dangerous animals, but actually we get more calls about cats," the man went on. "Statistically—"

"She was not a dangerous animal," the woman said.

"She was in a yard where she didn't belong. They had a legal right to request the trap." His voice grew softer, gentler. "If she'd been wearing a collar, we could have notified you."

"Collars can strangle a cat," the woman said.

"No more a cat than a dog," the director intoned. "Your case is a good example of the purpose a collar can serve."

"I can't see how—"

"Why, once we found a cat from clear over the other side of Allegany County, found it way up there on the mountain."

Marshall imagined the dogcatcher pointing and the woman

following the path of his finger. "That cat had got its foot stuck inside its collar. It was wedged so tight that the foot had actually attached itself to the chin—actually grew onto its jaw. And you know, the fact that the cat had its collar on, why we were able to locate the owners all the way up beyond Cumberland."

The woman was quiet.

"We all of us here love animals," the dogcatcher whispered. "I wouldn't have anyone work here who didn't." He might have been a father crooning a lullaby. "I can't tell you how many animals each of us has taken home because we couldn't bear to see them put down."

"I don't believe that about the paw growing to the chin," the woman said. "Even if I did, I'll tell you what. If it was me, I'd take my chances without the collar." Her voice grew scratchy, then cracked. "I'd take my chances."

"No need to— Here, now—"

A high, unworldly, strangled sound began then, drowning them out. It floated in from outside, too terrible to name. Marshall expected the receptionist to startle, to jump from her seat. She didn't even turn in its direction. He rose and followed the noise. He did not see the dogcatcher emerge from his office with his arm around a large, weeping woman. He did not notice the receptionist smile at them. Marshall was called by the sound. In a second the keening stopped, as horribly as it had begun.

He emerged into bright sunlight. The memory of the sound took him toward the outdoor runs. The barking dogs had fallen silent. They stood with their snouts pointed upward, sniffing the air. Beyond the runs, on the other side of the building, dozens of cats in their common outdoor cage froze like statues. Long seconds passed before anything moved.

The sound had come from a third cinderblock structure in the distance, not visible from the parking area or the office. It was a small windowless square about the size of a closet. A fat, uniformed woman emerged from behind it, walking fast.

"What was that?" Marshall asked.

Startled, the woman stopped and lifted a hand to her throat. Each ragged nail was rimmed with a dark line of dirt. He recognized her then as the one who'd given him the citations.

"What?" she asked.

"That sound. What was it?"

"We had a sick animal brought in. We had to put it down." She motioned toward the cinderblock square behind her.

The woman made as if to move beyond him. He stepped so as to block her way. "How?" he asked.

"I beg your pardon?"

"Gas? Injection? What?"

"It's an air-extraction chamber. It sucks out the air."

He did not move to let her around.

"It's a humane process," she said.

"It didn't sound humane."

"The dog was sick," the woman told him. She was sweating, a line of dampness across her pale forehead.

"No," Marshall said. He knew what he had heard. Not a yelp of pain. Not illness.

The woman began to fidget. She was coarse featured as well as overweight. Her skin was waxy. "It's unfortunate," she said. "We wish we didn't have to destroy any of them. But if there's no one to take care of them, they starve or get hit by cars." She fixed him with a stern expression he knew she had practiced. "You can't imagine what happens to some of them. This is better."

Marshall's attention went beyond her to the door of the death chamber. It was made of heavy steel, with no ornamentation or indentation, completely flat.

"I heard that sound before," he said.

"We have no choice," the woman told him.

"People make that sound, too. Right before dying. Not from a natural death." Marshall did not move. "I know what it is," he said.

In the sunlight, the woman's face froze into a stark mask of neutrality. "I'm sorry," she said.

"You think you're on a mission of mercy," Marshall told her, "but really you're on a mission of death."

The woman's expression remained blank. "You don't see the state we find them in," she said. "If you did, you wouldn't say that."

Sometimes Marshall repeated what he had heard before. He did not know he did this. He gestured toward the death chamber. "You really think it's better for them?" he asked. "I'll tell you what. If I were that dog, I'd rather take my chances."

It was evening before he got back. A thin scrim of clouds had drifted across the sky, but they hadn't made much dent in the heat. When he walked up the hill, he saw Ernie sitting on the steps of her porch. She wore a sweater over her blouse and hugged it to her chest.

"Been walking?" she asked.

"Went to animal control." He would not tell her about the summons.

"Getting a dog?" She knew he wasn't. She sounded out of breath.

"They're all the time playing kissy-kissy with those dogs

they're going to kill," Marshall told her. "All the time saying how much they love them."

"Bull." She took hold of the railing, pulled herself up, sighed.

"They got signs all over the place saying the problem is people don't get their animals fixed. I bet they don't spend one penny of their budget getting them fixed. Spend it all on killing them. How many you think they put down?"

"Couple thousand a year." Her words came in short little puffs.

"That many?"

"Maybe more."

Marshall thought of the pudgy woman in the uniform. "Humane. Shit."

Ernie stared beyond him at the mountain. The clouds drifted off and sun fell in a golden rectangle across the porch, but Marshall couldn't see her eyes. "I don't breathe very well, anymore, Marshall," she said. "I'm all the time thinking about breathing."

CHAPTER 9

If not for always thinking about her breathing, Ernie would never have listened to Veronica's plan. She hated the idea of going back to the doctor. But even more, she hated thinking about how she was going to draw her next breath, hated knowing that the main focus of her thoughts lately was how to make air move in and out of her chest. Above all, she hated knowing that living seventy years in this world hadn't made her a bit wiser or more confident, only more frightened. It seemed a long way to come for nothing.

So when Veronica suggested that Ernie allow Dr. Wilson to check her out again—after all, he hadn't seen her for months—and give her something to make her more comfortable, Ernie had to consider it. She had no wish to live as an invalid any sooner than she had to. She had a terror of ending up in some assisted-living prison or nursing home, under the control of strangers. If she had to be delivered into hands other than her own, Veronica's would do just fine. She'd make it as easy for her as she could. Ernie even imagined that seeing Dr. Wilson might in some way make Veronica a little less unhappy, the way coloring Ernie's hair and making her tea seemed to.

"Just a checkup," Ernie insisted. "No fancy tests." She didn't care what the genesis of her disease was or what they wanted to name it.

"Of course not," Veronica said mildly. "You only want some relief."

They seemed to understand each other. Ernie told her to set up the appointment.

By the end of the week, the doctor had prescribed oxygen in a portable tank with thin plastic tubes to carry it into Ernie's nose. She had no intention of using the contraption all the time, just when she was active. She also had medicine to keep her cough under control, though her lungs remained so sour and phlegmy that anything strenuous, even walking up the stairs, made her so breathless she had to stop two or three times. She could hardly put an unlit cigarette to her mouth anymore without feeling remorseful. And, sometimes, such a heavy veil of fatigue dropped over her that she felt separated from everything she needed to do.

Still, she was sure the oxygen would see her through these final days of harvesting and selling. It had to. While she still could, she made the necessary phone calls to get Simpson hired part-time at Valley Video, a store gradually losing business to movies-on-demand, but as yet open regular hours. Simpson worked evenings, giving her less time to spend with Owen Banner down by the barn. Then Owen started picking up Simpson from work and taking her to late dinners and movies in Hagerstown—and no doubt to his apartment—and bringing her in at all hours of the night. Veronica didn't seem to mind. Ernie supposed she shouldn't either.

"So you're dating now?" was all she said.

Simpson regarded Ernie with honest befuddlement. "Dating? You mean, are we going out? I haven't heard anyone call it 'dating' except on television."

"Going out, dating, whichever." Ernie was hurt, not to know the lingo, to be outdated, as it were—and to have her question dodged in the bargain. It was one of her cat-on-the-chest days, when she wanted more than anything to pluck the mantle of Simpson's youth and health and drape it over her own weary shoulders, just to remember what it was like. She forgave herself for that.

The Silver Queen corn was gone; late tomatoes remained, and winter squash and pumpkins. Then Veronica could clean up the garden and they'd be done. In the meantime, Simpson still loaded the van every morning and set up the vegetable stand, while Ernie and Lily candled Lily's eggs—an arrangement Lily accepted but resented, since she'd always before set out the vegetables herself. "Lord, girl, you done put that ratty-looking corn so it's first thing anybody sees," she'd grumble when she came down from the candling shack, or, "Lord, girl, them peaches has seen better days. You want to put me out of business?"

"What would you rather have in front?" Simpson would counter. "Those mushy old tomatoes?"

The two would snipe and parry, while Rita, tied nearby, watched with perked-up ears and wary eyes, terrified she'd have to defend her mistress. The poor dog flopped down and slept for an hour when Simpson finally drove off. Ernie kept out of it. How could she take sides between her best friend and the girl who chauffeured her everywhere? She wasn't sorry Lily found Simpson wanting. Someone had to. Not Ernie herself. Ernie wouldn't.

"Come on, girl, candle the eggs with us, I'll show you how

it's done," Lily demanded one day, enjoying as always the way Simpson bristled at being called "girl," when she so obviously considered herself a woman. With one quick flick of her wrist, Simpson caught the sweatshirt Lily threw to her and pulled it over a clingy T-shirt that left nothing to be imagined about her shapely breasts.

The candling shack, except for its new compressor, was the same shabby, refrigerated shed at the edge of Lily's yard that Ernie had first laid eyes on thirty years ago. She'd liked the place then and she still did. Cold air usually bothered her lungs, but in here the frigid breeze seemed to spur them into action, open the sluggish bronchi, let her breathe.

"The eggs come down this conveyor belt and in front of that bulb," Lily told Simpson when their eyes had adjusted to the dimness. "Look close and you can see if there's any blood spots inside." Passing the single point of light in the dark room, the shells grew so translucent that even the smallest imperfection inside showed up as a telltale black splotch. "Here, feed these eggs from the basket onto the belt." Lily guided Simpson into position. "I'll pull the bad ones off the line and Ernie will pack the good ones into cartons for the inspector." She threw the switch that made the ancient conveyor belt groan into action.

"Not very efficient," Simpson muttered.

"Maybe not. It's the same way they done it when Cain and Abel was still squabbling, but it don't cost hardly nothing and it still works. I reckon they got fancier methods on fancier farms."

Ernie wasn't sure if Simpson looked more irritated or more bored. The girl was probably thinking she could be setting up the vegetable stand now and then be out of there to take her swim. She couldn't be expected to appreciate that candling the eggs meant earning a carton of them to take home, with tiny blood spots that disqualified them for sale but were edible after Veronica cracked them open and picked out the bad spots. How else would they get such a bounty of free food?

Lily sorted eggs with the dexterity of a blackjack dealer. Ernie had seen her scratch, blow her nose, even crack her knuckles without missing a beat. Today, Lily looked up and impaled Simpson with a lengthy stare, while her hands worked on as if there were eyes in her fingertips. "How's your mama?" she demanded.

"Fine. You just saw her, didn't you? The other day?" Simpson sighed dramatically.

"Oh. Sure. Right." Lily was all innocence. "I spoke to her about what a good tan she got. A farmer's tan." She paused. "Not much of a farmer though."

"Now Lily—" Ernie began.

"Saw the remains of them collards she planted," Lily said. "One sorry sight."

"The soil wasn't right," Simpson said. "She didn't know. Everything else in the garden did fine."

"Natural for her to want collards," Lily said. "Everybody likes what they ate wherever they come from. Comfort food. Bet you miss collards, yourself."

"I never liked them."

"That don't mean your mama don't."

"She ate them now and then. They were never a staple of her diet. She's doing fine."

"Lord, yes." Lily lifted her hands from the belt, shook her fingers. "Doing tons better than when she first come here and wouldn't get out of bed."

"She's been out of bed now for a long time."

"Yes," Ernie felt the need to put in. "Veronica got out of bed and saved that garden from ruin. Nobody goes crazy working in a garden. Gardening's one of the great secrets of sanity."

Lily chuckled.

Simpson frowned. "If you think Mama's functioning only because you've got her weeding and hoeing, you're wrong. Mama isn't crazy. This is just a different life for her. She wanted a garden, but never had one. She always worked in stores. She's not some country-raised *farmer*." This with a poisoned glance at Lily. "She probably misses my dad. It's only natural."

"Sex." Lily plucked a bloody egg from the lineup. "She misses sex. Look at this." In front of the light, the egg was so opaque that the defect inside was not even a splotch of darkness, but a solid block of black. "Blood clear through. I'll give it to Rita." She set it into a basket. "Like I say, it's just sex. A woman that age, she gets addicted to it. Whether she likes the man or not."

Simpson dropped an egg onto the conveyor belt with such force that it cracked.

"Well, maybe I shouldn't of said that, being she's your mother, but it's true. She's not even forty. She'll grow out of it in another ten years or so."

"As if you're the expert. Who probably hasn't had sex for thirty years."

"I know about missing sex because of when Ronald died. I wasn't forty yet, myself."

Simpson opened her mouth to reply, then shut it.

"I remember real well," Lily went on. "Yup, an addiction all right. All them hot juices put you in a daze, sort of like a disease. Then zap, you go through the change and you come out of it." She winked in Ernie's direction and smiled a wide, lewd, deliberate grin that made her gold tooth flash, even in the dimness.

Simpson stopped working and wiped her hands on a rag. "Count me out of this conversation, will you?"

"You know it's true, girl. I mean, not about the change— you got a lifetime before all that happens to you. But about wanting sex. Missing it if you don't get it. Don't tell me you don't know."

Simpson flung the rag onto the conveyor belt. "I'll unload the vegetables and come back for you later," she told Ernie. She slammed out so fast that a brief hot beam of sunlight shot in and disappeared like a mirage, plunging Ernie and Lily into darkness, broken at first only by the sharp crack of their laughter.

Ten minutes later, the two women were sitting in their folding chairs at the vegetable stand, in front of piles of produce Simpson had thrown haphazardly on the tables before making what must have been a quick departure. "Coward," Lily said. "She was afraid to face me."

"Probably afraid she'd pound you to smithereens."

"And then get eaten by Rita." Lily stroked the gentle dog's decidedly ungentle face, tracing the dark stripe that ran down the length of her long snout, like a thin dusting of soil atop snow.

"In a fair fight, I'd bet on Simpson," Ernie told her.

"Against a vicious beast like Rita?"

"Vicious, my ass." Ernie grunted dissent as she shoved her oxygen paraphernalia under the table. No one in their right mind would buy fresh, health-giving foods from a person who looked as if she might expire while making change.

The first customer drove up just as Ernie finished. Sovereign County was such a tiny, unnecessary county, tucked so shamelessly into the narrow neck of Maryland, just below the Mason-Dixon Line, that you could walk through it in a few hours to West Virginia on the south or Pennsylvania on the north, a feat Ernie and Knox had once accomplished, just to say they had. Then, as now, Lily's stand had been in the strategic location that forced every local farmer to sell at her place instead of their own, at the crossroads visible to every car heading east to Hagerstown, west to Cumberland, or north or south to a neighboring state. The stand had been busy even before the coming of the ski resort and antique hunters and expatriates from Baltimore and D.C.

For the first hour, Ernie didn't miss the steady, automatic puff of oxygen the hidden container might have provided. She bagged so many bushels of apples and weighed so many pounds of acorn squash that she didn't have time to note when she grew winded, or even that it was getting worse. But by the time Simpson returned at noon, Ernie was so breathless and anxious that her every inhalation was a yawn or a sigh, and she had forgotten completely the fun she and Lily had had at the girl's expense. With a kind of mute gratitude she wouldn't have expected from herself, she let Simpson hook up her oxygen, while she fought a fog of exhaustion so thick she was afraid she wouldn't be able to stay awake long enough to get into the van.

So it was as if from a distance that Simpson's voice came to her as they drove, and only gradually that she realized the girl was still fuming.

"You know what I don't understand?" she spat. "I don't understand how you and Lily can be such good friends. You talk like someone who had a decent education. Lily talks like a hick. She doesn't know when to back off. I don't see what you two have in common."

"Thirty years of living out here and growing vegetables, for one thing."

"She talks like she never even learned to read."

"She reads."

"You know what I mean."

Wrenched from the comfort of her half sleep, Ernie said, "Most country people talk exactly like city people. Knox did. Lily would, too, if she didn't work at keeping her accent." She stopped, waited for air. "Lily just knows people from the city like their peasants to sound earthy."

"Oh, I see. The best vegetables are grown by people who talk rough as the soil."

"Something like that." Ernie didn't add that Lily had nearly had her gold eyetooth cap replaced with a white one once, and then decided against it because of what she judged she'd lose in sales.

"She's run that farm solo ever since Ronald died," Ernie said. "Chickens are a nasty business to begin with." A yawn, a long sigh. "She's not as dumb as you think."

Simpson squeezed her full lips into such a narrow line that Ernie felt there was no point pursuing this, though she would have liked to. Thirty years ago, she'd been a newlywed in a strange place, come to live with a man she loved and an eleven-year-old boy she didn't. Thirty years ago, Lily was the one who'd welcomed her by saying Knox's son, Kevin, was a little brat, sparing Ernie from having to entertain that idea all by herself. And later, after Kevin was killed, it was Lily who said, "Lord, forgive me, I never meant my thoughts about him being bratty would be a curse." It was a statement that left Ernie feeling absolved for her own dislike of the boy. Who knew what harm you truly wished a person you didn't like? Who could live with having their darkest wishes granted if they didn't know their friends were harboring those same notions themselves?

But Simpson's dislike for Lily was so palpable that she would have no appreciation of this story, no more than she had for the woman herself. Ernie was fully awake now. It galled her to let Simpson dismiss a thirty-year relationship so easily. She and Lily had their ups and downs, and sometimes Ernie hated the way Lily would lord it over people who sold produce at her stand, but lately Lily was the only one who could make her laugh. It occurred to Ernie that she wouldn't mind shaking Simpson out of her complacency. It occurred to her that now was the moment to bring up a subject that had been on her mind for weeks. "It's time," she told the girl abruptly, "for you to learn to become a dowser."

"A dowser!" Simpson jerked the wheel and skidded around a curve.

"Hey, take it easy!"

"What makes you think I want to become a dowser?"

"I've had three calls asking me to spot wells. I don't feel up to it. We need the money."

"I thought you didn't take money for it."

"I don't. Some people do. *You* could."

Another curve loomed ahead. Ernie braced. Simpson slowed down. "Ernie, I don't believe in dowsing. It makes no sense to me."

"Don't believe water has a draw for people? What about those wells I spot for Buck, and the water turns out to be right underneath where I said? What about your mother forever staring east, like if she looks hard enough she'll get a glimpse of the ocean?"

"Then teach my mother to be a dowser. It's something she ought to be good at."

"I need her in the garden."

"It doesn't take all day to weed a garden and straighten the house. I'm the one who drives you around and then goes to a job."

"Huh," Ernie huffed. "How many videos do you rent in one evening? They're doing you a favor letting you work any hours at all."

"I'll get some other job, then. Not dowsing. You can't learn to do something you don't believe in."

"Anybody can learn."

Simpson lifted her hands from the wheel in a gesture of disbelief, then dropped them back. "First it was a man had to teach a woman or vice versa. Then it was only the ones who have the gift. Now anybody can learn no matter who teaches them?"

"More or less." In fact, Ernie wasn't sure about this. "The pay is better than you think," she said.

"How much?"

"A couple days' salary at the video store."

Simpson pressed her foot on the gas. She did not say no. Ernie closed her eyes and drifted into the sweet motion of the car, and slept all the rest of the way home.

Simpson would have taken a harder line except for Ernie's pallor. Beneath the old woman's touched-up silvery mane, beneath her speckled skin a dozen shades of brown and pink from the sun, she looked just awful. Maybe Simpson should have kept quiet about Lily. Maybe she should have picked up Ernie earlier. Back at the house, Ernie took two bites of the gazpacho Veronica had prepared for lunch, then excused herself and slept for two hours on the lumpy living-room couch. Simpson hoped Ernie would forget about dowsing by the time she woke up, but she didn't. Ernie's first conscious act was to flip through the neat files Simpson had created and hand her an article that said dowsing had been an accepted practice for at least eight thousand years.

"Eight thousand years!" Ernie exclaimed. "We know because somebody painted a picture of a dowser on the wall of an African cave. And it goes even further back than that." Excitement brought a flush of pink to Ernie's face. "In the Bible, Moses strikes his rod on a rock and water gushes forth."

"*All right,*" Simpson said. "One try. I'm serious. Not ten. Not two."

"Deal," Ernie told her, and gathered up her oxygen canister and marched outside.

Ten minutes later, Simpson found herself holding out the forked twig that Ernie had instructed her to cut from a wild cherry tree. Simpson's hands were sweating. It wasn't even hot.

"Relax," Ernie said. "You're going to strangle it." Taking the sprout from Simpson, she turned her palms face up and made loose fists over the ends of the forked branch. "Like this." She handed the limb back to Simpson.

"This feels weird."

"You'll get used to it." She walked beside Simpson, rolling the oxygen behind her across the grass, its transparent tubes snaking out and up toward her nose.

"What's wrong with holding the branch the other way?"

"Probably nothing."

"Then why—?"

"I don't know. That's how Knox taught me, is all. Just walk. This is not some satanic rite."

Simpson wasn't so sure of that. As she walked away from Ernie into the yard, two of the usually wary cats threaded around her feet, rubbed at her ankles, nearly tripped her. She held to the sprout for dear life.

"Wait a second," Ernie called. "You're choking it again."

Simpson stopped. She'd failed. It was over.

It wasn't. Ernie caught up with her and reached out. "Give me one end. You hang on to the other." Now that the old woman had napped, she no longer looked as sickly as she had earlier. She looked as if she could keep this up all afternoon. Ernie took one branch of the stick from Simpson and kicked at the cats, who scattered. "We'll go this way."

They walked side by side, nearly touching. Considering her youth and health, Simpson assumed she'd be the one to set the pace, but it seemed to her that she was drawing energy from Ernie. She fought the urge to break away and flee. They weren't doing anything, after all, but walking across a yard she traversed at least two or three times a day.

This is perfectly ordinary, she reminded herself. Perfectly fine. *Relax.* Dowsing is hokey, anyway. Her mind began to lodge on this, to slip beyond her own reticence. This wasn't so bad.

Then the stick began to bend.

Simpson was so startled she would have dropped it if she could. She felt the pull the way she might have felt electric current. Invisible, undeniable. Magnetic. She and Ernie both held on.

The stick tried to point straight downward; it might have

had its own will. Such a frail, green portion of stick that you would not imagine the force of the pull could make its bark begin to peel off as it did.

Ernie took another step forward, dragging the oxygen and Simpson with her. As suddenly as it had started, the downward thrust stopped.

"See? You can't be next to the vein of water, you have to be right over it. Even an inch or two away from it, there's no pull." She sounded satisfied. "Now you try it yourself."

"What?"

"Try it yourself. I've been over this yard a thousand times. I know where the water is already."

Simpson meant to protest. Instead, with her empty hand, she grasped the end of the stick Ernie had dropped. She walked over the water vein again. Nothing.

"Once more."

She did as she was told. The branch stayed steady. The electric current must have come from Ernie.

"It gets easier. Try again."

It didn't get easier.

"I didn't believe in this myself, once. I believed in facts."

Simpson dropped her arms, but Ernie motioned her to continue. "I didn't believe you had to plant leaf crops in the light of the moon, either," she said. "But it works. Maybe that's why your mother's collards died."

"I thought the soil was wrong."

"That, too." Ernie reached toward her mouth with a languid hand, as if to puff on a cigarette, then must have realized she didn't have one. "Scientists say something doesn't exist and then they find an explanation for it and suddenly it does exist. But really it was there all the time."

Simpson lowered her arms, let the limb dangle from her hand. If Ernie was right, she didn't want to know. "I can't do this, Ernie," she said.

Ernie hated the way the girl looked at her then. As if seeing right to the heart of her and deciding she was a fake, not just about dowsing, which she was damned good at, but about everything else, too. Fake farm wife because she'd never raised a single animal, but only grown a kitchen garden…fake reporter because she'd never done more than write obituaries for the *County Crier*, which let's face it had been more of a shopper than a newspaper…fake… Then it occurred to her, Simpson didn't know or care if Ernie had ever raised a farm animal or done any of the rest of it. Simpson plain didn't care. It wasn't the girl saying, Fake! Fraud! Charlatan! It was Ernie herself. And there was no time to fix any of it—unless maybe she could stop Simpson from casting the stick away as she was about to do. "Try one more time!" Ernie yelled.

The girl stopped and turned back toward Ernie. For one luminous second, Ernie remembered how Knox had taught her to dowse on an afternoon not unlike this one—an event no more logical than her falling in love, at age forty, with a man who lived on a farm in the middle of nowhere…a man who came into the office to place an ad in the *County Crier*, moving with such effortless grace that Ernie couldn't refuse when he asked her to go out with him for a drink.

Simpson came toward her slowly, the branch limp in her hand, her expression slightly slack and stupid.

"Try one more time," Ernie said again, pointing toward the wide vein of water that ran beside the cornfield. Simpson seemed too listless to protest. Ernie didn't feel sorry for her.

Simpson was young and wanted to be practical, but there was nothing practical about the way she and Owen Banner sniffed around each other or the way she reacted when Lily talked about sex. Logic did not explain the important things. It hadn't for Ernie and wouldn't for Simpson. The girl would be a dowser yet.

CHAPTER 10

The first time Veronica had laid eyes on Guy Legacy was the cold, late-January day he came to the Long house, the home of her eighth and final foster family, to repair a cabinet in the kitchen. The evening before, Elaine Long, who took in foster children for money, had brought home a stale, day-old cake from the grocery store, on which she'd written in colored icing Happy 17th, Veronica. The half they hadn't eaten at dinner—the half with the writing—sat on the Formica counter where Guy had seen it, covered loosely with plastic wrap, a few burnt-down candles still poking out of the icing.

"You must be Veronica," Guy had said, when the sound of hammering drew her into the kitchen.

She'd been startled to find such a beautiful, muscular boy there—well, a man, really—and not old Johnny, who usually did the repairs. "Veronica. That's me."

He'd given her such a slow, easy smile that her heart had stopped for moment, and she'd put her hand to her throat to make sure the pulse had started again.

"Aquarius," Guy said.

"Pardon?"

"Born under the sign of Aquarius, the water bearer. Aquarians like to live near the water."

"Don't I wish." She vaguely recalled a house near the ocean and the man who may have been her father. She remembered a trip with her mother away from that house and far into the country, where the hills rolled so high you couldn't see from the one to the other, and you couldn't hear the sound of the ocean no matter how hard you trained your ears. That was the beginning of the sadness, the inland towns, the foster homes.

Then Guy had appeared in Elaine Long's kitchen, his winter-pale biceps nearly bursting the seams of his too-thin T-shirt, and he had been all the sweetness a girl of seventeen could stand. Watching him that first day in the kitchen, Veronica had felt so light-headed she'd had to place a hand for balance onto the white enamel edge of the stove. She'd held herself up that way the whole time they talked. Later, after Guy had left with a promise to return, Veronica had finally lifted her hand from the stove, only to see the whirled splotch of her fingerprints permanently etched into the whiteness, burned there for all the world to see.

Guy laughed when she told him that later. He said it couldn't possibly be true, Veronica was talking about temperatures in the range of spontaneous combustion and lookee here, she hadn't combusted after all, she was right here in front of him, he would prove it by tickling her ribs until she laughed and begged him to stop and admitted that everything he said was true.

But that imprint of her fingers was what Veronica remembered.

Guy made her finish high school before he took her off to the ocean. He intended to stay by the sea the rest of his days, he said, now that he'd found what he was looking for, inland. He persuaded her case worker that someone ought to sign the papers to let Veronica marry him once she was out of school, given that she was still underage. Only Billie, one of the Long's other foster children, came to the courthouse for the wedding. Elaine must not have seen the point, now that she'd be losing the income Veronica brought in.

So the newlyweds moved to the seaside, where Veronica thought they would settle down. They swam every day after work, then went home from the beach and made love. Veronica was amazed that pleasure could start so specifically in one place and then spread out in such powerful waves that it was like riding the crest of a swell, until she was not just *in* the ocean, she *was* the ocean. It was the happiest summer of her life.

Sometimes, they forgot to eat until night fell and their stomachs growled with real hunger. Then they cooked the most wonderful dishes: omelets with fresh tomatoes and spinach, fish from the seafood market, cheese toast when they were too tired to think of anything else. It was all delicious, the best food they'd eaten in their lives. Veronica's brittle, ever-splitting fingernails grew long for the first time in her life. Her dry skin grew silky. When fall came and Guy wanted to move farther south, Veronica didn't think a thing about it because she'd been selling T-shirts anyway and could do that anywhere.

From that sweet beginning, how had they gotten to where they ended up? How had she gotten so tired that all she wanted to do was sleep, or at least languish among a stack of magazines, in the confused days before yet another move? How had they gotten to Beaufort, all cross-purposes? After so many years of easy chatter, how had they gotten to the place where a silence lay between them even when they were talking—

maybe especially then? Guy would be in the middle of answering some question Veronica had thought to ask about his day and she'd already be thinking, *Good Lord, what am I gonna ask him next,* terrified she wouldn't be able to think of anything and she would smother under the blanket of his silence.

Veronica had known for some time that the family she dreamed about every night in Maryland was her own family, years ago—the Legacys, jumping the breakers, happy as whales. She knew the reason she couldn't reach them no matter how fast she ran was that they didn't exist anymore. They weren't happy and they weren't a family, except in the dream. She'd known that since the day she'd found herself trying to reach Guy by phone.

What she didn't know, until the night of the storm, was the other thing.

The dream was different that night. She wasn't sure why. It started, as always, in the ocean under a moonlit sky. She was farther out than usual. As sometimes happened, the night sea frightened her, gave her a little shiver of fear. Then Guy touched her arm. It pleased her to see he was right beside her. He'd been there all the time. They floated together on the swells. After a while, he began to do the strong crawl he'd learned as a child, heading straight out to sea. He beckoned Veronica to follow. She started to call him back, but a splash of water poured into her mouth, and she spit and tasted salt. She paddled in his direction, but he was too fast for her. He was gone. The sound of the ocean was loud. She opened her eyes. Her face was wet, and the sound was not the sea, but rain, and the salt she tasted was tears.

She wiped her face and sat up in bed. Outside, the rain pounded, and inside her head the dream was very clear. The real reason she'd left Guy, she saw now, was not because of his wanderlust or his refusal to settle down, or even to make a stable home for Simpson—though that was part of it. No: the main reason was that she didn't want Guy to be the one to swim away. If she made a preemptive strike so he couldn't find her, even if he tried, he wouldn't have that chance. Veronica had left because after the terrible year they'd had together in Beaufort, with him aching to get moving every second of the day, she was afraid he wasn't coming back.

She had abandoned him. To save face.

She wept, not just because she missed him, but because she had done him wrong. You did not abandon someone you had lived with more than half your life, no matter how inconsiderate they'd been. It was mean. You did not abandon the people you loved.

"Veronica!" Ernie's voice rasped from down the hallway. "I think we need the buckets."

"What?" Veronica wiped the tears away, blew her nose.

"When it comes down like this, it comes in. The buckets are in the basement."

"Just let me get dressed and I'll get them."

"I'd get them now."

"Where's Simpson?"

"Still at the barn feeding the cats." Ernie appeared in Veronica's doorway, pulling her oxygen tank with one hand, clutching her terry bathrobe to her chest with the other. The set of her expression said she was angry, but not at Veronica. Ernie wore the furious pallor of helplessness, of someone no longer able to get the buckets herself, no longer able to stop the gray, insistent tap of rain from coming into her own house.

Quickly, Veronica fetched the buckets from the basement

and placed them where the old woman instructed—"Just to the right of the bed in Simpson's room. At the foot of the bed in mine. In the hallway at the top of the stairs. And next to the toilet in the bathroom. Your room doesn't leak. It's the only one."

A minute later, Simpson returned to the house soaked and breathless from a fast dash from the barn. The wind shrieked. With a loud bang, it tore Ernie's planter boxes off the upstairs front of the house and flung shreds of pink geraniums all over the yard. By the time it was over, it had dumped three inches of rain on Whisper Springs and flooded some of the roads. Inside, each of the buckets had been emptied several times, and the yellowed wet spots on the ceilings, to which Veronica had paid no attention before, were sagging so badly she feared they might cave in. She pulled down the rickety wooden ladder to the attic and went up to investigate. Most of the floorboards were rotted. The insulation was lumped into a nasty pink mat. In one spot, the hole in the roof was so obvious that, if Veronica squinted, she could see out to the clearing sky.

"This is no new leak, Ernie," she called down.

"Understatement of the year."

"If you knew, why didn't you have it fixed?" Veronica descended the ladder and faced Ernie on the landing.

"Marshall's patched it for me a couple of times. It's to the point I need a whole new roof. They're expensive."

"I imagine so." Veronica knew nothing about house repairs. She and Guy had never owned anything but a truck, a car, some tools, and their TV and clothes. Guy said he wouldn't own a house if you paid him, would never play Harry Homeowner after working construction all day. But what did you do about a leaking roof if you were stuck with one, and you were broke?

Simpson was the one who had alerted Veronica to this. She'd tackled Ernie's finances with the same gusto she'd applied to sorting Ernie's papers. "Her Social Security barely pays the monthly bills, Mama," she'd explained. Most of the money and land Knox had left her had been spent or sold. And now, it appeared, she could not afford to fix her roof.

"Or the furnace, either," Ernie confessed.

"The furnace!" Veronica exclaimed.

"It's not so bad. Last winter I just bundled up."

"In your condition! Just bundled up!"

"I'm still here. The house is still standing."

"Why didn't you tell me? Why am I spending my time hoeing your garden when I could be working?"

"Doing what?" Ernie narrowed her eyes. "What will pay you more than the garden brings in at this time of year?"

Just about anything, Veronica thought. But then who would cook the meals, tend to the house, check Ernie's breathing and fill her prescriptions? "Simpson can work full-time, too."

"Not in Whisper Springs. There's no jobs here. Not in summer. She's lucky to be at the video store part-time. Besides, I thought you wanted her to go to college."

"That can wait." Veronica could feel her heart squeeze at the sound of these words. From the moment they'd arrived and gotten settled, she'd vowed that eventually they'd establish Maryland residency so Simpson could continue her education. The idea of Simpson going to the University of Maryland four full years, or even taking courses at Hagerstown Community College for two, pleased her enormously. Even an associate's degree might keep the girl from working in cheap T-shirt shops on the southeastern coast as Veronica had done.

Ernie sighed, forcing air into her lungs and hugging herself against the damp. "The buckets aren't so bad. It could be worse."

Veronica didn't think so. She was so shocked, so muddled, that she began to shiver as if the breeze coming through the window were the dark wind of despair. Then something occurred to her. She was not helpless. She had something valuable to offer. It had been bad enough to leave Guy to save face. It would be worse to abandon Ernie.

The salesman at Whisper Springs Motors, east of town on the old road to Hagerstown, quoted her such a low figure that she wasn't sure she'd heard right. She made a strangled sound she tried to pass off as laughter.

"Lady, you think you know what the car is worth just because it's a Mercedes, but you don't. Believe me, this is the best I can do. Even then, I'm being generous."

"Generous!"

"More than generous." He looked pointedly at his watch, though it was only three in the afternoon. "Take it or leave it," he threatened.

Veronica walked out.

When she got home, she told Ernie what she was planning to do. "With you not driving much anymore, there's no reason we can't all share the van. None of us need a Mercedes."

Ernie said Chester Vaughn had always been a crook. It was a good thing Veronica hadn't dealt with him. The place to go was to that dealership where Lily's daughter had bought her car, from the fellow just over the river in Martinsburg.

"You mean in West Virginia?"

"Sure. It's not far."

The Martinsburg salesman introduced himself as Ed, smiled

winningly, and examined the car closely, like a doctor trying to rule out a fatal disease.

"She's pretty," he admitted finally.

"She is."

"But high miles. Anything over two hundred thousand, we consider it high."

"It runs like a dream."

"These cars usually do," he agreed. "Did you bring your service records?"

"It never had any service to speak of. I mean, no problems. Just the usual oil changes and stuff." She didn't add that a person who moved several times a year had every square inch of the car filled with possessions on each trip, everything from an old TV set to bottles of aspirin to ward off a migraine, each of them far more important than nine years worth of service records.

"I can't offer you as much if you don't have your service records," Ed said. A dank smell of tar rose from the hot blacktop as he squinted at the sleek navy exterior of the Mercedes, the creamy palomino leather interior. The car looked so appealing, she was sure the threat about service records was a bluff.

She'd always known the Mercedes was worth a fortune. She wanted at least enough to pay for Ernie's roof. They'd worry about the furnace later. By then the garden chores would be finished for the winter and she would have a real job.

Ed lowered his voice and spoke with what sounded like kindness. "If we can make a deal, I'll drive you back home myself," he said. "But book value's not that high. And with no service records…" He let his voice trail off.

"How much?" she whispered.

They negotiated for another half hour, but in the end, she

saw she had no choice. When she signed the contract, her hand was steady. She was doing the right thing. But in her mouth, even as she accepted the check, there was a tinny taste of fear, as if she'd been sucking on her keys.

CHAPTER 11

Owen was drunk, but not as drunk as his roommate, Cappy, and not nearly as drunk as Simpson. The plan had been to spend the day at Greenbrier State Park outside of Hagerstown, where they would picnic and swim. But Cappy's girlfriend, Rae, was sick when they reached her house, so instead of going to the park, Cappy drove them to this fallow field—why this particular field, Owen wasn't sure or pleased, but didn't want to draw attention to the fact by asking. In the shade of the bordering hickory trees, they ate the lunch Simpson had packed and started on the screwdrivers Cappy had brought in his cooler.

Always a loquacious drunk, Cappy couldn't stop talking. He talked about his brother in real estate, his sister in college, and when he'd exhausted those topics went on to the Grand Scheme, about which Owen had already heard too much. "The Grand Scheme?" Simpson asked, eyes wide with mock—Owen hoped it was mock—fascination.

"Extremely grand. *Beyond* grand." Cappy leaned over to refill her paper cup. "I was planning to go to law school, should have done it before I got stuck selling computers—" this with a hooded glance at Owen, who *enjoyed* selling computers "—but I didn't take the entrance exams. The— Bear with me here. The L-Sats? L-Cats?" He grinned at not being able to remember.

"L-Cats." Simpson giggled. "Like the A-Cats and B-Cats we have in large numbers at Ernie's farm." She slipped off a sandal and put her foot on Owen's, allowing Cappy a view of her sleek, tanned leg. She recited the alphabet of C-Cats and D-Cats all the way to L.

"No M-Cats?" Cappy asked.

Simpson caressed Owen's ankle bone with her toes. She laughed mindlessly.

"What he means," Owen said sternly, "is that you take the M-Cats before you apply to medical school."

"Right." Cappy pointed to Owen. "I mean what he says."

Owen's irritation wasn't quite strong enough to cancel out the mellowness of the liquor. He didn't think Simpson was interested in Cappy. He thought she was punishing Owen for not taking her to bed. *The best-laid plans*, he thought. If he'd been a little drunker, he would have carried her off.

Or maybe not.

This felt like it had been going on forever.

More than a month ago, they'd finally jumped the no-touch barrier that had paralyzed them during those first weeks, when they were meeting at the barn. Then they'd decided not to "consummate our relationship," was the way they had put it, until Cappy went away to a wedding he had to attend, and they had Owen's apartment to themselves. No fumbling around in the barn ("Oh Lord, think of it, we could literally have a roll in the hay"), although Owen had hidden a soft blanket there, just in case. No awkward tangling in the back of a car. No tryst in silence in Owen's room with its paper-thin walls. No! In anticipation of the time they'd have together soon, they had clung to each other like teenagers (Simpson *was* a teenager for a few more months, Owen had reminded himself), clutched at body parts, held on until Cappy's planned departure. They were cautious, practical, sensible even about sex.

Cappy's cousin was getting married in Atlanta. He was to have been gone for three days. As Owen bent to unlock the door the evening of Cappy's scheduled departure, Simpson was so agitated that she giggled, which was so unlike her he knew how nervous she was, and whispered, "My blood feels so fizzy I might as well have champagne running through my veins."

"Stick with me, woman. It gets better." Owen opened the door.

Cappy lay on the couch, his head atop a cloud of pillows. Rae dropped an afghan over his legs. "I know it's summer, but I think he has the flu."

Cappy sneezed.

Back out in the hallway after their hasty retreat, Simpson said in a wry tone, "I guess the oldest living virgin from the Carolinas doesn't get to be deflowered tonight after all."

"Your virginity. Don't you wish."

"Oh, sure. Desperately." Her voice was so high and false that all at once Owen understood she actually *was* a virgin and hadn't wanted him to know. He rejected the idea of taking her to a hotel. It seemed too sleazy. They ended up doing nothing.

Except for their maddening craving and clinging, they'd done nothing ever since.

Two days after that first fateful night, Owen came down with Cappy's virus. He wouldn't let Simpson visit. Flu wasn't romantic, he said. Simpson got it anyway. Between the two of them, they were laid up for weeks. "Is this the Fates playing with us, or what?" On the phone, she sounded nasal and feverish. He had had the sense they were waiting for something, adhering to some skewed vow of abstinence neither of them remembered taking.

Maybe, at the moment, they were simply waiting for Cappy to pass out here under the hickory tree and leave them alone.

Owen wished he were drunker.

Cappy threw back the last of his drink. "Heard Ernie tried to get you spotting wells," he said to Simpson.

"She tried to teach me dowsing." Simpson's lips curved into a long, lazy smile. "I was a failure."

Oh, she was drunk! She must be. Failure was not a word she usually applied to herself, not a word she allowed. Right now it almost made her laugh. If she was going to fail at something, let it be dowsing! Raise our cups, make a toast. "That's me," she said. "Simpson Legacy, failed dowser." She let *failed* rest for a moment on her tongue.

Owen scowled, but Cappy appreciated her humor. Simpson had no great fondness for Cappy, but today she didn't mind his sunny russet-haired looks against Owen's gray-eyed stormy ones, or the way Cappy regarded her as if she were a ripe apple begging to be plucked from a tree.

An apple begging to be plucked! What a notion. Oh, she liked the way this vodka made her feel. Two years ago, she'd sampled every alcoholic beverage she could get her hands on, to help her forget she was the oldest high-school junior she knew. She couldn't stand the taste of her father's beer. Her mother's wine gave her a headache. Bourbon upset her stomach. Gin made her so dizzy she had to hang one foot over the side of her bed and let it touch the floor, just to keep the room from spinning. But vodka, even a lot of it, gave her only this warm buzz, this glow from the inside out.

"Now, how do we know you were really a failure, Simpson?" Cappy asked. "How do we know you're not just putting us on?" His head bobbed a little. He'd begun to slur his words. "I see you as a person who can do anything she has a mind to."

"Trust me, Cappy. In my hands, a twig is just a twig, not a magic wand. The day of my dowsing lesson, it wouldn't do a damned thing, unless Ernie had hold of it, too." The memory seemed funny now, drunk as she was. At the time, standing in front of the house with that ridiculous forked branch, she'd felt as queasy as she would have if she'd had to hold a séance. The yard on all sides of her had been so still and dry, it couldn't possibly hold water, even underneath. She'd tried to picture underground streams running through rocks, a labyrinth of waterways connected at once to the mountains in the near distance and the Carolina shore she'd come from, hundreds of miles away. "There's water under there, you just have to sense it," Ernie had kept insisting. But Simpson couldn't, or wouldn't, and finally Ernie had let her be.

"Well, I'm not sure I believe you." Cappy waved his cup in her direction. "You better give us a demonshra—" He struggled to get his tongue around the word. "A demonstration."

"In your next life, maybe," she said.

"C'mon, Simpson," Cappy said. "You scared?"

Owen leaned his head against the gnarled bark of the hickory tree they were sitting under and closed his eyes to slits. He reached his hand down to squeeze Simpson's foot. "Sure, show us Ernie's technique." She couldn't tell if he was being sweet or daring her.

Well, either way, why not? It was a game; they had all afternoon; her head was swimmy and warm. "I need a forked stick." She listened to her own voice, nearly as thick and slurry as Cappy's. Pleasant. When she brushed off her lap and stood, a kind of singing started in her head.

Cappy pointed to a little forked twig on a sapling that grew nearby. "What about that?" She nodded and he rose unsteadily to cut it with a knife from the picnic basket. The way he stared at her made her aware of her breasts pushing against her T-shirt, her shorts hugging her legs, the bareness of her feet as she pushed them into her sandals. His look made her feel satisfied with herself, the way women are when they are drunk and desired.

In front of them, the field was overgrown but not high. Its lush summer growth had been bush-hogged a few weeks before. Now, much as it tried to resume its rampant progress toward wilderness, it was too late. The short, sweet season of green was waning; already the season of yellowing had begun. A little wobbly, Simpson held the stick out and walked.

The hickories they'd picnicked under were at the top of a rise. Below was an unkempt field, not fit for cultivation, rocky and bumpy and steep, dipping to a draw thick with locust trees. Beneath the locusts, dogwoods grew in an oval, so neat they looked as if they'd been planted. Simpson listened to the singing in her head as she moved forward—a drunken singing to go with her drunken weaving as she propelled herself down the hill toward the dogwoods.

This was not the way she'd felt at Ernie's. Then there'd been sweat under her arms and a worm of nerves in her belly. This was better, shuffling through the undergrowth with singing in her head, more like a calling. She felt detached, almost asleep. Under the dogwoods, under the overhanging locusts, that's where she was going. Toward the cool, cool shade.

She wasn't sweating, wasn't even hot, so she didn't expect the shade to call her so strongly. She hardly noticed the snap of burrs against her legs, the hum of insects. Then she was under the locusts and the stick was bending, almost jumping out of her hand. The electric buzz she'd felt in Ernie's hand was in her own hand, so strong that she would have been frightened if she hadn't been so full of vodka, so sure of herself and warm. Her dreaminess wrapped over her like mist. She might have been in a trance, given that the stick was dipping so hard. See? See?

Then Owen loomed in front of her, big and angry. He snatched the stick away.

"That's not funny, Simpson. Not even close."

"What?" A storm brewing in his eyes. A spell ending. Confusion.

Cappy came into her line of sight then. Put his hand on Owen's shoulder. "Take it easy, man. Somebody must have told her."

Owen shook free.

"Told me what?" Simpson asked.

"About the car."

"What?"

"Don't act like you don't know," Owen said.

His voice harsh. His face tight as a block of wood. Simpson was suddenly so sober and heavy that her eyes ached, way back behind the eyeball. She wanted an aspirin. "What car?" she asked Owen, who was already walking off. "Know about *what*?"

Ernie watched Owen drop Simpson off. He drove away so fast that she let Simpson sit on the porch nearly an hour before she went out to her. By then she'd decided it wasn't normal, her sitting on the steps more statuelike than the recumbent cats, except for her right hand peeling paint chips from the post. If she didn't want company, she could damn well go sulk in her room. That kind of stillness in a girl of nineteen was too unnatural to let be.

Simpson didn't turn when Ernie came out. She was staring beyond the overhang of the porch, into glittery air, darkened in the distance by a gathering of storm clouds that gave a mournful, eerie quality to the light.

"What's wrong?" Ernie asked.

"What's down in the field? The one with the dogwoods." Simpson pointed in the general direction.

"Where's your mother?" Ernie asked.

"How should I know?"

"Probably in town looking for work," Ernie muttered. Veronica wanted a part-time job to go along with finishing up in the garden and managing the house. The money from the Mercedes was nearly gone, what with the cost of fixing the roof and the furnace.

"The field," Simpson persisted.

Ernie clung tight to her oxygen tank. Seeing no alternative, she said bluntly, "There's a car buried there." Inside her chest, the phlegm slithered around like a snake.

Simpson's eyes, usually a soft hazel, were hard now. "That's what Owen said."

"It was one of those old farm cars with no tags on it. Old junkers. Everybody had them. To use in the fields."

Simpson squinted at Ernie as if the sun were in her eyes.

"It's the car Knox's son, Kevin, was in when he died," Ernie explained. "It was the car Kevin got killed in."

Simpson averted her eyes. She examined a long strip of

paint she'd peeled from the post and thrown onto the porch. She seemed to be holding her breath. "That car is buried there," she repeated finally, as if not quite able to grasp Ernie's meaning.

"Kevin was driving it." Ernie made it sound as if this would explain something.

"I thought he was only eleven."

"That field was never any good for planting. Too hilly, and with all those rock outcroppings. I don't think they even used it to graze cattle. It was mainly a place the kids took those old junkers." Ernie inhaled as deep as she could.

"An eleven-year-old? Driving?" Simpson's voice grew shrill.

"He wasn't by himself. He was with an older boy. A boy of fifteen. The other boy was always good with equipment. Not just cars, any kind of machines. He helped his folks on their farm and he worked part-time for a backhoe contractor. That was how good he was." Ernie was reciting a tale. It had been in her head so long it wasn't hard to say out loud. "That boy could operate any kind of equipment. A front-end loader. A baler. Anything."

"If he was fifteen, he wouldn't have had a license, either."

"No." Ernie listened to the puffs of air spewing out of her oxygen tank; regular, like a heartbeat. "Nobody cared about having a license. People did what made sense to them. Not necessarily what was the law."

"I see."

"The kids liked to race those old cars up and down the hills on that field. It wasn't all that dangerous. Most of those kids were used to driving some kind of machinery or vehicle from the time their feet could reach the pedals. They'd help out with the baling and such." The oxygen puffed into her, making a coldness at the back of her throat. "Knox wouldn't let Kevin go out joyriding. He told him two or three times. But Kevin was a wild kid. Anything you told him not to do, he'd do it." She did not mean to sound callous, but this was true. "Kevin probably talked the other boy into letting him drive. He was probably showing off, trying to impress the big kid."

Simpson reached for one of the cats sleeping at the top of the steps, a half-grown calico. Instead of bolting off, the cat let her hold it.

"I don't know if he hit a rut or one of those rock outcroppings. I don't think anyone ever knew for sure. The police figured he lost control of the car and it flipped and rolled down the hill. That gully was steeper than it is now. Afterwards, the other boy buried the car."

"Buried it," Simpson repeated dully.

"The accident probably happened so fast— Later the other boy said he should have grabbed the wheel. He says he jumped out instead. I don't think he could have—grabbed the wheel or jumped out, either one. I think he got flung out. They both did. I don't think he remembers."

Ernie sighed deeply. Then went on. "Kevin died before anybody else came. I don't know if he was conscious for a while or if he was killed on impact. A couple of hours later, the older boy showed up in one of Lou Burke's orchards. He was covered with blood. He said to one of the hands, 'I killed Kevin Truheart.' He kept saying it over and over."

Simpson stroked the cat in her lap mechanically, her hand rubbing the top of its head and its ear.

"They didn't get a wrecker out there till a couple of days later. By then the car was buried. The boy had gotten a backhoe from the guy he worked for and a huge lot of fill dirt—

ten, twenty truckloads worth. Nobody ever knew whether he paid for it, somehow, or if he traded the dirt for labor. He dug a hole and pushed the car in, the way you would a dead horse. He covered it over and filled up that draw with the dirt. They say he worked one whole day and a night without stopping. And into the day after. I don't know."

"That's crazy."

"The boy was never the same after that. The field and the car both belonged to his family. After the car was buried, they said let it be. Later the kid planted those dogwoods in a ring around where the car was. I think the locusts grew up by themselves."

The gathering clouds were filling the sky and the air had grown so silent that the only sound Ernie heard was the oxygen tank, *shhht, shhht, shhht.*

"The boy blamed himself, but he shouldn't have," she heard herself say. "Most of the kids around here would have been able to drive that car, even at eleven. Most of them were around farm equipment more than Kevin was. Knox wasn't really a farmer."

"Not a farmer?" Simpson's eyes swept the landscape, the barn, the fields. The cat was purring in her lap.

"His parents farmed, but Knox didn't take to it, except for the dowsing and the garden. His brother had already moved away. He leased the fields to tenants and did some buying and selling of land. He enjoyed the farm as recreation—digging the lake and all. He was mostly a businessman."

Simpson stared at the clouds.

"I know what you're thinking," Ernie said. "Nothing's the way you thought it was. It never is. Who told you about the field with the dogwoods?"

Simpson shifted the cat from one knee to the other. "Owen and I had a picnic there with his roommate. They asked me to show them dowsing. They knew I couldn't. It was a joke. I showed them what you taught me to do. I guess I found the car."

Ernie nodded. She was not surprised. "You're not a water dowser. Some people are better with metal. Lots of people are."

Simpson looked up, bewildered.

"The car's made of metal. Some people find metal. Metal dowsers. It's not an exact science. People find all sorts of things."

"Christ," Simpson said. "That's too weird."

"It's true, though. I've known dowsers who find all sorts of junk, just about anything that's buried."

"You told me this was about water."

"It is and it isn't. I don't know. There's some force there, maybe lots of forces, and sometimes they draw you to other things. If we knew what it was, I bet we'd find out it's all related, like the knuckles of the same hand. Like I said before, not everything makes sense like a straight line." Ernie could feel the rain coming in all her joints. Simpson looked like she was about to cry. "I guess Owen was pretty upset," Ernie said.

"Angry more than upset. I guess it's creepy, having your girl-friend find a car she didn't know was there."

"It's more than that," Ernie said.

"Isn't that enough?"

"Listen to me, Simpson. The reason he was upset was, there's more. The older boy I said was with Kevin, the boy who buried the car…it was Marshall. Owen's father."

Simpson didn't move. "No," she whispered.

"Marshall still owns that field," Ernie told her. "It belonged to his aunt, and when she died, it was sold for taxes. Marshall never had much money, but he saved up and bought that field with his wages. Not anything else, just that one field. He's never used it for anything, and it's nearly thirty years."

"Even when you first look at him," Simpson said mechanically, "you know there's something wrong with him."

"Yes. It started after that accident," Ernie said. "Even in high school he'd wander off sometimes, you'd never know where. A couple days later, he'd come back like nothing had happened. Some people said he was crazy and some people thought he was having a kind of spell, like a sickness. I don't know. He could never keep a regular job."

Simpson stared ahead, her hand still nuzzling the sleeping cat. Ernie didn't add that there'd been other theories about Marshall Banner. That he'd been strange, even before. That from the beginning, he'd been a boy who could never carry any weight, who refused to wear heavy clothes even in winter, whose mother had to go clear to Washington to find garments of the gossamer material he could tolerate, which would put no pressure on his skin. Or that still later, after he married Rose and Rose died and Marshall buried her in his garden, the real reason he'd never move her to a real cemetery was that the idea of such a thing would have weighted him down more than he could bear.

Simpson put down the cat she was holding, which suddenly seemed to realize it had endured a kind of taming, and scurried off.

"If he was crazy, why did you give him that land up there?" She nodded toward the hill.

The heaviness of the gathering thunderclouds had come to settle on Ernie's chest. It took effort to get the words out. "I didn't give him the land at first, just rented it to him. He was so odd by then that nobody wanted him as a tenant. He couldn't afford to buy a place. He'd gotten married, and Rose was pregnant with Owen. Even Knox felt sorry for them. I thought if we helped him, it would show we didn't blame him for what happened to Kevin. I thought it would help him. Knox wasn't so sure. But I convinced him. So we rented him the land. And I think it did help. For a while."

Back then, Lily had said what turned out to be true: there were some people who, no matter how high life raises them, don't ever feel on top of the heap. Marshall had never been all right, then or later. In the end, after Knox had died, Ernie deeded Marshall the house he lived in and two acres of the land it was on. She did it, not out of sympathy, but because, as terrible as it had been at the time, it was Marshall who had delivered her from Kevin and set her free to enjoy her marriage to a man she loved.

"You're tired, Ernie," Simpson said, standing up.

Ernie was. The phlegm shifted inside her lungs. It hurt. It scared her.

"Let me help you inside," Simpson said.

Usually Ernie wouldn't, but just then she was so weary that she did.

Simpson walked up the lane to the Banner house. Owen hadn't said a word to her after their abortive trip to the dogwood field. He'd driven her home in Cappy's car because Cappy was too drunk, dropped her off in the driveway and spun his wheels trying to make his escape, spewing chinks of gravel at Simpson's retreating legs.

Now he was on his father's porch, waiting for her as she'd

known he would be, his gray eyes a match for the lowering sky. He must have taken Cappy home and come right back. He looked like he'd been sitting there for a while. In the dogwood field, his anger had been flamelike, glittering with heat. There had been the possibility, then, that it would spark and burn itself out, but that seemed out of the question now. Simpson felt it as soon as she entered the yard, a slow, simmering, anguished thing.

"I should have known you'd find it," Owen said in a flat voice as he came down the porch steps into the yard. "My father buried a car in that field almost thirty years ago. After Ernie's stepson died."

"I know. Ernie told me the whole story."

"Did she?" A clipped, sarcastic tone, and the anger hanging between the words. In spite of the clouds, it was so hot that the air and their clothing and the sky itself seemed glued to their flesh.

"So. She told you the whole story. About the car? About crazy Marshall Banner? About giving him this house as charity, so he could raise his pathetic little son?"

"She didn't put it that way at all. She didn't—"

"Didn't she?" He grabbed her arm, held it tight.

"Owen, stop."

"*Dowser*. What a joke." He spat the words, let her go, flung her away from him. "Why don't you dowse *this*, then—" flinging his hand out to indicate the yard.

Where his fingers had pressed into her arm, the blood came rushing back, throbbing. How dare he? "Well, fine! I think I will dowse your yard. Why not? Dowsing your yard is about as nutty as you are!" She marched over to a little tree and found a forked branch, brittle enough to wrench from its mooring

with a flick of her wrist. "You want me to dowse, here goes."
The car was big and metal. This yard was small, some grass and
a patch of flowers. There was nothing here. There was no
danger. There was nothing to dowse.

Her hands and feet felt tingly, vodka-sopped, though she
was sober now, had been for hours. She thrust out the branch
and walked across the flower garden, a rectangle filled with
zinnias and marigolds and sunflowers and asters, no vegetables,
which seemed odd, just this long plot with a trellis at the far
end, covered with climbing red roses. She held the stick out
and walked. Nothing happened. Nothing *would* happen. And
nothingness, the ordinariness would heal them: yes.

Then suddenly the calling came, the silent melody pulling
her across the yard, holding her in its path the way an electric current would, so she could not even run away. When the
branch dipped as she walked under the rose trellis, she saw that
she had nothing to do with it; she was the conduit, nothing
more. Watching, as if from a distance, she saw the frail little
twig in her hand lower itself mightily toward the ground, compelled by a force as powerful, as unmistakable, as love.

This was how it had been in the dogwood field, exactly the
same. Her heart pounded; she was sick and jelly-limbed. She
moved out of the force field and threw the stick away.

Owen moved toward her, no trace of anger in his eyes now.
She didn't understand it. "Oh, God, Simpson," he murmured,
folding her in his arms. "I'm sorry. Oh, God."

"What is it? Under the roses?" Her voice the unsteady
thread of a child who had been weeping.

"My mother's grave," he said. "My father buried her there."
And more softly, "Her name was Rose. She always loved flowers."

Simpson shivered in the hot air. Owen kept his arm around her and walked her down the hill. She knew where they were going. She let him lead her, needing to submit, not wanting to be in charge, not wanting to pull away. As they entered the barn, several cats came running, but Owen shooed them off and pulled shut the door. The air was heavy and silent, full of rich-smelling hay and the scent of the truth that had burst between them: that the reason she had recognized Owen from the first was that somewhere inside her, hidden and unaware, she had known his secrets, all along.

In the gray daylight that seeped through the broken roof, Owen pulled Simpson's T-shirt over her head, the same striped T-shirt Cappy had stared at, and undid her bra and slid her navy shorts down over her tanned legs. He made love to her on the blanket he had placed in the barn weeks ago, thinking she didn't know. He moved so skillfully and so slowly Simpson forgot where they were. He did not say he loved her. What they were doing had nothing to do with love. Simpson lay on the blanket in the sticky air and felt neither pain nor pleasure. What she felt was more like the slaking of thirst.

When it was over, he held her for a long time. They didn't talk. Then he was asleep, and Simpson twisted from his embrace, put on her clothes and left the barn. She had wanted this for so long. She wasn't sure she wanted it now. At the price of finding his father's car? His mother's grave? She did not notice the cats licking themselves frantically, signaling the coming storm. The clouds were lowering and the air was thick. Alone, she walked across the cornfields to the edge of the lake. Her breasts and limbs felt heavy, as if the earth's gravity had increased. A terrible lassitude gripped her. She feared she would sink to the ground.

She waded into the water, across the mucky bottom, until it was deep enough to let her float. The clouds grew blacker and hung at the edge of the water. After a time the sense of heaviness eased and Simpson began to swim. Breaststroke at first and then freestyle. Soon the dull weight of her breasts and limbs began to wash away, along with the musky smell of the barn. She swam across and back, then across again. The water was cool against her skin. When she finally waded back to shore, the clouds had darkened, but remained in the distance. She was at the top of the ridge when the sky went from gray to purple and a streak of lightning split the air, leaving a sharp smell. There was another odor, too. At first, she did not recognize it, and then she did. Neither the water nor the exertion, nor anything she had done, had washed away the feral, gray-eyed scent of Owen's skin.

She walked faster. At the crest of the hill, she saw the lightning hit the lake. She remembered something her father had told her once about the ocean. A fact that had nothing to do with today, or maybe everything. Her father had told her that every time lightning hit the water, it killed a thousand fish.

CHAPTER 12

Guy Legacy had spent only three days in jail that summer, which was more than enough to make him swear off drunkenness forever. Then his bail was reduced because Parker Dean was taken off the critical list. This was standard procedure. Guy paid the bondsman most of his remaining cash and agreed not to leave the state of North Carolina before his court hearing in ten days.

Right, he thought. *Don't leave the state.* He walked to the bus station and bought a one-way ticket to Beaufort, South Carolina.

What choice did he have? Veronica had been upset with him before, but this was the first time she'd cut off communications completely. She'd had their phone disconnected; she hadn't answered either of his telegrams. Let him rot in jail, she was probably thinking. Do him good. The only way to make amends was face-to-face. It didn't occur to him, until he found strangers in their duplex, that she and Simpson might actually have left Beaufort without a word or a forwarding address.

Guy went to all the neighbors to see if Veronica had left a message for him. She hadn't. He went to Tammy's T-shirts, where Veronica had worked, until she decided they didn't need her salary. Lucy, the owner, said, "Lord, honey, she never called me once since the day she quit her job."

Veronica had closed their bank account. There wasn't much in it, anyway. According to the people across the street, she'd left the landlord red-faced and fuming about midnight movers.

Guy began to feel the way he did when he was about to get the flu—not sick, but not normal, either. In twenty-one years, this was the longest he'd ever gone without speaking to Veronica. They had had their low moments, but eventually they always made up. Was this some kind of practical joke? To punish him for all the times when he'd wanted to move on and she hadn't?

By his third day in Beaufort, he knew it was no joke. Veronica had left him. By the fifth day, his desire to hear her voice was almost like fever.

For lack of a better idea, he took the bus back to Wilmington. It was the only place he could think of where he still had something left to do.

He arrived shortly before midnight and walked from the bus station to the hospital. From the graveyard-shift information clerk, he learned that Parker Dean had been moved to a regular room. He was told that visiting hours had been over for some time. But no one interfered when he headed for the elevator, or even as he walked the corridors of the boy's floor or, finally, located his room and entered.

In the bed, Parker Dean lay bandaged and motionless, no longer attached to as many tubes as he had been, but otherwise not looking much improved. Guy stood watching him for a long time. Now and then, the boy's half-closed eyes darted from side to side as if he were not asleep but keeping some painful, private vigil. Guy's shoulder throbbed and a dull ache settled in the pit of his stomach. He was barely aware of saying, in a singsong, chanting tone, over and over again, "Wake up, son. Wake up. Wake up."

"He will, eventually," a woman's voice interrupted. Guy jumped. Parker's mother was standing in the doorway. "Most of the time it's not like you see in the movies. They don't just open their eyes and start talking. It happens in stages. It can take months." Her voice was controlled, cold, rigid, like the steely points of a blade.

In the dim light that came in from the corridor, she looked too insubstantial to carry so much anger. Her dress hung loose as if she'd been crash dieting; her skin was ghostly. Even from across the room, the dark circles under her eyes made her look as if someone had punched her.

"Right now they're giving him medicine to make the coma deeper," she said. "To alleviate some of the pain you caused." She crossed in front of him and dropped onto a recliner between the bed and the window. Probably she had been sleeping there. She fixed him with her withering glare for a moment. Then her face crumpled and she pressed a thumb and forefinger to the bridge of her nose to keep from weeping.

"I'm sorry," Guy said. Even to himself, he sounded stupid.

"Sorry doesn't change it."

"I have a daughter. Almost his age."

The woman looked up. "A daughter?"

"Yes."

"Here?" She sounded incredulous. "With you?"

"No."

"Where, then?"

"I don't know."

She slipped off a sandal, curled into her chair, composure restored. "She ran away." Her tone was arch.

This had not occurred to Guy, but he supposed it was true. "Serves you right," she told him.

A week later, he was convicted, found guilty of driving while impaired, fined a thousand dollars and court costs, and sentenced to seven days in jail. The sentence was suspended. He was put on supervised probation. Since he had no money, he was to find a job and pay his fine in installments every two weeks. He was to attend an alcohol-abuse program. His driver's license was revoked for a year.

He was leaving the courtroom, had almost reached the massive swinging doors at the back, when he noticed Parker's mother coming toward him from one of the benches that looked like church pews. Her hair had been cut, her skirt ironed and she appeared almost normal except for the hateful fire in her eyes.

He pushed open the door for her and they stepped out into the wide corridor. "You think I should have gone to jail," he said.

"Execution would have been preferable, but I didn't expect it." Her expression didn't soften.

"Then why did you come here?"

"To study the American justice system. To see what punishment it would mete out in exchange for a college student's life." Her voice was so low no one would have guessed she was angry, unless they saw how she impaled him with her gaze.

A muscle tensed in Guy's shoulder, as sharp as if she'd jabbed it. "I didn't take his life."

"You've been to the hospital. You saw how he is." She lifted her chin higher. "Would you call that a life?"

His probation officer was a middle-aged man named Lester, whose voice dripped boredom. Mechanically, he recited to Guy the address of the employment office and told him to report the next day. He handed Guy a copy of the *Wilmington Star-News*, open to an article about a TV series that was filming in town. "Try their production office," he said. "There's an open casting call for extras."

"Extras?"

"You're a carpenter, right? Not a lot of work available for a carpenter who can't move his arm. Employment-office listings are mostly for busboys, dishwashers, laborers. You can't do any of that, either."

Guy weighed his options and decided to go to the casting call. It was either that or leave town. He could become a fugitive from justice, hitchhike out of the state, search for Veronica and Simpson. But where would he begin?

To his surprise, he was hired as a stand-in for one of the actors whose height and coloring were the same as his own. He was told working as a stand-in was better than being an extra because it was steady work for the duration of the series. His sole responsibility was to sit on the set between takes and let the lighting crew take meter readings off him while the camera crew set their equipment for the next shot.

Mindless as the job was, it distracted him from his troubles. They worked twelve-hour days, sometimes longer, five days a week. The show used three of the nine soundstages at the movie studio and moved often to locations around town. Guy tried to make sense of the filmmaking process while the cameras rolled—of actors saying the same lines over and over as a scene was shot from three or four angles, of the director bellowing, "Cut," of the first assistant director echoing, "That's a cut," into her headpiece, thirty, forty, fifty times a day. He couldn't understand the appeal.

He studied his co-workers. The stand-ins were mostly out-of-work actors looking for a break. The gaggle of young production assistants who rushed on and off the soundstages and seemed to want nothing more than to look important. The assistant directors and line producer, all women, spoke with curt, professional efficiency that was startling in contrast to their clothes—ragged shorts and T-shirts that made Guy wonder what had happened to the career types in the magazines Veronica always left open, to pages featuring women in tailored power suits and bright lipstick. Only the stars were both polite and presentable—but distant, too, venturing onto the set briefly for shots, then returning to their spartan dressing rooms. Guy found it all unfathomble. When the camera and lighting crews scurried around him—ordinary, unglamorous workers like himself—he felt so jealous, being reduced to a spectator, that he found himself always testing his shoulder, imagining how it would feel if he were swinging a hammer, but finding the muscles not healed.

He avoided the long banquet table at the end of the soundstage, always laden with food, where the others congregated when they could. Guy was used to having no one to talk to. Working construction, there'd been times when he didn't say a word to anyone all day, just listened to the radio. He'd never minded. But now—what would he say, in any case? That he was a criminal on supervised probation? He might have been working on the moon.

One day, an actress wandered onto the set to play a bit part, a tall woman with short, unruly hair. Even from a distance he could tell she wasn't beautiful, not even pretty. Yet the sight of her filled him with a stab of more desire than he had felt in months, an unbidden jolt of yearning. It wasn't until she walked up to the director that Guy realized what had drawn him: the particular, lanky, loose-hipped stride he had never before seen in any woman except Veronica.

At night, he took up running. He had never much admired runners, had been contemptuous of their deliberate, pretentious sweatiness. When he had worked construction, he'd gotten all the exercise he needed. Now, it didn't matter how late he left the set. His furnished apartment was spare and sterile. If he didn't run, he couldn't sleep.

His route took him to the hospital, four miles. "Wake up, son," he'd tell Parker, over and over. Sometimes the boy thrashed from side to side, restless, as if trying to throw off his yoke of sleep. Other times he actually opened his eyes, staring at Guy dull and unseeing. But when Guy squeezed his hand, Parker squeezed back.

"I'm still not sure why you feel obligated to make these nightly visits," the boy's mother said. "If you see them as penance, don't. Don't feel forgiven." At first she'd told him to stay away, but he came anyway, unable to stop himself. Now she tolerated him, perhaps because he was the only one who visited with any regularity. The aunt, the friends, the young woman who must have been the girlfriend…they all found more and more reasons to stay away.

"My name is Guy," he told her.

"I know your name. It's in the accident reports." He knew hers, too: Millie. If she minded his arriving in sweaty shorts, she didn't say so. Neither did she suggest he wash up at the sink, perhaps change his shirt. They were not friends.

One evening when Guy arrived early on his way to an AA meeting, a man was in the room, dressed in a gray suit, maroon tie loosened at the collar, five-o'clock shadow.

"This is Parker's father, Oakley Dean," Millie said.

"You're the one who hit him," the man accused.

"Yes."

The man narrowed his eyes. "You have a nerve, coming here."

"I'm sorry," Guy said, and wondered why, every time he tried to apologize, he felt more ineffectual than the time before. This was the first he'd seen of the father. If it took nerve for Guy to visit, wasn't it equally nervy for Oakley Dean not to?

"We've been divorced four years," Millie explained when Oakley Dean had left.

"Does he live out of town?"

"No. His family owns a furniture store here. He's the third generation." She sounded bitter. "He works long hours."

"He should come more often," Guy said.

Millie shook her head. "He can't bear to see it. That's how it always is, isn't it? The men can't bear it, and the women do."

Guy had been too distracted at first to pay much attention to the sets. Now they intrigued him: full of careful details he wouldn't have expected, and skillfully, even cleverly, constructed. A mock-up of two rooms of a house, the interior of a drugstore, the reading room of a library. The walls could come down in five minutes' time to make room for the cameras, and often did.

"Who puts these up for you?" he asked the designer once when they happened to be standing in the same corner.

"Different crews. You'd be surprised how many crew people move here just to work on these shows. North Carolina used to make more films than all but three other states. Then most of the work started going to Canada."

"Six weeks ago I didn't know there *was* a film studio in North Carolina," Guy said.

"I guess a lot of people don't."

"In the library," someone cued Guy. He sat at a reading table and studied the construction of the library-set stacks—authentic-looking but not difficult. He could do this. Even the elaborate, permanent street scene on the lot outside wasn't that complicated. A set would go up in a couple of weeks. Then he could go somewhere else, work on another job. It would suit him. They'd been shooting a film in Beaufort when he lived there, he recalled. Not all the work went to Canada. They probably filmed all over the South. A good carpenter could work as much as he wanted, take off when the mood hit, travel, come back.

The camera and lighting people buzzed around him. Guy rolled his shoulder, tested it. Beginning to mend, he told himself. At first, his evening runs had sent a ribbon of pain through his shoulder every time his foot hit the ground. Now it hurt only a little. If he lifted a few weights, exercised every day, by the time this series had finished its season, he'd have his full range of motion back. He'd have his strength. He could buy some tools.

"All right, ready for the first team," the assistant director said, referring to the actors. Dismissed, Guy wandered outside into the daylight, forming his plan. Now that he had a few connections, he should be able to get set-building work when he was ready. Veronica would like Wilmington. It had its share of T-shirt shops, but also Kmart and Wal-Mart and Target and a bunch of upscale department and clothing stores. She might like working in Belk or Ann Taylor for a change. She'd be good at it. And for Guy, it would be a nice break from building houses. Already he had begun to form in his mind how he would tell his family: slowly, carefully, the way he always did. And then, like a slap, he remembered Veronica and Simpson weren't there.

It flashed into his mind then, like a switch being thrown, that August was the month Veronica's car registration came due. This was a problem when you moved from state to state. Did you transfer the title, or not? Where did you pay the taxes? Their solution had been to keep the Mercedes registered in North Carolina, since Guy had been working in Atlantic Beach when he'd acquired it. They'd had the paperwork mailed every year to their "permanent" address in Atlantic Beach, actually the home of a woman Veronica had been friends with at the time, who kept in touch with them and sent the registration renewal forms to them each year, wherever they happened to be. Guy didn't have time until the weekend to go to the library and use the computer to pull up the woman's phone number. When he called her, she said the paperwork had come, yes, but she hadn't heard from Veronica since last Christmas. She'd sent the papers to Beaufort a few weeks before.

The next morning, Guy phoned his probation officer, Lester. "Can you trace a set of tags? I mean, find out where and when they were renewed?"

"I thought you didn't have a car. Just the truck."

"I don't. It's my wife's car."

"In just her name?"

"What difference does it make?"

"What reason would I have to run a check on something that belongs to someone else? Much less to tell you what I found out?"

"I put the car in her name because it was a gift."

"Then it's hers, not yours." Lester sounded sleepy.

"Yes, but it would be good for me to trace my family, wouldn't it? Therapeutic."

Lester grunted.

The next day, Guy called him again. "Listen," he said. "I have a job. I'm going to AA. Don't you think I'd be more likely to stay legal if my wife and daughter were with me?"

Lester mumbled something unintelligible. But two days later, he called back. "Tags weren't renewed at all," he told Guy. "The car was sold."

"Sold?"

"That's right. To a dealer in West Virginia."

"Well...thanks." Guy had trouble imagining this. He and Veronica had vowed once, over a bottle of merlot his boss had given them for Christmas, never to venture above the Mason-Dixon Line. Did West Virginia fall into that category? Guy wasn't sure. If Veronica had gone there, even in a frame of mind angry enough to leave him and sell the car he had given her, she wouldn't stay there long. She couldn't. Not in a cold, gray, landlocked place like West Virginia.

CHAPTER 13

September was always an unsettling month for Veronica. It was the prettiest time on the beach in some ways, but the height of hurricane season, too. She spent the month in watchful anticipation as storms came in waves off the coast of Africa and tracked across the Atlantic, powerful and so unpredictable they could easily turn in any direction at all.

There was certainly no threat of hurricanes in western Maryland. But the days were noticeably shorter and the nights so crisp that Veronica's memory of the hot, green Septembers of the South made her feel displaced in a way that had nothing to do with the ocean. Although the leaves had barely begun to color, there was a dry, chill sense of completion in the air that extended far beyond the garden. Each day, Veronica cut down spent stalks and pulled up dying vines as Ernie instructed, and raked them into piles to be burned. Veronica was grateful when it was time to go inside and change her clothes. It was time—long past time—to get some sort of paying job. She'd been looking for a month.

By now, they'd had to replace the old washing machine as well as the furnace and the roof, and they were very short of cash. Ernie was no longer strong enough to help regularly at the vegetable stand, so Lily took a heftier cut of the few pumpkins and squash Ernie still wanted to sell. To Veronica, this seemed a bit uncharitable for someone who was supposedly a dear friend.

Frightening as all this was from a financial standpoint, there was also Veronica's growing alarm at realizing she couldn't possibly work full-time. Ernie needed her too much at home. The old woman was sick, yes, but not *deathly* sick. Above all, lately, she simply needed Veronica to be close by, to urge her to eat her soup, to help her to the bathroom or up the stairs without making her feel needy or embarrassed, as Simpson's offers always did. The only help Ernie would accept from Simpson involved driving or selling vegetables. Beyond that, her relationship with the girl varied from day to day: sometimes warm, sometimes strained. And the truth was, in the deep, empty well of Veronica's days, Ernie's neediness was a form of sustenance.

To Simpson's credit, she announced in mid-September that she'd left Valley Video to work full-time at Fudge's, the only grocery in Whisper Springs. She would contribute most of her salary to "household expenses," she declared, and keep just a small amount of spending money for herself.

"I only wish I had a car to drive, Mama. It's not that I mind walking to work, but I worry about when the weather gets colder," she said in an even, reasoned tone. "If you had traded the Mercedes for some little junker, I might have gotten a job in Hagerstown for double the money I'm making here."

What Simpson actually meant, Veronica believed, was that with a car she could have spent more time with Owen. Veronica didn't begrudge her that, though there was no chance of another car right now. Veronica was happy—wasn't she— that her daughter had found someone to care about who also cared for her? Veronica was happy—wasn't she—that Simpson was putting down roots?

Her uneasiness would lift, she was sure, as soon she was bringing in a little income.

There was nothing in Whisper Springs equivalent to the cheap T-shirt shops that dotted the coast. Veronica went instead to the Burgermeister and the Pizza Tower, where it was clear they wanted younger waitresses. At the hardware store, the owner rejected her application with hardly a glance. Ernie told her later that he never hired anyone who hadn't lived in Whisper Springs for at least ten years. The best openings, Ernie assured Veronica, were at the antique stores that lined the main street. But Veronica didn't want to work in an antique shop. It had always seemed to her that each discarded item of old furniture, no matter how valuable, had a sad story of aging and decay that hung about it like a gloomy aura. As much time as she spent in the dark cave of Ernie's house, she hated the idea of even another minute surrounded by old furniture and knickknacks.

So on the following Friday afternoon, when she was finally hired to clerk at the gift shop attached to the Springs at Whisper Springs, Veronica was thrilled. The job suited her: selling souvenir bottles of spring water, engraved mugs and key chains, colorful postcards featuring the springs, the ski resort, the mountainside covered with snow. She would ring up cash sales on an antique-looking cash register and process credit-card purchases on the not-so-antique electric scanner. It was exactly the kind of work she knew how to do. The closest thing to working at Wings or Eagles or Wal-Mart—the closest thing to home—since South Carolina.

Happier than she'd been for months, she left the office determined to celebrate. She would buy something—yes! So what if she couldn't afford anything extravagant? She would splurge on some cologne, or some scented lotion for her cracked skin.

Outside the Springs, she sat on one of the wrought-iron benches Ernie sourly dubbed "early-American chic" but Veronica thought were cute. In the shade of the overhanging eaves that made the entire block a gigantic front porch, she slipped off her high-heeled pumps and reached into her purse for the pair of sneakers she'd brought for walking home. She'd been giving Simpson the van as often as she could.

A pickup truck pulled to the curb just as she was tying her right shoe. For a second, she saw it only at the edge of her vision. Her heart slammed into her throat so hard she might have been hit by a baseball.

Guy!

He'd found her!

Of course!

Then an unfamiliar voice asked, "Need a ride?"

It wasn't Guy's truck, what was she thinking? It was just the familiar truck she saw going up and down the farm lane every day. The man inside was Marshall Banner.

"No thanks, I don't need a ride, I'm going to do some shopping."

Marshall turned off the ignition. He slid out and stood on the sidewalk, towering above her. Hadn't he heard her refuse? "I still have a couple of errands to run," he told her. "I could pick you up later."

"No. That's okay." Veronica didn't see Marshall up close very often. After his summer outdoors, his hair was straw and his bleached eyebrows were platinum slashes against his bronzed face, but otherwise there was nothing in his craggy features or bland expression to suggest there was anything wrong with him. Yet just looking at him made her uneasy.

He grinned and pointed to her outfit. "Job interview?"

"They hired me," she said.

"Well, congratulations." He offered his hand. She had no choice but to take it. She made herself meet his eyes, which were every bit as gray as his son's, the disconcerting color of rock outcroppings.

"Where?" he asked.

"Pardon?"

"Your job."

She nodded in the direction of the wooden sign that read The Springs At Whisper Springs.

Marshall laughed. "Our famous springs."

"Is it funny?"

"Until a dozen years ago, those springs dribbled out of the ground, with a metal pipe sticking up so people could get water if they wanted it. They were exposed to God and everybody." He arched an eyebrow. "Then they built the ski resort and the town had the springs enclosed and built a whole little scene around them. They brought in rocks so the water could spill down them like a waterfall. They put in all those plants."

"Lucky for me, I guess." The springs were in an airy, sunlit atrium, separated from the gift shop by a glass door.

"I guess they figured the skiers might not buy trinkets if it meant being exposed to the elements. Riding the ski lift was an adventure, but if you drove all the way into Whisper Springs, you wanted to be comfortable."

He gentled his sarcasm with the hint of a smile, sounding

nowhere near as bitter as Ernie was on this subject. Even so, he gave her the creeps. Veronica slipped on her other sneaker and tied it quickly. "I don't know how long I'll be," she said. "I don't mind walking."

"I could help you," he said.

Help her how? She looked up at him because his tone had changed. His expression was painfully earnest. This wasn't about offering her a ride. Then, what? Was he was trying to pick her up? The man probably hadn't gone out with a woman for years.

"No, Marshall. I'm fine. It's kind of you to offer." She slung her purse over her shoulder and stood. "Thanks anyway." She waved and fled across the street into Franklin's Sundries and Drugs.

Wandering down the cosmetics/fragrances aisle, Veronica examined gift sets of lotions and cologne until she was sure Marshall was gone. She felt adult and professional, wearing a dress instead of gardening garb, shopping like a woman about to go to work the next day, even if only for a few hours. She strolled into the men's section, began toying with the samples. Idly, she picked one up and sprayed it on her wrist.

The heady familiarity of the scent stopped her short. If a moment before she'd been a thirty-eight-year-old woman about to embark on gainful employment, the fragrance wafting into her nostrils made her once again the seventeen-year-old lying in bed with the only boy she had ever loved, listening as he crooned into her ear, "Veronica," as if the name were a mantra with powers she could never know. "Veronica," he'd whispered over and over, while his hands caressed her body and the spicy scent of his aftershave whirled through her brain. She grew dizzy from the aroma, warm from the heat of his breath. For months afterward, as she and Guy had traveled south in his pickup truck and settled in their first apartment and begun their intertwined lives, his aftershave had been forever on her hands and in her hair, as inseparable from that time as salt spray and beach sand and the pure, unalloyed joy of their union. As Veronica stood in Franklin's Sundries now, at the end of the long, convoluted web of events that had brought her to thirty-eight, she remembered all of this as if it were yesterday. She took a bottle of the scent from the shelf, because she was powerless not to, paid for it, and started walking back to the farm.

Already the sun had dropped low in the sky, though it was still afternoon. Even with autumn upon them, the light might have seemed brighter if it hadn't been absorbed by the mountains. The road was mostly empty of cars, but filled with the shifting shadows of trees along the fence lines. With effort, Veronica pushed her mind beyond the sourness threatening to overtake it. She had a job! Everything was fine. Truly. Everything.

Back at the house, she cooked a supper of butternut squash and late tomatoes from the garden, and stewed apples from Lou Burke's orchard and an omelet from Lily's eggs, which she broke into a bowl one by one before carefully picking out the blood spots. To Lily's credit, even though Ernie no longer helped with the candling, she still supplied them with eggs.

By nine o'clock, Simpson had gone out with Owen and Ernie had gone to bed. Veronica turned on the TV. They didn't get many stations. She turned it off, restless and suddenly hungry. Prowling the kitchen, opening cabinets filled with nothing more exciting than flour and salt, rejecting the uninspired spaghetti left over in the refrigerator, she decided there was nothing here to eat. She wanted a bowl of seafood chowder. And not just any seafood chowder, but the kind with the clam-broth base they sold on the Outer Banks. She and Guy always argued about this because he thought cream-based chowders were the only ones worth eating and would dismiss the clam-broth varieties as if it they were nothing but water. If she couldn't have chowder, she wished she had something to do. She imagined herself inside a movie theater, stuffing herself with the buttered popcorn Guy always liked to buy. The idea of watching a first-run film thrilled her even more than the idea of popcorn. So when someone knocked on the door, Veronica didn't stop to wonder who it was or dwell on the fact that her summer in the garden hadn't lent itself to a wide social life. She rushed down the hall and flung the door open.

"Why, Marshall." He was standing on the porch, shuffling his feet, looking sheepish.

"I think I upset you earlier when I said I could help you."

"No, not at all."

Before she could motion him inside, a cat leaped onto the porch from out of the darkness and scrambled into the door. Veronica caught it just as it tried to scoot past her. Ernie was adamant about keeping the cats outdoors. "Shoo!" she said, spilling the cat back outside, not before it had extended its claws.

"He got you." Marshall touched the scratch on her wrist with the tip of a long finger. Startled, Veronica snatched the hand away.

Marshall retreated a step backward. "This afternoon when I said I could help, what I meant was—"

"I appreciated your offer of a ride," she said—evenly, she hoped. "It's just that I like to walk sometimes."

"I didn't mean just giving you a ride. What I meant was, I know the money problems you must have. Many times I've had enough of them myself." He chuckled lamely. Under the porch light, he looked ungainly and menacing. "With Ernie the way she is," he said, "it must be hard for you to take an outside job right now."

"Oh, no. I'm glad to have it."

"Yes, but to work outside and take care of her, too. Anyone can see how weak she's getting." He paused. Veronica couldn't read his expression. "What I'm saying is, a job right now really isn't necessary—at least for the time being."

Oh God, he was going to offer money.

"Can I come in?" he asked.

Did he owe Ernie money? Rent, maybe. No, Ernie had deeded him his house. If he offered cash, he would be offering it to Veronica directly. What would he expect in return? With the darkness behind him, he hovered in the doorway like Bigfoot or the Incredible Hulk or the homicidal maniac he probably was.

She held up her hand to hold him off. "It's just that Ernie isn't feeling well," she said. "I was about to go up to her."

His expression went flat then, or rather the light went out of his eyes. "Some other time, then." He turned without another word and walked woodenly down the porch steps into the night.

Veronica shut the door behind him. She stood in the hallway. Her hands were shaking. Why? Nothing had happened. Was she upset because he desired her? But no—Marshall's expression hadn't once degenerated into that raking leer men had when they were coming on to her. She knew that expression well enough from dealing with male tourists all those years. Whatever Marshall had come here for, it wasn't sex.

Then—what? In the drafty hall, cold from letting in so much night air, Veronica locked the door and checked the bolt twice before heading upstairs to her room.

The Franklin's Sundries bag sat on the bed where she'd thrown it when she'd changed her clothes. Reaching in, Veronica took out the aftershave in its glossy red-and-black package. She opened the bottle and held it to her nose. Odd, how a scent could bring back everything. Guy at twenty. Guy at thirty-five. Next to Guy, no wonder Marshall looked so clumsy. Marshall had none of Guy's agility. None of Guy's grace inside his own body. She'd watched Guy dance around on flimsy two-by-fours twenty feet above the ground, just to scare her. In all their years together, he'd never fallen. Men like Marshall looked cloddish by contrast. It was just a fact.

Dabbing a touch of aftershave on her pillow, Veronica lay down to breathe it in. She was asleep before she thought to get undressed. She dreamed that she and Guy lay on silky sheets, beneath an open window bringing in warm air and the whooshing, sucking breath of the sea. Guy was whispering, "Veronica," with his lips against her ear. She dreamed this for what seemed many hours. And when she opened her eyes, for the first time since she'd left South Carolina, Veronica felt young.

It was the cat that made Marshall remember about going to court. The cat trying to rush into Ernie's house from off the porch and scratching Veronica's arm. Damned thing was probably one of the same cats he'd had vaccinated all those months ago. It reminded him how he needed to tell the dogcatcher that he'd gotten the cats their shots and paid the money for them. That he didn't need to go to court. It had been over a month since he'd walked to the shelter and heard the cry of the dog in the death chamber. He had wanted to forget. All the same, he needed to go there again. Wasn't his court date sometime in October? He needed to straighten this out.

The next day, he drove to the animal shelter late in the afternoon. He got there just before closing, when he knew they wouldn't be doing their killing. He did not want to hear the animals dying.

There were few cars in the gravel parking lot. Everything was quiet, even the dogs. The animals were probably worn out from people coming and going all day. When Marshall stepped inside, the place seemed deserted. There was not even a receptionist at the desk.

"Be there in a minute," a male voice called out from somewhere in the back. Marshall stood at the counter. On the wall in front of him was a placard announcing the shelter's hours and the fees charged to adopt an animal. Marshall frowned as he looked at the numbers. They were high.

Another car crunched into the parking lot, and there was the sound of a door being opened and shut. Presently a woman came in, holding a forlorn and bedraggled-looking cat. It was black and white, probably about half-grown. It gave out a plaintive meow.

"Hush," the woman said. She wore shorts and a sleeveless top. It was too cold for such skimpy clothing. Her arms were too heavy for the top and her legs were too skinny for shorts. She held the cat with one hand under its shoulders so its hind legs dangled, as bowed and skinny as the woman's own.

"Isn't there anyone here?" she asked Marshall.

"Will be in a minute."

The woman's eyes darted in this direction and that. "I need to drop this cat and get going."

"You're sentencing it to death," Marshall told her.

She gave him an uncomprehending glance.

"The cat. You leave it here, they'll only kill it. It'll be dead by this time tomorrow."

"I don't think so. I brought it here so they can find it a home."

"Look." Marshall pointed to the list of fees on the way. "See what it costs to adopt them? You pay for the shots. You pay for neutering, whether they've already been neutered or not. You pay a fee to the county. Most people can't afford it. No wonder they kill so many."

"They won't kill this one. It's not even grown." She scratched the top of the cat's head. "Somebody might want it."

"They won't. It's too ugly, pardon me for saying. No one will take it. Look at its skin." He pointed out some scaly patches where the cat had licked off its fur.

A young, uniformed man came out from a door to the back. He was about Owen's age. He looked familiar. A circle of keys hung from his belt.

"I'm telling you the truth," Marshall said to the woman.

"I can't keep him, though. I can't." She gave him a beseeching glance.

"Help you?" the young man asked.

Abruptly, the woman handed over the cat, which tensed and bared its claws. The clerk petted it and said, "It's okay, fella, it's okay." They all knew it wasn't. With his free hand, the young man pushed a release form and a pen across the counter. "I just need you to fill this out and sign it." The woman started to pick up the pen and then must have thought better of it. She turned and fled.

The young man shrugged. "They do that. Be right back."

He carried the cat down a hallway to what must have been cages for the death watch. Before he disappeared, he reached for the keys at his side. Marshall remembered then who he was. His name was Billy Tuggs. He'd gone to high school with Owen. He'd never been any good.

"Didn't know you were working on this side of the law," Marshall said when he returned. He gave the boy a false smile and Billy Tuggs returned it.

"Security guard, four to midnight." Billy sounded proud. "I got stuck at the desk this afternoon because the receptionist is out. We close in a few minutes. How's Owen? Married yet?"

"Not yet. You?"

Billy Tuggs held up his left hand so Marshall could see his gold wedding band. "Baby boy born in May."

Which explained why the little jailbird was gainfully employed. "Congratulations," Marshall said.

Outside, a dog began to bark. "Gonna put them in for the night in a minute," Billy told him importantly. "What can I do for you?"

Marshall meant to ask for the dogcatcher, but a better idea occurred to him. "They pay you good here?" he asked Billy.

"Could be better." Billy's bemused expression said he knew what was coming.

"I know how you could make a little more."

"Yeah?"

"Yeah. You could lend me your keys." Marshall pointed to the ring of them at Billy's waist. "Just for a night."

"I'd lose my job."

"No you won't. You've got a wife and kid, I wouldn't get you in trouble. You get tied up by a perp, who can blame you?

Maybe you work your bonds loose and call the police. When the story comes out the next day, you're a hero."

Billy Tuggs considered that for a long moment. "I couldn't, Mr. Banner," he said.

But when Marshall gave him a hundred dollars, he did.

The night was warmish, and there was a three-quarter moon. Marshall left his truck half a mile away. He could hear the dogs barking inside the shelter as he walked up. They didn't leave them in the outdoor runs at night. They quieted once Billy let him in. Marshall took the keys that Billy gave him and tied the kid up good, bound his ankles to the legs of a chair and his hands behind his back.

"You were going to leave me a way to get loose," Billy complained.

"I will. Let me do this first."

"There's a gray tabby in the holding area," Billy said. "Supposed to be sick. Better leave him there."

The holding area turned out to be a twelve-by-twelve room stacked on every side with cages less than a foot high, where a single cat could only crouch. The cats were locked up tighter than the prisoners in the county jail. Some of them mewed or pawed the doors of their cages when Marshall entered, but most of them just eyed him. If there was a sick gray tabby, he couldn't tell. A lot of them were tabbies and a lot of them were gray. The cats mostly looked sad; maybe you'd say they looked hopeless. None of them looked exactly sick. Marshall unlocked the cages, one by one, and then walked down to the communal cat cage at the other end of the hall and unlocked that, too. Then he turned to the dogs.

They were on the other side of the building, in smallish

indoor runs that smelled. Most of them didn't bark when he turned on the overhead light. They came awake and stood upright, staring at him with what Marshall thought at first was confusion but then decided was terror. They probably thought he was their executioner. He walked down the line, opening their doors. Only the bravest ventured out right away. At the end of the runs, a single exit led to the outside. He shoved it open to the night. The dogs stayed where they were, sniffing the air for danger. "Shoo," he said, waving his hand. "Shoo!" Blinkingly, slowly, they seemed to realize they were free.

Back in the office he found the cats wandering around aimlessly. He opened the front door long enough to shoo them out. Then he turned to Billy Tuggs, tied securely into his chair. He contemplated not loosening his bonds. What kind of person would take a job as a security guard for helpless animals? Any creature ought to have the right to walk free in this world, even a dog.

But in the end, Marshall decided it best to stick to his plan. He felt fine-tuned and sharply focused, suffused with a wide-awake certainty. Before he loosened the thick rope that bound Billy's wrist, he repeated, once again, the story he had concocted and they had rehearsed. Billy had been overpowered by two masked, wild-haired white men, one dark, the other a red-head. From their voices and the way they walked, they didn't seem very old, some of those young environmental-terrorist types. They had tied Billy up, freed the animals and fled. Billy thought they'd come on foot. He hadn't heard a car.

Marshall was sweating as he made his way back to his truck. He thought Billy would tell the story the way they'd planned. He was too dumb not to. If he screwed it up, it didn't matter.

He'd be too scared to involve Marshall, afraid Marshall might give him away. After all, he had a wife and a kid.

All the same, Marshall didn't think he'd venture back to the animal shelter anytime soon. He could have talked to the dogcatcher, but freeing the animals was better. He guessed he'd have to go to court.

CHAPTER 14

In the middle of October, Ernie let Veronica drive her into Hagerstown to buy some winter clothes.

"Everything is falling right off of you. You have to have at least one or two outfits that fit," Veronica insisted.

Ernie knew they couldn't afford it, with her Social Security and Simpson's salary barely paying the bills, and Veronica's pathetic fifteen or twenty hours at the Springs, which created more aggravation over who would get the van than help in the way of cash. But she didn't argue. She'd always liked October. That morning, she'd stumbled out of bed just at daybreak. From her window, she'd spotted a full moon hanging in the turquoise sky, looking so perfect that she almost forgot how hard it was to breathe. The trees were dark against the pale dawn, a bit blurred by a slight mist. Then it was day, and the mist lifted, leaving the distant fields all green and gold, rich with rolls of hay, except for the places where the equipment hadn't reached and the hay lay new-cut, touched white by a light frost. Ernie thought then: later on, this is what I must remember, how it was this October morning. This is how it is possible for it to be.

She didn't mind the prospect of a drive into town.

But Veronica did not take Ernie directly to the mall. Instead, on the outskirts of Hagerstown, she parked beside a small complex of medical offices.

"What's this?"

"A pulmonary specialist I want you to see." Veronica sounded firm. And then, apologetically, "Ernie, I know you wouldn't have come if I'd told you."

"I'm not coming now, either."

"You know you ought to. That bronchodilator pill Dr. Wilson prescribed made you throw up. A pulmonary specialist would know to give you something gentler. And what about that inhaler you won't use? A pulmonary specialist might—"

Ernie held up a hand. "It was *heart* specialists that killed Knox," she said.

"Now, you know—"

"I do know. I know he was having a 'routine' heart catheterization. I know it dislodged a piece of plaque from an artery and sent it straight to his brain. And that was that."

"Things like that are very rare."

"Before that, he wasn't even particularly sick."

They argued for five more minutes before Veronica gave up. By the time they got to the mall, Ernie's pleasure in the day had drained. The effort of trying on slacks exhausted her. When she caught sight of herself in the three-way mirror outside the dressing room, she nearly fainted dead away. The woman staring back at her was as skinny as toothpicks, her arms so devoid of fat or muscle that the flesh hung from them like folded draperies, and her hair was so thin that, on the back of her head, a patch of shiny scalp was visible beneath the strands.

"Thin hair, that's a sure sign of dying," she said. She hoped her words would make Veronica squirm, and they did.

"Your hair is thin," Veronica finally managed to say while

the salesclerk was ringing up the slacks, "because you pull it back so tight all the time. It cuts off the circulation. Anybody's hair would get thin. All you need is a good cut, it would do you wonders. You could get it styled right here in the mall."

But by then Ernie felt as weak as string. "Too expensive," she murmured. "You can cut it for me yourself."

"What?"

"Cut my hair. Maybe you can do it tomorrow."

"Oh, Lord, Ernie, you don't know what you're asking."

"I'll sign the hold-harmless clause," Ernie told her.

"I guess you'd better."

The next day, sitting in a kitchen chair with a towel wrapped around her shoulders, Ernie listened to Veronica snip away at her hair and watched the thin, unhealthy-looking strands fall to the floor. She felt somewhat revived.

"I've kept my hair long since I married Knox," she said.

Veronica stopped for a moment, panic on her face. "I just hope this is going to be all right. If I'd had any talent at this, I probably wouldn't have spent the last ten years selling trinkets and T-shirts."

"Don't worry. When you're terminal, style isn't the main consideration."

"I wish you wouldn't do that."

"What?"

"Refer to yourself as terminal."

"Well, you might not like the phrasing, but it's accurate. I doubt I'll make it through the winter."

"Stop it, I said!" Veronica folded her arms in front of her chest, burying the shears inside the folds of her baggy black sweatshirt. She looked like a pouty, older version of Simpson, with messier hair—but not all that much older, except for the two deep lines etched between her eyebrows. "Someone who's terminal doesn't flush her medicines down the toilet," Veronica said. "Someone who's terminal doesn't boss everyone around."

Ernie tried to suppress her smile. On the floor beside her chair, a substantial pile of hair had begun to collect. The sight of it cheered her. Surprising, she thought, that getting rid of something so ordinary and taken for granted could be such a release. "Humor an old lady," she said. "Cut."

Veronica unfolded her arms and uttered a deep, dramatic sigh. She resumed working. Ernie gave her a few minutes to settle into the task, then said, "I guess after it's over, you'll go."

"This haircut won't scare me away. Remember the hold-harmless clause. Besides, it's you who has to wear it, not me."

"I mean after my illness is over."

"I'm serious, Ernie. Don't do this." She kept on cutting.

"Even if you stayed in the house, what would you do? Keep that part-time job and try to raise a cash crop of vegetables every year? No offense, Veronica, but I've never seen anybody with less feel for it than you."

"Well, thanks a lot." Veronica opened and closed the scissors in front of Ernie's face. "For all you know, I'm giving you a Mohawk."

"Don't take insult. You can't help it. Not everybody likes to farm."

"That makes me feel a hundred percent better," Veronica huffed.

"I mean it," Ernie said. "Some people have good gardening instincts and some don't. You're born that way. You can't help it."

Veronica rolled her eyes.

"I'm serious," Ernie insisted. When she'd first come to the farm, despite forty years of living in town, she'd picked up gardening right away. Warm gray days in spring, she couldn't make herself work indoors to save her life. Nothing satisfied her except grubbing in the soil. And sure enough, after she'd transplanted seedlings or put in a few hills of squash, next thing she knew a soft rain would fall, as if she'd known all the time that it was coming, and everything she'd planted would flourish. By contrast, Veronica wanted to set out seedlings when any good gardener could feel a drought in the very movement of the air.

"Best thing for you, when this is over, is to go," Ernie advised. "You can't always live in the home of your heart, but if you're lucky you can go back."

"I'm not going anywhere for a long time," Veronica said. "There is no 'home of my heart.' There is no 'home,' period. Except right here. Stop talking that way." She flung the scissors onto the kitchen table and thrust her hands into the pockets of her jeans. "Kick me out if you want to. I'll get an apartment. I'm planning to stay so Simpson can go to college."

"She could go to college anywhere. Assuming she *wants* to go to college, which I doubt. Whatever she decides, *you* could go wherever you want."

"Oh, I think she can still use a mother."

"Or not. She's at that age." Although it was perfectly clear to Ernie, Veronica refused to acknowledge that Simpson was spending more time at work or with Owen than anywhere else. She might move in with the boy before the year was out. That's what young women did these days. There was nothing you could hold on to, your grown children least of all.

"She's at 'that age,'" Veronica mimicked. "I see what she's

up to. I'm not as clueless as you think. That doesn't change the fact that she needs to get her education."

"That's her decision, not yours," Ernie said. Veronica didn't seem to grasp that Simpson's childhood was a thing of the past. She had just turned twenty. She wasn't even a teenager anymore. When something was over, the best you could do was put it behind you and continue your journey. In the light of such thinking, Ernie had once convinced Knox to rent the house up the hill to Marshall Banner, arguing that even a man with his mental problems might be able to put his past behind him, now that he had a wife and a child on the way. She'd never been sorry.

As if realizing suddenly that arguing with Ernie about Simpson's future was a lost cause, Veronica shook her head and retrieved the scissors to make a few more swipes at Ernie's hair. "Finished," she proclaimed. "Go look."

It took Ernie a while to hoist herself up and make her way to the bathroom mirror. What a shock! White spikes of hair shot up from her crown and made uneven bangs along her forehead. Not a bad effect, though. Almost…punk. She lifted the hand mirror and positioned it so she could see the back of her head. One glimpse and her euphoria vanished. Why, anyone who looked at her would know the whole truth. Underneath the feathery white spikes were yellow-white patches of scalp and sickness. Her approaching demise was written across her head like a map.

Maybe it was only the fluff of hair in the air everywhere that set her coughing, but it lasted so long everything around her started to go dim, even the constant burning that lived in her chest now like something alive. She slumped on the toilet seat until, mercifully, the fit was over. By then such a nasty film of exhaustion had settled over her that it took her a while to register Veronica's anxious call: "Are you all right, Ernie? *Ernie?*"

"Fine, fine," she managed to say. But the words came out so slowly, and from so far away, that she wondered whose voice she was hearing.

Sitting next to Owen as they drove to Marshall's hearing in small claims court, Simpson smoothed her skirt and fingered the vest she'd worn because it was woven through with all the colors of autumn. The very sight of it made her happy—but so did most everything else lately. She'd taken off work on the pretext of offering Owen moral support, but the real reason was so they could go back to his apartment afterward and make love. Much as she tried to reflect on the seriousness of the moment, sex was the main thing on her mind, even now, in the car, on the way to a legal proceeding, with the late-October sunlight pouring over the mountain and illuminating everything they did.

Owen dropped his hand from the steering wheel onto her leg and regarded her with eyes so full of love that they no longer reminded her of sorrow, as they had when they'd first met, but of the lightening sky just before dawn, which was the most intimate time to make love. She smiled and closed her eyes at the memory.

"Tired?" Owen asked.

"Just cozy." She leaned over and nuzzled her face against his coat. In spite of her job at the grocery and the errands her mother was forever sending her to run, Owen was the only thing that beat in her blood with any sense of urgency. Because of him, the bright blue days of October had flown by, with the exact crisp weather she'd always longed for in autumn in the

South but often didn't get until Christmas. Because of him, the leaves on the mountain had seemed to burst with such shades of yellow and crimson and burgundy that she had to swallow hard at the very sight of them, after living so long in the green monotony of magnolias and pines. For weeks, she'd found herself rushing down to the lake just to soak up the colors: blue water against a backdrop of leaves too beautiful to be real. It was almost a relief when a hard rain stripped the trees to a sober brown and the mountain began settling into dormancy.

"Well, here goes," Owen said, pulling into a parking space. Owen was worried because he thought his father was in for a rough time. A month or two ago, his fines might have been excused. But ever since someone tied up a guard at the animal shelter and freed all the dogs and cats, the animal control department had been on the warpath. Officers were forever canvassing the county on the pretext of protecting people from disease—although what diseases and whether there had been more of them than usual, no one would say. There had been no cases of rabies even in wildlife. For a time, Owen had tried to talk his father into skipping this court date entirely. A lawyer who had an account with the computer store had told Owen the worst the county could do to Marshall was issue a judgment against him, which didn't mean he actually had to pay it until he sold property—and even then only if the county remembered to renew the judgment every so many years. But Marshall was determined to have his day in court.

"I'm going," he told Owen, "because the longer I'm in that place, the longer those animal people have to be there, too, and the longer they'll be off the streets."

Behind a frosted glass door etched with the words Small

Claims Court was a large anteroom where the defendants sat waiting for their names to be called. To Simpson, the long dark benches looked like church pews, not that she ever went to church. They spotted Marshall alone, in the back, sitting next to a window. He wore khaki trousers much like Owen's, an open-collared shirt and a navy blazer with sleeves too short for his long arms.

"You didn't have to come," he said to Owen when he and Simpson joined him.

"Moral support," Owen said.

Marshall seemed not to hear this. He pointed to an unattractive woman in a beige uniform, sitting with a short, bearded man a few rows in front of them. "That's her. Netta Brabham," he whispered. "And him, the dogcatcher, Don Murray. Probably grew the beard for hunting season. Doesn't surprise me he'd be a hunter."

Every few minutes a voice over the PA system announced the name of a defendant, who would then be accompanied through a door into the courtroom. The dogcatcher and Netta Brabham looked quite comfortable, waiting there. They spoke to each other in low voices now and then, but mostly sat silent, staring ahead at nothing in particular, as if this were an accustomed and rather pleasant part of their job.

When they were finally escorted into the courtroom, the magistrate sat at a long table at the front, a tall man with a round, red face that made him look as if he'd been drinking. He swept his arm in the direction of two more tables where the others were to sit, gesturing more widely than necessary, Simpson believed, to call attention to his flowing black robe. This was not a formal proceeding, he said. He read the charges and asked Marshall to present his defense.

Marshall stood.

"You may stay seated," the magistrate said.

Marshall seemed confused. Owen touched his arm. He sat down. "These fines are for seven cats not having rabies shots," Marshall said loudly. He tugged at the too-short jacket of his blazer. "But all seven of them do have their shots. This lady—" he pointed to Netta Brabham "—said we had five days to get the shots and we did." He pulled a handful of silver-colored tags from the pocket of his blazer and scattered them noisily onto the table. "The vet gave us these as proof."

The magistrate looked at Netta Brabham. "Is that true?"

It was the dogcatcher who answered. "Yes, Your Honor, but it doesn't matter," he said in an amiable, unthreatening tone. "We give people five days to get the rabies shots so they can avoid being arrested. But there's no grace period for paying the fine."

Marshall frowned. "You arrest people for not vaccinating *cats?*"

"There's the danger of disease," Don Murray said in a deliberately low and soothing voice. "Especially when you have vandals freeing even the animals in the shelter."

"If you have to pay a fine anyway, why tell people they have five days?" Marshall's voice rose. He looked around as if the solidity of the room had begun to slip away from him. He stood. The magistrate pounded his gavel. "Sit down, Mr. Banner." Owen tugged on Marshall's sleeve again. Marshall finally sat. For the rest of the proceeding his gaze was vacant, as if he heard nothing more than a harshness of noise, saw nothing but a blur of color.

"He found for the plaintiff," Owen whispered to his father when it was over. Marshall blinked. Reality might have been at the end of a long hallway, the wrong end of a binoculars, too far away to touch. Don Murray rose slowly, studying the wood grain of the table. Netta Brabham, the plump animal control officer, looked at Marshall directly and smiled.

"It isn't just animals they want to control," Marshall suddenly shouted. "I mean they do, but—"

The magistrate pounded his gavel again. "You have the right to appeal to district court," he said. "If you have a problem with the verdict here, you should appeal."

Marshall stood as if at attention, trying to regain some of his dignity. "I intend to, Your Honor," he replied.

Owen kept a death grip on his father's arm as they left the chamber, guiding him as if he were infirm. Simpson followed.

"I didn't ask you to come," Marshall said, pulling away from Owen when they were back in the anteroom. Then, abruptly, he stopped walking, apparently mesmerized by the sight of Don Murray recognizing someone and shaking hands.

"If it isn't the dogcatcher," the other man said jovially, patting Don Murray's shoulder. Both men smiled and showed white teeth. Both might have been running for office. Simpson wondered if Marshall was fascinated because the men had social graces he himself lacked.

"You're not really going to appeal," Owen said as he opened the door and propelled his father into the hall.

"Of course, I am." Marshall looked at his watch. The whole procedure had taken five minutes, not counting the half hour they'd waited.

"There's a filing fee for appeals, Dad," Owen persisted. "Fifty dollars."

Marshall ignored his son. To Simpson he said, "Is your mother enjoying her job at the Springs?"

"Yes, sir," Simpson replied. She could see Marshall didn't like her practiced *ma'ams* and *sirs*. Owen had made a point of telling his father she couldn't help it, this was the way Southerners were brought up.

"I doubt it," Marshall said.

"Sir?"

"I doubt she's enjoying it. I tried to tell her she didn't have to take the job, but she didn't let me…" He trailed off.

"Let you what?" Simpson asked.

"Because of the furniture," Marshall said.

"Sir?"

"The furniture in Ernie's house. It's all valuable antiques. More than she needs. If you sold a few pieces your mother wouldn't have to work."

Owen and Simpson exchanged glances. She could see he was as surprised as she was.

"Your mother could take care of Ernie and pay the bills," Marshall explained. "I tried to tell her, but— Actually I never did tell her. I started to. I meant to." He looked vacant for a moment and then seemed about to speak again when the dog-catcher and Netta Brabham came into the hallway and raised their eyebrows at Marshall, as if to say, "You see, after all, who's in charge here." He glared at them as they turned their backs and walked away.

"Your mother doesn't have to work," he repeated to Simpson when they had gone. "Tell her she doesn't have to work."

Owen could sense right away that Simpson was distracted. Probably upset by Marshall's outburst, as she had every right to be. Maybe it had been a mistake to ask her to come along. But his father needed him, and Owen needed Simpson. By now, she ought to realize that Owen was nothing if not steadfast and wouldn't ask her a frivolous favor.

He guided her along the sidewalk toward the car, hand beneath her elbow. She might as well get used to his father. She'd have to. When Ernie died, he intended to ask Simpson to marry him. It wouldn't be long. The old woman couldn't last another year.

Stop. Callous to think in those terms. But he couldn't help it. When Ernie died, Simpson and her mother would have discharged their obligation. When Ernie died, he'd have Simpson to himself.

"Antiques," Simpson muttered, clutching her jacket to her neck. "I should have known. All that solid wood. I didn't even think."

A brisk wind came up, carrying her voice into blowy sunshine.

"You sound upset."

"No, of course not." But her face was pale except where the breeze had painted a circle of red on her cheek, and her eyes were glassy. "Ernie has twice as much furniture as she needs. She ought to be willing to part with it."

"You can use the money."

"No kidding."

"Simpson, what's wrong?"

"Nothing. Why?"

He opened the car door, let her slide in. He pictured himself teaching her to ski this winter, swimming in the lake next summer, fixing up the home they would buy. He pictured her tending their children, three or four of them, enough so none of them would feel as lonely as he had, growing up.

He got into the driver's side and paused before starting the car, but Simpson stared at her fingernails, wouldn't face him.

"You okay?" he asked again.

"Fine."

They had never talked about marriage, couldn't have, considering Ernie's health. But ever since Simpson had discovered his father's car and his mother's grave beneath the western Maryland clay, he'd known it was inevitable. She'd plumbed his history, had known it in her bones. They'd been joined even before they'd met.

Still tense, Simpson let her jacket fall open in the warm car and picked at a nubby orange thread that wove through her autumn-hued vest. Owen steered with one hand and slid the other into her coat sleeve, stroking the underside of her arm. Gradually, he felt her softening, relaxing her muscles. She turned toward him and smiled an unfocused smile. This was something Owen understood.

"Cappy won't be home until six," he said.

The dreamy grin spread across Simpson's face, like a flush.

Two hours later, Simpson lay in Owen's bed, thinking how, until recently, she had never fathomed how people could be so irresponsible, much less get pregnant or contract AIDS when they had the means to prevent it. Now she understood. The yearning for sex was more powerful than whatever logic said to hold back. Well, of course, it was powerful! Sex accounted for the survival of the species. And yet, for her own part, she hadn't expected it to be so all-consuming.

She shifted so that her hip touched Owen's. In a minute he would kiss her and it would start all over. Maybe sex was exactly as Lily had said, a kind of sickness. Simpson didn't care. If Lily was right that you recovered in your forties, she was glad she had twenty years to suffer.

Owen rolled toward her, as she knew he would. His body was longer, harder, heavier than hers. She became its cushion, its receptacle—terms that six months ago would have appalled her. Afterward, as they drifted off to sleep, something dark niggled at the edge of Simpson's mind, but she was too content to deal with it. She slapped it away, a pesky, inappropriate, flealike thing.

An hour later, she awakened with a start. A dry, sour taste lodged at the back of her throat. Beside her, Owen slept on.

She had been dreaming. Walking through a furniture store, checking prices on velvet-upholstered chairs, oak tables. The same stab of fear shot through her that had jolted her earlier when Marshall had announced that Ernie's furniture was valuable. Antiques. Hundreds of them. How could she have forgotten? This would change everything.

It wasn't just that she loved every piece of furniture in Ernie's house, or that each item they sold would be like giving up a little part of herself.

It was more that, if they had enough money, they could leave. For two months, Simpson had been pestering her mother about getting another car, and Veronica had been very sympathetic. "I promise you, honey, the minute we have two cents to rub together, that's the minute we buy one." Now they would.

And once that happened, who knew how long Veronica would stay?

It was not that Veronica didn't mean well. Not that she didn't intend to nurse Ernie through this final illness, as she'd said she would, no matter how long it took.

It was rather that her mother probably had no more power to remain in one place than her father did—especially a place like this, far from the ocean, with weather that was already getting too cold for Veronica's tastes. For all her grumbling, except for the year in Beaufort, Veronica had always been willing to move on. It was true that after she quit whatever job she'd taken, she'd mope around for a week or two, engaging in the usual histrionics. But then she'd start packing, idly at first and later with fervor. It had happened in fifty different towns. By the time the car was loaded, Veronica was good humored, cracking jokes, impatient to be on the road.

Simpson was pretty sure nothing had changed.

Veronica would convince herself that Ernie would be better off in the hands of professionals who'd been trained to handle a serious illness. She'd tell herself that, with the vegetable stand open only on weekends, Lily would probably check on Ernie every day. A good friend and a real nurse: just what Ernie needed—not two strangers who'd moved in on her all those months ago, using her house and eating her food. Simpson knew too well how her mother's thought processes worked. Veronica would be on the move as soon as she could arrange it.

And if Veronica went, Simpson would have to go with her. Left to her own devices, her mother was as helpless as a child. If Simpson allowed her to set off alone, she would never forgive herself.

She wasn't ready. Not this time.

Yet if she had to, she would.

Lying in Owen's bed, with the shades pulled against the daylight, she reminded herself that often, after they made love, she was so unwilling to leave him that she almost wept. But after he dropped her off, she went for hours without thinking of him. Perhaps she'd forget him just as quickly after she and her mother drove away. Perhaps it would be no worse than leaving the friends of her childhood, reluctant and wounded at first and then, before she knew it, fine.

In the dim light, Owen groaned and rolled over. He squinted at the clock. Cappy wouldn't be home for another hour. "Come here," Owen said.

He touched her breast and pulled her toward him. And she was happy. Happy! So much that she forgot, for the moment, that in a lifetime of moving from town to town, she'd discovered that happiness was a bubble set in the palm of her hand, intact only so long as she stayed perfectly still—which was impossible—and as soon as she moved, shattered.

CHAPTER 15

Hire a nurse! What an idea. No sooner had Simpson revealed how valuable Ernie's furniture was than Ernie brought up the subject tentatively, almost shyly, as if she thought it was the only polite thing to do. At first, Veronica could hardly bring herself to respond. Did Ernie really think Veronica wanted them to hire some efficient stranger who'd come in to take Ernie's vitals and give her a bath? Some stranger who'd look at the self-help rituals in the well-thumbed library book Ernie had renewed three times, and say, "No, dear, I don't really think they'd help. Here, let's take your blood pressure."

No, a nurse in the ordinary sense wouldn't do at all. Ernie hated doctors and everything associated with them, except maybe the pills that helped her breathe. Look what happened to Knox, she'd always say. Veronica rejected the idea of a nurse out of hand.

The relief on Ernie's face was unmistakable. It made Veronica feel that, in an odd way, she was becoming someone she should have been all along. Not a nurse, that went without saying; and certainly not a *caregiver*. She hated that word. She was more like Ernie's coach. Yes. She was coaching her through her illness.

"Well, if you're going to be with her all the time, then at

least you'll have enough money to quit your job at the Springs," Simpson said.

"Quit my job?" Veronica was more and more befuddled by Simpson's line of thinking. As Ernie often pointed out, going to work was the only change of scenery Veronica got. And why should they sell off Ernie's furniture any faster than they had to? That first week alone, they sold a mahogany secretary and several small pieces to buy the second car that Simpson had been whining about for so long, an old Ford Taurus. At that rate, they'd be down to the bare walls before they knew it. Veronica's current work situation suited her fine. She never went in to the Springs before noon. She was with Ernie every bit as much as she needed to be.

In the mornings, after Simpson left for the grocery store, Veronica would prop Ernie up on the living-room couch so she could do the "pursed-lip breathing" her self-help book described. To Veronica, it looked like one of the Lamaze exercises she'd learned when she was pregnant with Simpson, but she didn't mention that. A good coach had to be supportive. Veronica nodded encouragement as Ernie sucked in air through her nose, puckered her lips, and then breathed out through her mouth for a long, long time.

"It keeps the air in the bronchial tree longer," Ernie explained. "The book says it's something you can do anytime you feel the need."

But both of them knew Ernie would never "feel the need" in front of anyone but Veronica.

The second exercise was called "postural drainage"—"because everything flows easier downhill." Ernie lay facedown on the floor with her belly propped on three fat pillows, her head lower than her chest so the fluids in her lungs could run downhill.

"Okay, tap," she'd command, signaling Veronica to cup her hands and pound on Ernie's back with light, staccato strokes, to get the fluids running. Then Ernie would sit up and hold one of the pillows to her belly, sniff the air like a dog, then bend over and practice "therapeutic coughing."

No nurse from the health department would help with *that*, Veronica bet. Sometimes, the exercises took thirty or forty minutes, with Ernie having to stop to rest after each one. Veronica had never imagined before that a person could use most of her energies trying to clear her airways. When they were finished, the trash would be full of tissues soiled with Ernie's thick yellow-gray sputum. Veronica would empty the can and then wash her hands for a full four minutes, so as not to spread germs. Then she would turn her attention to fixing some kind of lunch Ernie might actually eat.

Ernie's growing distaste for almost every kind of food was a real problem. Veronica experimented with recipes constantly. It was Lily, dropping off a basket of eggs one day, who suggested the idea of baked custard. She even showed Veronica how to make it. Eggs and milk and sugar, and a long, slow bake in a pan that had been placed inside a second pan full of water. The dish came out warm and soft and sweet, maybe not ideal for Ernie because dairy products thickened the mucous in the lungs, but clearly something she enjoyed. Would a hired nurse care about something like that? Not likely! In matters of nutrition, you needed a dedicated coach. Those mornings, it never occurred to Veronica to look at her watch. She was always startled to peer up at the kitchen clock and realize she had only a few minutes to change her clothes and head for work.

As long as she had important tasks to occupy her, she told herself, she was more or less content.

But not on Thanksgiving—oh. Simpson and Owen had taken over the kitchen before breakfast, and there wasn't a single thing Veronica had to do. Ernie refused to practice her breathing exercises with so many people buzzing around the house, even up in her room. What good was a coach without a student? By midmorning, Veronica's idleness was driving her crazy. The smell of roasting turkey permeated everything. Simpson and Owen were preparing the traditional feast that each of them had always yearned for, but had probably seen only on television. They'd been studying recipe books for weeks. Last night, they'd cut up celery and onions and boiled them until the very air had made Veronica's eyes water. Then they'd fried a pound of sausage and mixed the meat and celery and onions with seasoned bread cubes to make stuffing. After a heated discussion about the safety of putting the stuffing inside the turkey, they'd spooned the whole concoction into baking pans. Now, they were making mashed potatoes for Owen and yams for Simpson; creamed onions from Owen's grandmother's recipe; canned peach halves filled with cream cheese; green beans; crescent rolls; and two kinds of cranberry sauce: jellied and whole-berry. Lily had dropped off a pumpkin pie and an apple pie, along with a plastic bowl of homemade whipped cream. Marshall had been invited to eat with them, but even so, how much could five people consume? Ernie would manage only a few forkfuls, except maybe for the pumpkin pie. In the kitchen, something crashed to the floor, followed by Owen's booming laughter and Simpson's giggle trilling behind it. Until Owen came on the scene, Simpson had never giggled in her life. The two of them acted as if cooking the meal together were the beginning of some grand new family custom.

Spare us, Veronica thought, and suddenly wished she were engaged in her own family tradition down in North Carolina, which had nothing to do with food. Almost every Thanksgiving, she and Guy had made a pilgrimage to the Outer Banks so they could climb Jockey's Ridge. It was the highest sand dune on the East Coast, a mile long, twelve thousand feet wide, more than a hundred feet above the sea, a summit of sun and light.

Not that she cared about that now except as ancient history. Their first Thanksgiving there, she and Guy had climbed up through such a thick fog that they might have been lost in a desert, wandering through shifting shades of beige and white, unable to see more than a few feet ahead. Then, just as they reached the highest ridge, the haze had burned off to reveal everything. Below them, across the ocean highway, beyond the roofs of shops and houses, the long blue stretch of ocean had sparkled in the sunlight; and on the other side, to the west, the Roanoke Sound had spread out like a great, flat pool. They had stood so high that the roads and buildings seemed miniature and unimportant. All that mattered was the heady expanse of dunes, the light reflecting in their faces, and a wind so brisk it had lifted curls of sand into the air and sculpted patterns into the hills beneath their feet.

They had grinned at each other, pleased the day had turned out so well. Then without warning Guy had dropped to one knee and asked Veronica to marry him. Veronica had been so startled that for long seconds she'd stood mute. "But we're already married!" she'd finally blurted through a rising bubble of laughter.

"I know." Pleased with himself, Guy had stood up and brushed sand off his legs. Then he'd kissed Veronica hard on the lips, in the sudden sunlight, in front of all the other tourists. At the time, she'd wondered if it was possible to stay this happy forever.

"I read in a guidebook," Guy had told her later, "about a legend saying the woman you take to the summit of Jockey's Ridge will soon be your wife. So, just in case you weren't already, I wanted to make sure."

That clinched it. They went back to Jockey's Ridge every Thanksgiving they could, and often on other holidays, as well, or anytime they were close enough to make the trip. When the weather was nice, hang gliders soared off the cliffs, curving and dipping like multicolored kites. After Simpson was born and grew old enough to appreciate the place, she'd often followed the nature trail, guided by a brochure that showed where wild grape and bayberry grew, and where you could see tracks of deer and hognose snakes. As long as they were at Jockey's Ridge for the hundredth time, Simpson had said, she might as well further her education. But Guy and Veronica had just walked the high dunes, burrowing their toes into the sand. What Veronica always remembered afterward was not plants or snakes, but height and sand, and water on either side below them, and nothing in front of them but wind and light and sky.

Compared to that, Ernie's stuffy house made Veronica think she would smother. She would have gone for a walk if it hadn't been so cold and cloudy, but the clean-swept look she'd almost enjoyed after the leaves had first fallen had given way to gloomy bare mountains that made the whole landscape look as if it were in mourning. Ernie was so engrossed in the Macy's parade on TV that Veronica thought she might actually scream. Owen and Simpson hadn't even asked her to set the table. At the exact moment she finally decided to put on her coat, the clouds began spitting a cold, nasty rain that rebuked her. The very atmosphere was against her.

Veronica went to her room and changed her clothes for dinner, wondering if Guy, too, was thinking about Jockey's Ridge just then. Well, of course, he was. He hadn't seen Veronica for almost six months, but he had gone up there with her for twenty years. He was probably desolate at this very moment, wondering where she was.

Not that she cared.

Maybe it was true that your blood thinned, living so long in the South, or maybe Veronica would have shivered through the month of December anyway. It occurred to her the very first week that she already hated venturing out to drive to work, and especially hated the cold wind that assaulted her between the curb and the gift shop. Compared to this, the somber russet fugue of November hadn't been so bad. It occurred to her that the weather would only get worse.

In Wal-Mart at this time of year—this was where she always tried to work during the off-season at the beaches—she wouldn't have had a minute to herself. In the Whisper Springs gift shop, time was all she did have. The store was not exactly a prime destination for Christmas shoppers. Ski season wouldn't begin in earnest for another month. Even the pleasant, junglelike sight of the springs beyond the glass door and the bubbly sound of the waters trickling over their little fall didn't cheer her, though Ernie assured her it should.

"They said on TV that the sound of running water increases the endorphins in your brain," Ernie maintained. "You ought to feel better, just being in that place."

But Veronica didn't. Not with the gray chill of December looming outside.

Ernie also reminded Veronica that the springs came from the same underground streams that flowed everywhere, making their way to the sea, so connected to each other that Veronica might just as well be living ten feet from the ocean. "We're all daughters of the sea," Ernie asserted. "Doesn't matter where you are." But Veronica wasn't fooled. The only ocean she believed in was twenty degrees warmer than these springs, and hundreds of miles away.

The first Saturday in December, just before Veronica left for work, Lily drove up to the house, hauling boxes of pies and homemade breads she'd been baking all week to sell at the annual Christmas bazaar at the middle school. The back of her truck was so full that Rita was confined to the front seat, where she pressed her nose to the frosty window.

Lily lowered her own window a crack. "I come for Ernie," she said.

Veronica regarded Lily skeptically. Didn't she know Ernie had no energy to go to a Christmas bazaar or anywhere else?

"Don't worry. She's gonna sit right here while I unload this stuff. She don't have to do no work."

"Still—"

"We'll say hello to a few folks and I'll bring her home."

Veronica began to protest, but Ernie emerged from the house with her coat on, oxygen tank in hand, and got into the truck next to Rita. She didn't ask permission.

Not a soul came into the shop for the whole first hour. Ve-

ronica sat on the tall stool behind the counter, and for lack of
anything better to do, slipped her shoes on and off and wrig-
gled her toes against the cold tile floor. She wouldn't even mind
the cold, she decided, if every now and then she could hear the
sound of the tides or rest her eyes on the open ocean.

The chimes announcing a visitor brought her up with a
start. She literally jumped to her feet when she saw Ernie and
Lily shouldering their way into the door.

"Ernie! What's wrong? Are you all right?"

But on closer inspection, it was Lily who appeared to have
been crying, whose face was streaked and swollen. The two
women had linked arms. It was Ernie who seemed to be sup-
porting Lily.

"They took Rita," Ernie explained.

"*Who* took Rita? Took her where?" Veronica dragged her
stool out from behind the counter and helped Lily sit down.

Fat tears welled in Lily's eyes. "Some lady from D.C. came
up with her kid," she whispered. "He stuffed a raisin up Rita's
nose." She sniffed and Ernie handed her a tissue. "And then
Rita—Rita—" Her voice lost itself in a tangle of sobs.

"Rita snapped at him," Ernie finished. "Rita was tied outside while Lily was unloading the truck. Then she went in to
price the pies when this boy started messing with Rita. A
nasty little kid, maybe eight or nine years old." Ernie's voice
grew breathless, but she kept talking. "I was in the truck, but
I wasn't paying attention at first. The kid put the raisin in
Rita's nose, and she snapped at him and he started screaming."
Ernie stopped to let the oxygen work its magic. "I'm not sure
Rita actually bit him. The mother made a stink. There was security all over the place. Animal control came and took Rita
away."

"To kill her," Lily sobbed.

"Surely not to kill her," Veronica said.

Lily shook her head. "She's a wolfdog," she sobbed.

"But if she didn't bite anyone—" Veronica was puzzled. "They won't kill her, Lily. Why, they'll call you up in an hour or two and tell you to come get her."

"No." Lily sniffed and tried to stop crying, but she couldn't.

"They told her you're not allowed to keep a wolfdog," Ernie said. "They say it's because they're not sure rabies vaccinations work in them. Because of their breed. You can only keep animals you know won't get rabies."

"I ain't never gonna see Rita alive again," Lily muttered.

Veronica wanted to say, "Yes you will, of course you will," but Ernie caught her eye and shook her head no.

On the local news that night, the bearded chief of animal control, Don Murray, stood next to his officer, Netta Brabham, and spoke in a serious tone meant to convey his deep concern for the public welfare. "We've been especially vigilant about diseased animals ever since someone vandalized the shelter and let the animals out. Some people don't realize the danger a wolfdog can present to an innocent child."

"And what measures are you taking now?"

Don Murray clicked off his answer in brisk, competent-sounding phrases. "The dog was destroyed immediately and its brain sent to Baltimore for testing. As a precaution, the boy will get antirabies treatments until we know the results."

Ernie, on the sofa, huddled into her afghan.

"Several witnesses say the dog only snapped at the boy because he provoked it," the reporter said. "They claim the dog didn't actually bite him."

"Doesn't matter," Netta Brabham put in brusquely.

Don Murray glared at her, then shook his head sadly for the camera. "Wolfdogs are illegal because you can't immunize them for rabies. The owner could have been arrested, especially for bringing the animal into a public place." He segued into a confidential whisper. "In this case the owner is an elderly woman, so we decided not to make the arrest, pending the rabies findings."

"As if that's a kindness," Ernie spat.

Veronica turned off the TV.

The tests came back negative, as they had all expected. "Them rabies shots work just fine," Lily asserted, and then refused to speak of the incident further.

In the following days, every evening, Lily came to the door carrying an offering of a casserole or a pie, and said without a trace of her usual spunk that she'd "set with Ernie a while." Before losing Rita, she'd visited mainly during the day. Now, for hours, the two old women sat side by side, watching television and dozing. Occasionally, one of them would awaken with a start, Ernie to cough, Lily to groan or even sob briefly when she realized where she was and why. The sight of them made Veronica feel so lonely she thought she'd burst into tears herself.

One night, Veronica's need for something to look at besides the ever-droning TV pushed away her every other thought. She was long past the point of brewing a pot of tea, settling in front *Jeopardy*, sipping her little cup of comfort. "I'm going out," she called upstairs to Simpson, who had just come in from the grocery.

"But, Mama, I'm only here for a minute. I'm meeting Owen in Hagerstown."

"He'll have to come here. I need somebody to stay with Ernie."

"Lily's here, isn't she?"

"I want you here, too."

Simpson appeared at the top of the stairs, hands on her hips. Veronica wasn't sure if she looked more irritated or more worried. "Where are you going, Mama?"

Veronica had no idea.

In town, most of the stores were closed. Only the restaurants, Pizza Tower and the Burgermeister, beckoned with lights and Open signs. But Veronica had already eaten. She pulled into the parking lot of the library. What was she doing here? The last thing she wanted was reading material. She'd gone through about a thousand magazines on slow afternoons at the Springs. Wandering toward the bank of public computers, she watched a student taking notes in front of a text-filled screen and a woman playing an electronic game of what looked like bridge. She hadn't used a computer in an age. She sat down at an idle one and found an old game she used to like, Jezzball. After ten minutes, capturing the endless tiny balls that bounced around on a grid and isolating them into smaller and smaller spaces, the frantic trapped things began to remind her of her own narrow life. She closed the window, already knowing why she had really come here and what she needed to do.

She logged on to Google. She typed in the words *Find someone.*

Under the sponsored links, there were *Locate Old Friends and More,* and better yet, *Free People Finder.* The site asked only for the person's name and a state. She typed in *Guy Legacy.* She typed in *Georgia.*

No matches.

No matches, either, for South Carolina, North Carolina or Virginia.

She surfed the Web a little, liking the phrase *surfing the Web*, which she hadn't used for a long time. One of the interactive missing-persons sites allowed you to communicate directly with other users. *I am looking for Guy Legacy*, she typed. *He is a carpenter, probably living in a coastal town between Virginia and Georgia. Probably South Carolina or Georgia at this time of year.* She didn't know what else to say. She clicked on Submit.

Sorry, kid, came her first reply.

This was probably crazy. Guy was not interested in computers.

But most people were. Someone might know him.

She still owed him an explanation, didn't she? Or maybe she didn't. Either way, at least he deserved to know that Simpson was all right. *More* than all right, she thought, now that she had a boyfriend. What would Guy think of *that*?

If nothing else, maybe she could get a message to him by e-mail.

CHAPTER 16

By the week before Christmas, Guy knew his arm was healed. Parker Dean was healing, too. Back in the summer, the boy had been moved from the hospital to a rehabilitation center, where at first he was awake only in a blurry, not-quite-focused way. Day by day, he grew clearer headed and stronger. After a few weeks, they sent him home.

It was Guy's suggestion that Parker's mother sue the umbrella insurance policy that Simpson had made him buy a few years ago. "Anything that doesn't cover, I will," he had said, though he had no idea how. That softened her some. She tolerated his visits even after the boy went home.

The first time Guy went to Millie's elegant house to see Parker, he realized she didn't need to work. She wanted to. After spending her days driving her son to endless outpatient therapy sessions, she probably relished her nights away, working as the quality-control manager for a local chemical plant. A nurse named Beverly stayed with Parker while she was away— not that he really needed a nurse.

All that autumn, it was Beverly who let Guy into the house as if he were a member of the family and not the criminal they both knew he was; Beverly who befriended him; who updated him about Parker's condition. "They know exactly what to do to treat the body—the broken ribs and the pelvis," she told Guy. "But the brain, that's another matter. It seems to heal at its own speed." Beverly was red-haired, freckled, a few years older than Guy. She wore polyester pants and smocks that became a kind of casual uniform, and tortoiseshell glasses that made her look like a schoolteacher. She liked having someone to lecture.

"Waking up from a coma happens in ten stages," she told him—or did she say a dozen? Guy hated medical facts, couldn't hold them in his mind. Parker's gradual return to consciousness and functioning sounded alarmingly like the twelve-step AA program the court had ordered him to attend. Guy didn't understand AA, either. He wasn't an alcoholic, never had been, hadn't had so much as a beer since the accident, probably never would.

"Makes no difference," warned Lester, his probation officer. "The judge orders AA, you go." Guy figured, okay, it's only six months, for six months he could do anything. Besides, Parker's mother monitored everything. If he quit AA, she might make the visits to Parker history, too.

Most nights, Guy left the studio lot around ten. If Parker was awake, he'd greet Guy politely and then retreat to his room, as if he believed Guy was a benign but unimportant friend of Beverly's. "He knows who you are," she told him at last. "He knows what you did."

But it seemed to Guy that if Parker really knew, he would be angry enough to say something—unless he was too damaged, in some way, to care.

Often as not, the boy was already asleep when Guy arrived. "There was a time," he told Beverly, "when I wouldn't have been able to imagine anything worse than being Parker's age and going to bed every night by ten o'clock."

"It's a long process," Beverly said. "The therapy wears him out." Parker was learning to walk properly again, to talk, to read. His short-term memory was unreliable. He wouldn't be ready to go back to school for at least another year, maybe two.

"I took away two years of his life," Guy said ruefully.

"Not really. He's doing remarkably well," Beverly reassured him.

"This is 'remarkable'?"

"Some people take a year to get where he is right now. Be patient."

"You're getting better," he'd say to Parker's sleeping form as he stood in the doorway to his bedroom. In his sleep, the boy seemed younger than his years, not more than twelve or fourteen. "They say you're doing really well," Guy would whisper. "Get all the way better, son. Get all the way better."

Guy chanted the words *get all the way better* the way he'd once chanted *It'll be fine* to seven-year-old Simpson, who hadn't wanted to leave Manteo Elementary School where she'd had a friend. He'd chanted the whole car ride to Pawleys Island, watching her calm down little by little…but not entirely, no matter what he did, until they'd settled into their apartment and she'd made her first friend in the new town. Guy feared it would be the same for Parker: that he would not relax until his journey was complete.

At work, after the heat lost its bite in the fall, they began to shoot less on the soundstage and more on location. Guy was glad to be outdoors. They spent days at one particular dock beside the sound, and on the deck of a trendy waterfront restaurant. For a whole week, they shot scenes in the backyard of the sort of house Veronica had always longed for, flanked by azaleas and pines.

Hurricane season brought its usual share of storm scares, but most of them came to nothing. Even the ones that got close eventually headed north toward the Outer Banks. Only once was there a threat of a direct hit. For three days, the system skirted the coast, blanketing the town in a steady, humid wash of hot wind and rain. Filming was canceled for the duration. Guy had nothing but time. He would have gone to Parker's, but he wasn't sure he'd be welcome there in the daytime, with Millie at home. Before the accident, he would have spent his idle hours in a bar. Now, he stayed in his apartment and watched TV. He made his way through endless six-packs of Pepsi and then walked to the convenience store for more. He spent hours stretched out on the uncomfortable couch that came with the apartment, the TV turned low so he could listen to the wind.

Once, only an hour south of here, he and Veronica had weathered a storm on the little island of Sunset Beach. An evacuation had been ordered, but they hadn't left. From their deck, they had watched the wind whip the surf into a noisy gray froth, closer and closer to the house. Simpson, ten at the time, had been thrilled. When the hurricane had neared and the wind had grown more ferocious, they'd covered the ocean-front sliding doors with sheets of plywood and had lain on the living-room carpet, listening to the tempest outside. Anyone else might have worried that the storm surge would engulf the piers that held the building steady, flood the cottage, sweep them away. But such thoughts had never entered their minds. By the time the tempo of rain on the roof had slowed and the wind had stopped howling, all three of them had been lulled to sleep. They'd woken up to a morning so clear and bright that the churning surf was the only reminder of danger. Neither Guy nor Veronica had gone to work. Down on the beach, they'd collected big whelk shells the storm tides had washed up. Veronica's hair had been long then, and had blown into his face, smelling of indolence and salt.

With this memory churning in his head, Guy fell sound asleep for who knows how long, and was awakened by someone knocking at the door. It was Beverly, the nurse. Her red hair hung straight and damp around her face. Her raincoat was beaded with water. She held out a covered dish. "I thought maybe you were sick. I haven't seen you."

"No, just lazy. Laid off for a few days because of the storm." Guy took the casserole, motioned Beverly in. The dish was still warm.

"Moussaka." She followed Guy to the kitchen, dripping water onto the floor. "Not very Southern."

"I like moussaka. You probably didn't know this, but Legacy was originally a Greek name." It wasn't much of a joke. Guy's mind was still in Sunset Beach.

Beverly smiled awkwardly, as if not sure whether to laugh or take him seriously. Guy guided her into the living room, where they plunked down on opposite ends of the ratty couch.

Beverly looked around. She took in the door to the bathroom and the short hallway to the bedroom. Not much of an apartment, she was probably thinking. Guy didn't care.

"I thought maybe you were sick," she repeated after she'd finished her inspection. "I'm glad you're only off because of the weather." Her eyes were blue behind the glasses, clear, open to something more than chitchat.

Guy took this as a signal to move closer, but he didn't. The tan cloth of Beverly's raincoat matched the furniture. Gray light poured through the window. Everything seemed unbearably drab. Guy frowned. Seeing his expression, Beverly suddenly jumped to her feet. "Oh, I'm getting your sofa all wet!"

"It might be an improvement." He knew his next move was to pat the seat beside him, urge her to sit down again. He didn't do it.

She looked at the damp outline she'd left on the couch. "Well. I just stopped by. I have to go to Parker's anyway."

Guy looked at his wrist. He wasn't wearing a watch. All the same, he knew she didn't need to be at Parker's for hours. "I don't want to make you late," he said.

She walked fast toward the door. He opened it for her. "Thanks for the food," he told her. "I'll bring the dish back to you at work."

"Oh. No hurry." From the look on her face, he might as well have said, don't call us, we'll call you.

The rain let up after she left. Guy put on his jacket and walked the block to the convenience store. He bought two packs of Big Red gum and a six-pack of Sprite. Maybe it was the Pepsi that was making him so jittery. The air was heavy with water. If Beverly had come some other time, not during his reverie about Sunset Beach, he might have been friendlier. Even at its fiercest, that other storm had never made the beach house look as dreary as the sky looked now. He was married. Beverly knew that. He wanted to go home.

Not in the usual sense. Not to some physical place. A home was something he and Veronica hadn't needed, at least until she changed her mind. They were home, together. *She* was home.

He guessed he was ready to settle in one place if he had to. If she insisted.

But not in West Virginia, if that's where she was. It was hard to believe she'd stay there. Maybe she'd only been passing through when she'd decided to sell her car. Maybe she'd continued her journey by train or on a bus. He twisted the puzzle around his mind like a tongue on an aching tooth, and still couldn't imagine what she'd been doing in a place with cold weather and mountains and no beach. Eventually, she would go somewhere else. The wind howled, kicked up debris the way storms kicked up sand from the beach. He mulled it over. He thought he knew where she'd be.

He could not go at once. Sometimes, you couldn't. This was something he had learned. Although the series wouldn't wrap until March, there would be a long break at Christmas. It was the logical time to say he wasn't coming back. Just in case he had a chance to build sets someday, he wanted to make a clean break. He wanted a few references.

He saved his money, waited until his probation was over in December, avoided Parker's house for a few weeks after the visit from Beverly, and then went back, carrying the casserole dish. Beverly seemed glad to see him. They pretended nothing had happened. Guy said nothing about his plan. He pretended he'd go on like this forever.

On the last night, he rode over on the bike he had bought. He parked it at the side of the house. He attached the note he had written.

"Parker's asleep," Beverly said as she opened the door. It was barely eight o'clock.

"Asleep already?" Lately, Parker had been awake more, gone to his room later, worked on his computer instead of sleeping. He was improving rapidly. Guy was puzzled.

"They had him running today," Beverly explained. "Good progress, but it wore him out." She pushed her glasses higher on the bridge of her nose.

"I came to tell him goodbye," Guy said.

Her eyes widened. "Your job is over?"

"Yes," he lied.

"And your probation?"

"That, too. I've even been sprung from Alcoholics Anonymous."

Behind her thick lenses, her gaze was level, assessing. "Where will you go?"

"To look for my family. It's been six months."

Setting the dish on an end table, she gave him her full attention. "You know where they are?"

"Not right now. But I think I know where they'll end up. This one particular place."

"And?"

"I'll go there and wait. I'll get a job for the winter." He rotated his shoulder. "Arm's better. I ought to be able to do carpentry. I've saved enough to replace some of my tools."

"Going south for the winter," she joked.

"No, north."

"North. Now *that's* dedication." She smiled, and what was left of the awkwardness between them evaporated. "Millie will be here any minute," she said.

"She's not at work?"

"No. Christmas shopping. It's all right. She's used to you. Nobody else visits anymore, not even Parker's father."

"I remember." Guy felt suddenly ashamed. He sank onto a couch. "I thought it would be over by now," he said. "That he'd be recovered."

Beverly toyed with her glasses and stared down the hall at something Guy couldn't see. "It's never really over," she said.

"You said he'd be the same."

"In a way, but it might take years. And even if he's the same, his mother won't be." She reached out and touched his injured shoulder. "Neither will you."

"No," Guy agreed.

He went into Parker's bedroom. "Wake up, son," he said, as he had back in the hospital and so many times since. "Wake all the way up." For a time, Guy knew Parker was sleeping, and then, although Parker's eyes remained shut, Guy knew he was awake. They stayed that way for a long time.

Millie's voice came from behind him, cold and clipped. "Beverly says you're leaving." He hadn't heard her come into the house.

"Yes. I have to—"

Millie put a finger to her lips to stop him and motioned him to follow her out of the bedroom.

"You have to go back to your family," she finished for him when they were in the hall. "To whatever life you had before. How nice to be able to walk away."

It was true. There was nothing he could say.

"I suppose I'll be glad to be rid of you," she said after a time. "It'll be like getting rid of—I don't know. Some *stalker*."

"You could have asked me not to come. I would have—"

"You would have come anyway. Like in the hospital."

"Not if I knew you really thought I was a stalker." He would have said he was sorry, but every time he did, it made things worse.

"Go on," Millie said to him. "Go tell Parker goodbye."

Inside the room, Parker was waiting for him, sitting up in his bed. Guy noticed how very thin he was, how pale. "Get better, son," he said. "Get all the way better."

"I'm working on it," Parker said. "My memory isn't worth shit."

"Do you remember the night I hit you?

"Not a clue."

"You were riding a fancy bike that costs about as much as a small tropical island."

"So they tell me."

"There's a new one propped up by the side of the house. A Christmas present. Do me a favor. Get so you can ride it."

Parker nodded. His eyes seemed clearer than before. "You're leaving?"

"Yes." Beneath the boy's T-shirt, the newly healed ribs jutted out from too little flesh. "Get all the way better, son," he said.

"I will."

Guy would not forgive himself for what he had done. He never would. But Parker offered his hand, and Guy shook it, and the boy let him go.

CHAPTER 17

Christmas passed, and a frigid, cloudy New Year's. But it wasn't until the end of January that everyone realized Maryland wasn't having a normal mid-Atlantic winter. "More like upstate New York," an anchor on the Weather Channel declared, citing the snow every few days and temperatures rarely out of the teens. When the mercury finally soared toward freezing, Lily appeared at the door in only a windbreaker and said, "I didn't ever think thirty degrees would feel warm, but compared to ten below, danged if it don't."

Even Simpson, who loved the novelty of the first snows, soon tired of the bitter weather. Maryland was not that far north. Yet the winter light was so thin that she could almost understand why her mother said it made her shiver just to look at it. The evergreens were bronzed and blued instead of green, as if they were huddling into themselves to keep warm. And they'd sold so much furniture that even inside the house, everything looked bare and chilly.

But none of that would have bothered Simpson if it weren't for the fact that she hated skiing; hated it more than she loved swimming. She was as slow to learn as she'd been quick to pick up waterskiing and riding a Jet Ski and even windsurfing, which not many girls tried. She was pretty athletic, too. In the fall, she and Owen had spent whole days backpacking on the Appalachian Trail, where she could hike as far and as fast as he could. When she'd learned he had a passion for skiing, she thought it would be another activity they could share. She never imagined that their future together might be predicated on something as superficial and frivolous as a winter sport.

Owen's Christmas present to her was a pair of snow goggles, plus equipment rental and a day's skiing at the Whisper Springs resort. In the rental shop, there was much discussion of boot sizes and bindings and pole lengths. Simpson was outfitted with more clothes than she'd ever worn at one time: long underwear, waterproof ski pants, a turtleneck beneath her wool sweater, winter jacket, bulky socks. Her gloves were so tight around her wrists that they cut off her circulation.

Outside, Owen took no notice of Simpson's discomfort. In a rush of enthusiasm, he showed her how to walk on skis, get up from a fall, sidestep up a hill, snowplow. She tried each task, mastered none of them. Owen treated her as if falling every few seconds were normal.

After a while, getting up began to require extraordinary energy. As cold as the weather was, she was sweating and exhausted. Owen paid no attention. No matter how clumsy her moves or how labored her breathing, he kept nodding approval and offering encouragement and moving on to the next skill. "You're doing fine," he said. "Doing really fine."

In the days that followed, Simpson was thankful for her heavy work schedule at the store. There were no free weekdays for another lesson and on weekends the resort was packed. "We can go in the evening," Owen suggested. "It isn't so crowded then. We can go every night if we want to."

The biting after-dark temperatures, low enough to turn any

exposed piece of skin numb and blue, didn't bother Owen. Neither did Simpson's lack of ready cash. He offered to pay for everything. On their fourth trip to the ski resort, Simpson started toward the tow rope on the beginner's hill—a rope she still couldn't hang on to without help, so that she usually ended up on her bottom in the snow. Owen followed as if to help her, but instead drew her away. "This bunny's slope's great for kids to play on," he said, "but you're ready for more."

"Be serious, Owen. I haven't felt for one second that I'm in control of any given part of my body."

"Oh, you'll be surprised." He teased and cajoled until she forgot how she plummeted down hillsides, how she was always cold or hot or frightened or wet. Sitting beside him on the chairlift, her legs dangled and her feet felt so heavy with boots and skis that, except for the restraining force of a tiny metal bar, she would have gone flying off into the dizzying, wind-swept sky. At the top, she flung herself off the lift and fell down the ramp like a fool. She looked down at an intermediate slope so steep she would surely have to maneuver it by crawling down on hands and knees. Somehow, that didn't turn out to be necessary. But after that, she stayed on the beginner's hill, no matter how Owen teased. She waited him out until he grew bored and took the chairlift higher.

It wasn't that she didn't want to enjoy skiing. She would have liked to be as proficient as Owen was, whizzing down the blue diamond slopes like someone in his natural habitat, olive skin flushed from wind, Scandinavian hair poking out from under his cap.

But she *wasn't* proficient. She hated it. Worse, she resented Owen's expecting her to change. Resented his hooded, pouting looks of disappointment. For the first time since she'd laid eyes on him in June, there were moments when the sharpness of her desire for him only irritated her rather than giving her pleasure. For the first time since they'd started exchanging secrets, she found it hard to tell the truth and easy to lie.

"I have to watch Ernie for my mother," she'd say, or, "I have to run into Hagerstown to get Ernie's prescription. They don't stock it here in Whisper Springs."

Owen wasn't fooled. "You just don't want to ski. You're making up excuses."

"Am I? Maybe because it's no great pleasure, clunking around in boots that make me lean forward so far I feel I'm going to fall even before I get my skis on. Maybe because it's no fun spending all my time on my butt or chasing runaway skis down some cliff. Or being deafened and blinded by grainy ice the snowblowers spit in my face."

"You won't feel off balance after you do it a while," Owen insisted. "Your skis only get away from you when it's icy. It isn't icy that much."

"Could have fooled *me*."

"If you don't like the snowblowers, we'll ski in the daytime. They run the snowblowers mostly at night."

"No," she said. *"No."*

Owen looked crushed.

"Listen," she said. "It isn't your fault. I grew up in the South. This is the first time I've spent a winter where it snows. Skiing isn't natural for me. Walking is. Swimming is. Even ice-skating. But not this."

"Ice-skating!"

"I used to roller-skate when I was a kid."

"Completely different."

"Not completely. On skates I don't fall every ten seconds." Her voice wavered. It was different. Who was she kidding?

"It's that same draw to water, isn't it?" Owen accused. "Whatever—*thing*—it is that makes you a dowser."

"I'm not a dowser! I don't find water!" The day she'd found his father's buried car and his mother's grave, she'd been drunk. Water had nothing to do with it. "Don't make me into some kind of psychic!"

"If water doesn't draw you, then why do you like fooling around at the lake even if it's ten below? And hate skiing down a mountain?"

"I don't know. Why do some people like red more than blue? Why do some people like classical music more than country? What kind of *question* is that?" But it was true that she dreaded the mountain and adored the lake, that she hated gritty, snow-covered hillsides and loved the sheltering ice that allowed the waters of the lake to keep flowing below. She clumped down there almost every morning before work, through the stubbly, frozen cornfield, just to look at the lake under the winter-white sky.

It hadn't been frozen so deep for years, Ernie said, though she was too weak to go view it herself. She said the lake didn't usually freeze solid at all. Simpson had always thought water froze flat, like the skating ponds in old movies. But the ice had formed into bumps and ruts, as if the waves had stopped in midmotion. The only smooth spot was the one Marshall had made, using scrapers and brooms. Except for that small skating area, the ice had such a ragged white crust of snow on top that Simpson could walk all the way across without slipping.

Besides, what was wrong with taking refuge at the lake

when the rattle in Ernie's chest made Simpson feel helpless and frightened? What was wrong with escaping there when Veronica seemed so distracted there was no talking to her? Why did Owen think he deserved an explanation? "It's perfectly rational," she told him, "to want to test the skates Ernie gave me for Christmas."

"Also rational to want to learn to ski," he sniped. But she ignored him. Flat ground and a body of water, these were quantities she trusted. Her first days on ice skates had been hard because her ankles ached, but they soon grew stronger. She learned to skate backward, stop, turn, all the things she seemed not to be able to master on skis. On skis, her body grew clumsy and rebelled.

She and Owen didn't exactly fight about this, but the tension between them grew. Then late one afternoon, practicing a turn on the ice, Simpson pivoted and saw Owen sitting at the edge of the lake, putting on his own skates. It was the first time he'd joined her there. She was so startled that she tripped and fell.

"See?" Owen said as he watched her get up. "Ice is hard. Falling in snow has got to be easier."

"No!" she shouted, angry that seeing him had made her lose her balance. "At least on ice you fall and stop and don't end up flying all over a mountain where a dozen people are likely to run you over."

Owen finished lacing his skates, glided over to her, offered his hand. She grimaced and waved him away.

"You can skate for an hour and be done with it. Skiing takes half a day. Skating doesn't cost anything. Skiing is expensive. Do you want me to go on?"

He offered his hand again. The third time she took it and

let him guide her down the length of the cleared ice. They moved as if they'd been skating together always, graceful as dancers. Then he swung her away from him and turned her to face the mountain.

"Look," he said.

Above them, the snowy peak was bathed in sunset light. Purple clouds floated across the sun, with streaks of pink shooting out into the graying sky. They stood and watched until the colors faded. Owen might have been offering the view as a gift.

"You'll learn to love skiing," he said when the light was gone. "When that happens, don't ask me not to say I told you so." He smiled winningly. Simpson smiled back because it was all she could think to do, or maybe because his enthusiasm wore her out. Their bond was not the way he imagined—not inevitable, not sure, not fated just because twice her forked branches happened not to light on water but to dredge up, instead, the Banner family secrets. When they skated off again, the bitter darkening air brushed their faces, and even through Simpson's heavy gloves, the pressure of Owen's hand was tight.

On the morning of his appeal in district court, Marshall awakened with the uneasy feeling that he was already separating from himself, watching the drama of his life from far off. This would be one of those days when he would have to tell himself repeatedly: This is happening right now. I am not dreaming. This is real.

Sometimes he could bring himself back with this talk, or else with his medicine or vitamin B-complex pills. But now and then, no matter what he did, he would finally lose track of himself. He did not want that to happen today, did not want to stop responding to what other people said, or wander along the highway or through the fields instead of going to court. He did not want to find out he'd missed his hearing, a few hours or a few days from now, when for reasons as incomprehensible as its disappearance, his mind would slip conveniently back into place.

He pushed back his covers and pulled his robe from the bed-post where he'd hung it. He made himself go through his normal morning routine. He brewed the strong black coffee that sometimes gave him the jolt he needed in order to function normally. He ate a bowl of instant oatmeal. *This is happening right now*, he kept saying. *This is not a dream.*

In the end, what helped most was not caffeine or vitamins or even his chant. What helped most was the sense he had, from the moment his bare feet hit the wooden floor, of the small, cold teeth of winter biting into his skin. It was enough to keep anyone inside their right mind, providing they wanted to be there at all.

He disliked putting on many layers of clothes. He didn't like the weight of them, even if it meant being chilly. But that day he wore a crewneck sweater over his shirt and an overcoat over his suit jacket, and was still taken aback when he stepped outside. Almost instantly, the morning air froze the small hairs in his nose and stung the back of his throat. Where the sun had melted the top layer of snow the day before, now a shiny, unnatural-looking crust had formed, like the glaze on top of a cake. Everything was so gray and frozen that his memory of blue sky and summer-green mountains seemed hallucinatory, false. He was startled when his truck started on the first try. He was elated when his mind remained clear and present.

Marshall didn't have to wait in court as long as he expected. Several other cases had been postponed because of the cold. He was disappointed, since his reason for being there was not to win, which he didn't expect, but to keep the dogcatcher and his cronies off the street a few extra hours.

The judge was a young woman with thick, dark eyebrows and a voice that radiated calm. Just as Marshall positioned himself at the defendant's table, Owen arrived and sat next to him. The dogcatcher, Don Murray, was at the plaintiff's table next to his officer, Netta Brabham.

Marshall noted the soft, plump bodies of the animal control staff and decided they would not be out seeking strays in this weather, even if they hadn't had to come to court. They would be in the office doing paperwork and eating doughnuts. The dogcatcher had even shaved the beard he'd grown at the beginning of hunting season, no doubt because he was afraid the physical discomfort of the cold would offset the pleasure he took in killing.

The judge listened to everyone patiently. Don Murray explained again that anyone who had an unvaccinated pet was fined fifty dollars per animal. Marshall argued again that if a pet owner was given five days to get the rabies shot, he should also get a five-day reprieve on the fine.

The young judge brought her thick eyebrows together in a thoughtful frown. "A bit of a paradox," she muttered. Then she turned to Marshall. "You have to understand," she said, "that it's not my function here to argue the validity of the law. Even if it seems unfair, it's not my role to decide. Do you understand?"

Marshall nodded. Owen put his hand on his father's arm to comfort him, but Marshall was not upset. He anticipated that Her Honor would uphold the small claims court and hand down a judgment against him for three hundred and fifty dollars. He'd already decided not to pay.

"All I wanted to do," he whispered to Owen, "was keep Officer Brabham off the street on a morning she wouldn't have been on the street anyway." Marshall sighed at his son's uncomprehending expression. The judge leafed through her papers.

A strained, gravelly voice interrupted the silence, rising from the back of the room: "Your Honor? I have something I'd like to say."

The judge looked up. Everyone turned toward the back.

It was Ernie Truheart.

Marshall had not seen her since Thanksgiving. In two and a half months, she had aged ten years. Her hair was short and matted to her head. She could not weigh more than ninety pounds. Her sweater and skirt hung from her as if they'd been purchased at the plus-size store. She was being supported by Simpson on one arm and Veronica on the other. Beside them, Lily Foster was carrying Ernie's purse.

Slung over Ernie's right shoulder was a soiled canvas carryall containing a small oxygen tank. Translucent plastic tubing ran from it up into her nose. The weight of the strap dragged her down and made her right shoulder ride lower than the left, creating the illusion that she was limping. Ernie didn't seem to mind Veronica's holding on to her, but she kept jabbing at Simpson with her elbow, trying to break free. Simpson held on.

"It happened on my property," Ernie rasped as she approached the bench with her entourage.

"Is this true?" the judge asked the dogcatcher.

Don Murray held up his hands and opened his eyes wide as if to plead ignorance. Netta Brabham stood up. "Yes, ma'am," she replied. "I spoke to this lady first—" she stabbed the air in

Ernie's direction "—and she said the animals weren't hers. Then Mr. Banner walked up and said they were his."

Ernie pointed to Netta Brabham in return. "Who is this woman?"

"You mean you don't remember?" the judge asked.

"Remember!" Ernie took a wheezing, crackly breath. "My memory is fine. I've never seen this person before in my life."

"Ask *him*," Netta Brabham demanded, pointing now to Marshall.

Marshall's mind swayed, but just for an instant. This was real. This was not a dream.

"Remember you're under oath," the judge told him.

"It was just me and Officer Brabham," he lied. "Mrs. Truheart wasn't there. We were down by her house, but she wasn't anywhere around. Not that I can remember."

"What were you doing there? Close to Mrs. Truheart's house?"

"I was on my way down the lane to my mailbox," he said.

"Then whose cats are they?"

"Mine."

"Mine," Ernie put in. "He lives all the way up the hill from me. The cats never go up there." She glared at Netta Brabham. "She probably didn't even ask him where he lived."

"Did you?" the judge asked Netta.

"I assumed he lived on the property," Netta said.

"What I think—" Ernie stopped to take a breath "—is that she wanted to write some citations." She stopped again to let the oxygen flow into her. "She probably had a quota to fill."

Ernie fixed Don Murray with a malevolent frown. The dog-catcher stood up, slightly stooped and humble. "If I may address the court…"

The judge nodded for him to go on.

"Your Honor, I'd like to point out that this incident took place some eight months ago. No one questioned whose cats they were until now. The point is, Mr. Banner said the cats were his. He still does. They weren't vaccinated. They were breaking the law."

"The cats were breaking the law?" Lily piped up. "The way Rita was breaking the law by being a wolfdog, which she could no more help than you can help being ugly?"

The judge pounded her gavel. Lily sat down. Marshall felt a bit muddled. The bailiff was ordered to swear in Ernie. Ernie clung to Simpson and Veronica as she hobbled to the stand to answer a few questions. Marshall didn't follow much of this. Next thing he knew, the judge was giving a short speech to the dogcatcher about departmental policies taking up the time of the courts. Then she was addressing Marshall and Ernie, using the terms *perjury* and *contempt*, but keeping her tone kind and unthreatening. By the time the judge turned to Lily, Marshall was seriously adrift. He came back when Owen seized his shoulder. "Good going," Owen said.

"What?"

He heard the judge, or Owen, or maybe both of them, say, "Dismissed."

For just a minute, before her body caught up with her, Ernie felt victorious. Victorious! And this in spite of the fact that she'd found out about the hearing by accident, when Simpson had come into the house to change clothes and the whole incident with the officer about the cats had come back to her in such lucid detail that she'd had to put down the cup of tea Lily had just brought her.

"They were never Marshall's cats!" she'd cried. "He shouldn't be paying for them!"

"I don't think he'll actually pay, Ernie," Simpson had said calmly.

"That isn't the point!"

"The point," Lily had said, "is that them shelter people who claim to love animals really hate them. They make all kinds of dumb rules that don't help nobody. Look what happened to my Rita."

"She's right," Ernie had said, and told Simpson she was going with her to court.

Veronica had come into the room then, looking worried. "I don't know, Ernie. Are you up to it? It's awfully cold."

It was true, Ernie didn't go out much anymore, now that her body ached all the time from the fluey feeling that had settled in her shoulders and the hot, infected nastiness that rolled around inside her chest, and the effort of coughing so much. She'd said of course she was up to it, what did Veronica think?

Ten minutes later, all four of them had stepped outside into air so sharp it had made Ernie wheeze. She'd pulled her scarf over her mouth and told herself cold weather would do the same to anyone with chronic bronchitis; in a minute her chest would settle down. The heater in the old van didn't work, but the courtroom had turned out to be as hot and soothing as a steam bath, and she'd perked right up. She'd perked up so much that the sight of Netta Brabham had made red-hot pokers of anger rise in her throat and burn every one of her fingers. It had occurred to her right then to say she'd never seen the woman before. What a brilliant strategy! And here she was, victorious.

Leaning on Veronica's arm as they walked out of the hearing, she almost laughed at the way Marshall was trying to rein in his long legs to keep in step with her slow shuffle. He thanked her over and over for helping him.

"It was nothing," she said. "I thought: Let them slap a lien on me, get a judgment, whatever it is they do. What are they going to take away from me? The house? A year from now I won't be here to care."

"Now, Ernie."

"Don't look at me like that, Marshall. They didn't slap any liens on either of us, did they? It's just that when you get to my age you think, what the heck? You're more worried about what you'll be remembered for."

"You're not so old," he said.

"Hmmph," she retorted, but was too breathless to say more. She'd never been much interested in history, but now that she nearly *was* history, it seemed the only thing. She wouldn't mind being remembered as an eccentric woman who'd spotted wells and harbored illegal cats.

"I'll get your coat," Simpson said, touching Ernie on the shoulder and disappearing with Owen down the hall. The two of them were arguing, she could tell. She was so absorbed in watching that she was startled when the door to the courtroom opened again, and Netta Brabham and Don Murray swept past, flanked by one of the young, pretty assistant D.A.s. The dogcatcher touched the attractive lawyer's arm, stopped her in the middle of the corridor, began a conversation. Netta Brabham stood beside them, but they ignored her. After a moment Netta grew fidgety and cast her glance toward Ernie. After another moment, she took a deep breath and strode in Ernie's direction. "Never saw me before in your life, did you?" she whispered.

"That's not a very professional tone of voice," Veronica said, stepping in front of Ernie to shield her.

Netta stepped around her. "I know they were your cats," she hissed at Ernie. "So does he." She jabbed a fleshy finger at Marshall.

"Then why did you give him the citations?" Ernie asked. She didn't know why they had to continue this now. She was tired; she had already won.

"I cited him because if he said they were his, I had no proof they weren't."

Ernie inhaled as deeply as she could and hoped her voice would hold. "You have some kind of quota system, don't deny it. You meant to give somebody a citation no matter who."

Netta Brabham's nostrils flared and she wiped her hand on the scratchy wool of her trousers. "If I were you, I'd have every cat on my farm vaccinated and wearing a collar from now on," she whispered dramatically. "I surely would."

"Is that a threat?" Ernie listened to her voice reduce itself to a whisper. Even with the oxygen, she wasn't getting enough air.

"Leave her alone," Marshall said. He stepped forward. Dwarfed by his height, Netta Brabham seemed momentarily struck dumb.

"I wouldn't come visiting anymore, if I were you," Ernie gasped. When she lifted a hand to turn up her oxygen, her arm felt like a fifty-pound weight.

"Ready, Netta?" the dogcatcher asked. He moved away from the pretty lawyer.

"Do you always let your officers threaten people?" Marshall asked.

"I beg your pardon?" The dogcatcher tried to switch gears,

but his expression was stuck on open and amiable, no hard feelings, no regrets.

Marshall and Lily and Netta Brabham all spoke at once. Ernie couldn't follow. All at once, she wasn't hearing them, she was listening instead to her own runaway heartbeat, thudding fast and uneven.

"...wasn't fair..." someone said.

Purse lips, exhale slowly, she told herself. Don't breathe shallowly, your airways will collapse. Inhale through nose. Exhale through mouth. She wouldn't black out like she had that time last summer, not in public.

Simpson and Owen reappeared at the other end of the hallway, holding bundles of jackets. Even in the garish fluorescent light, their faces seemed hazy and indistinct. The whole scene might have been happening through beveled glass.

Ernie's hands were shaking, she couldn't ever remember being this tired.

"...no time to argue..." the dogcatcher said.

This air hunger...it was worse than thirst. The walls of the corridor began to tilt inward. Something cold hit her in back of her legs. "Sit," a man's voice said. Ernie had no choice. It wasn't until afterward that she realized someone had pushed a wheelchair under her and she had slumped into it like a cripple.

Hell.

For a second, she closed her eyes. She didn't want to see them staring at her in this state.

"I'll get the car," Simpson said. Her voice sounded panicky.

Ernie was left behind with the others buzzing about her. Her chest was tight, her breath shallow and uneven. *Anxiety, that's all*, she told herself. She made herself open her eyes. She shouldn't hate this so much. She'd known what was coming; she thought she was prepared. But she couldn't get away from herself, from a heartbeat so uneven it couldn't possibly be pumping blood into the right places, from limbs so shaky she could not have made a fist if her life depended on it.

Even the dogcatcher and Netta Brabham were staring at her with what looked like pity.

Ernie glared back at them. I was not always an old woman, she wanted to say. I was not always this afraid.

CHAPTER 18

As soon as they got home, they began turning the dining room into Ernie's bedroom. Owen and Marshall did most of the heavy work, Marshall silently, Owen grumbling that Simpson and Veronica should have moved Ernie downstairs before this, it had been cruel to allow the old woman to attempt the steps, sick as she was, and on and on.

"She wasn't this weak until today," Simpson argued, thrusting her shoulder into a corner of a mattress they were lugging through the upstairs hall toward the steps. On the floor below, they had already set up Ernie's headboard and dresser and brought in lamps and end tables and the TV from the living room. Owen had been working furiously all afternoon, and now he lifted the mattress away from Simpson with so little effort that she thought he was mocking her. He hefted it over the banister, letting it flop onto the steps and slide down. He'd been angry ever since the judge had handed down her decision, and Simpson wasn't sure why.

"My father was trying to do Ernie a favor by claiming the cats as his own," he had said in an accusatory whisper as they were walking out of the courtroom. "If you knew Ernie was going to dispute his word, why didn't you tell me?"

"Do you think I knew in advance what she was going to say? She got your father off, didn't she?"

"He didn't want to be 'gotten off.' That's the whole point." In the hallway, he'd seized Simpson's elbow and hustled her in the direction of the cloakroom with such firmness that she'd felt she was being shoved. "My father feels he owes Ernie," he'd hissed into her ear. "He wanted to help her out. You should have left him alone."

"He doesn't look so devastated," she'd snapped back, disengaging herself from his grip. "Why is this such a big deal for you?"

"Ernie would have stayed home if you'd insisted. She looks awful. She's sick." They'd reached the cloakroom, where he pulled jackets from hooks with fierce swipes of his hand. "You and your mother shouldn't have allowed this."

"Allowed it! You don't know Ernie very well, do you? If we hadn't brought her she would have walked. We'd have found her frozen somewhere on the road."

With their arms full of outerwear, they'd started back down the hall. Even from that distance, they'd seen the color drain from Ernie's face and her whole body begin to tremble. Simpson had dropped the coats first, but it was Owen who'd spotted the wheelchair propped against the wall, kept on hand by the county for litigants who couldn't walk. It was Owen who'd unfolded it and shoved it under Ernie's sinking bottom just in time.

Now, Ernie was safely ensconced on the living-room couch, drifting in and out of sleep. When she wasn't dozing, she watched her house being rearranged, making so little protest that she might have been directing the operation herself. By the time Owen and Marshall finished, the dining room was transformed. Ernie's bed filled the big space that had once been dominated by the mahogany table and china closet that had been sold in return for a full month's living expenses. The TV sat on a dresser, formerly from upstairs, filled with Ernie's clothes. Marshall had lugged in two armchairs from the living room so Lily and Veronica would have somewhere to sit.

Ernie let herself be led to her bed so she could try out the angle for viewing the TV. "Not bad," she pronounced. A thick, sloppy rattle issued from the back of her throat. "I'll tell you what. Not much takes me out of my miseries anymore, especially in this weather. But for a little while, those animal people sure did."

Simpson decided then that the rattle must have been a laugh.

An instant later, Ernie was asleep. She had been so docile that Simpson feared Owen was right. The older woman's deteriorating state had been obvious all along, to everyone but Simpson and Veronica.

As if he'd read her mental admission of guilt, Owen said, "See, she doesn't mind this arrangement at all." His tone was warm and forgiving.

"Don't you think I see that? Don't you think I feel bad enough?"

He drew her close, so tenderly that Simpson felt powerless to protest. "I know how you feel," he muttered. "I'm sorry."

And she wondered why, at gut level, you did not stop wanting to touch someone even when you disagreed with him in the lofty high places of your mind. Why you carried your desire in some other, deeper pocket entirely, and your cool logic had no more power than ice in the heat of sunlight. Her aching need for him didn't disappear even when he was trying to impose his will on her. It was not tidy, not logical. It was not fair.

In the weeks that followed, as Ernie grew progressively weaker, Veronica found herself thinking about an event she hadn't dwelled on for years—the first time she'd left Guy, more than eighteen years ago, to have an abortion.

Simpson had been a year old then. The pregnancy had been a complete surprise. Another child was out of the question. The jobs Veronica had held in the various towns they lived in barely paid for day care, but they'd needed whatever extra she could bring in. With another child, she wouldn't be able to make anything at all.

She'd never told Guy she was pregnant. She'd just waited for a Friday night when he was in the shower and Simpson was safe in her crib, and left a note saying she was taking the weekend to think things over and would be back by Monday. Guy was a good father. Veronica trusted him to follow the feeding and nap schedule she'd taped to the refrigerator, and to take Simpson outdoors each day to the beach.

The clinic was two hours away, in a town over the state line. Her appointment was scheduled for early the next morning. Forty minutes into the drive, she'd been overcome by such weariness that it was all she could do to pull over into the nearest motel. She'd dropped onto the bed and instantly fell asleep, still fully clothed. At 3:00 a.m., she'd come awake to a sharp cramp low in her belly, to bedsheets soaked with blood. She'd turned on the light and watched the stain spread across a faded, flowered spread. Her heart had pounded, and the blood had come faster. No one could bleed this much and not be dying, she'd thought. In the end, when numbness had eradicated her terror, her one regret was that she would never again see her husband or daughter.

The bleeding had gone on for what seemed an eternity. Then the cramps had suddenly stopped and she'd known the pregnancy was over. She'd made her way into the bathroom, showered, changed her clothes. The bleeding had slowed to a trickle. She'd called maid service to change the sheets. Then she'd spent an entire day and night napping, while the TV had droned in the background. The next morning she'd felt well enough to drive. When she'd gotten home, Guy had asked if she'd thought through whatever was on her mind, and Veronica had said yes. Guy had begun to say more, but the words had died on his lips, and she could see he was afraid to ask further. They'd never discussed it again.

In the eighteen years since then, Veronica had been very careful about birth control. It was one matter about which she'd been completely practical. No one could live the way she and Guy did with a bunch of children in tow. But more, she had never needed another child the way some women do. Simpson filled Veronica with all the motherly pride, and motherly concern, and sense of motherly completion she required.

But now, as Ernie's condition worsened, Veronica's memory of her second pregnancy kept coming back to her. Would she have gone through with the abortion if she hadn't miscarried? She hoped not. As she watched Ernie fail, it suddenly seemed insane ever to have considered it. Why would someone choose something—anything—that would stop a life?

In just a few weeks, Ernie had begun to die in earnest. Before, she would have huffed her contempt at the idea of ingesting so many chemicals. Now, she was uncomfortable enough to submit not just to the antibiotics the doctor prescribed, but also to a diuretic to reduce her swelling, a bronchodilator for her breathing and a course of prednisone that finally put a stop to three days of constant wheezing. There were so many medicines that Veronica had to keep a strict schedule. And there were so many side effects that one day, not long after the hearing, Ernie woke up too nauseated to drink her morning tea.

"I'll just take my shower," Ernie said. "It always perks me up." Early in the day, she argued, she had enough energy to manage it. But that morning, Ernie had no sooner closed the door behind her, and Veronica had no sooner stacked a few dishes in the sink, than a heavy thump echoed from the downstairs bathroom, followed by silence.

When Veronica burst in, thanks to a latch that had never worked properly, she found Ernie sitting on the floor, naked, trying to get up.

"I slipped," the old woman gasped, her expression hovering between embarrassment and terror. She reached up for the bathrobe she'd thrown over the towel bar. At the same time, she huddled into herself, trying to hide her body.

"You're just worn out from all that medicine," Veronica said. "Here, let me help you." She offered a hand, which Ernie brushed away.

"I'm okay now. Go ahead. I'll manage."

Veronica had no choice but to haul Ernie up by the armpits and into a sitting position on the edge of the tub. Her hands came away wet from Ernie's perspiration. She put the stopper into the tub, turned on the warm water, and thrust her fingers beneath the tap, pretending to test the temperature while she washed away the other woman's sweat.

Ernie stared at the rising water through a long moment of indecision, then let herself slide down into the bath. Veronica wet a cloth, rubbed soap into it, handed it to Ernie.

The old woman began to wash herself: arms, neck, face. Veronica knelt beside the tub, eyes averted from Ernie, but ready to assist in an emergency. The tile under her legs was damp and cold. Outside, above a crust of new snow, the sky was overcast and dreary, and the light coming into the window had no color at all.

Ernie hadn't quite finished washing when, with slow, forlorn dignity she let her hand drop and the cloth float into the tub. There was such exhaustion on her face that she might have been wearing a mask. "I guess you're right. I'm just worn out."

Veronica picked up the washcloth and finished the job—ran the cloth over Ernie's wasted body, between folds of loose skin more speckled than white wherever the sun had touched. From her childhood, Veronica remembered Ernie as slender, strong, tan. Now, Ernie's breasts, never large, splayed down over her chest, and below that, as scrawny as she was, she had a bit of protruding belly. Her pubic hair, the few strands that were left of it, had gone as white and thin as the hair on her scalp. Veronica had never bathed another person in this way, except Simpson when she was very young.

There was an intimacy about moving the cloth over Ernie's body that would have embarrassed her once. Now, it pleased her. The motion of her hands seemed to soothe Ernie, to calm her. Veronica scanned the counters for a razor and offered to shave Ernie's legs.

"Not necessary," the old woman gasped. "No circulation in the legs, no hair."

Veronica understood then why Ernie's underarms had felt so smooth.

A draft swirled in from beneath the window sash. The old woman shivered. Grasping Ernie under her arms again, Veronica hoisted her out of the tub. She regretted not being more gentle, but could see no other way to lift her. When Ernie was standing, she tried to shrug Veronica off, but not until Veronica had pulled a towel from the bar and draped it around Ernie's shoulders. Next time, Veronica knew, the old woman would not resist at all.

Veronica quit her job at the Whisper Springs gift shop that same week. Ernie was no longer lucid enough to leave alone. The doctor said her mental state could be a side effect of the medications, but he didn't suggest any changes. Ernie dozed and woke up with a start a dozen times a day, reaching out for Veronica or for Lily, who now spent her afternoons in the armchair beside Ernie's bed, watching TV. Sometimes, Ernie did not know which woman answered her. Sometimes she seemed too far away to care.

"Is it June yet?" she cried.

"No. February."

"The color of June is pink and purple," she said.

"Pink and purple?" Veronica was confused.

"Pink for roses. Purple for thistle and clover."

"Hmm," Lily put in, as if grasping the logic of this. Veronica herself was not keen for thistles or clover; the mention of them made her long suddenly for glossy-leaved magnolias, for cream-colored saucers of bloom that smelled so sweet they could break your heart. For heat and springtime, and open air instead of this stuffy house surrounded by snow and ice.

Then Ernie came fully awake, clear headed, coughing, angry. "Eventually your body starts closing in on you," she rasped.

bringing up strings of green and yellow mucus. "When the world is through with you, it spits you out, one way or the other. Let me tell you, it's not always that much fun."

Lily's face began to crumple. Ernie caught her breath. "Don't start bawling on me," she said. "This is the last great adventure—dying. Your Frank and my Knox did it. It can't be so hard."

Frank was Lily's late husband. "And Rita," Lily added. Stone-faced, she clutched the arm of her chair.

"The last great adventure," Ernie repeated. "I don't believe in oblivion."

"No? Why not?"

"Look at the garden."

"The garden don't look so great right now," Lily said.

Ernie's voice was barely audible. "Wait till spring," she whispered.

Veronica did not weep, but at those times tears seemed locked in her throat. Beyond the dining-room window, lay not flowers, but layers of dirty snow. If Ernie didn't believe in oblivion, Veronica did. She thought about the child she had lost. She wondered if it was a boy or a girl. If it was a boy, would it have looked like Guy? That night, she wandered the house until well past midnight, unable to sleep. Then she lay in bed listening to Ernie tossing and coughing in the dining room below. Without thinking, she reached for the bottle of Guy's aftershave that had sat for months on her bureau and put a dab on her pillow. The scent emptied her mind at once. She slept long and deeply, transported to a place where she'd once made love with such energy that she was life itself, and immune to the possibility of dying.

* * *

As Veronica had predicted, Ernie soon stopped trying to wash herself. Her arms grew so weak that she couldn't dress without help, or even brush her teeth. Veronica squeezed out toothpaste and helped maneuver the brush around Ernie's mouth. "All my own teeth," the old woman mumbled as she rinsed. "All but one."

"Is this a matter of pride?" Veronica teased.

"Damn right," Ernie said, but the emphasis didn't come out quite right, and she didn't laugh.

It became too much for Ernie to shuffle all the way to the bathroom six or seven times a day, which the diuretic demanded. But when Veronica bought a bedpan, Ernie took insult and made her put it away. One night Simpson came home with a rented wheelchair from a hospital-supply house, and after that they pushed Ernie up and down the hall. Before long, getting in the wheelchair was too strenuous if she had to do it very many times a day. Veronica convinced Ernie there was no shame in having a sponge bath in the comfort of her bed. If Ernie had to go to the bathroom, Veronica promised, they would get her there as best they could.

For the most part, Veronica had no time to think of anything else. Never in her life had a task so consumed her. Gone were the sweeping tides of emotion that had once occupied her so. Now, all she felt, at the end of increasingly long days, was exhaustion. Her life had come to this: bathing and dressing another adult who needed her. And it was entirely satisfying, entirely useful. But once in a while, especially toward dusk, she would peer out to the somber sky above the snowfields and be seized with such terrible loneliness and melancholy that she had to turn away and brace herself against the wall until it passed.

"Can't no one stay in a house of dying twenty-four hours a day," Lily always said to her then, as if she had felt the monster emotion herself. "Go out a while. Go somewhere. I got Ernie well under control."

Grateful, Veronica did go. She went to the library, turned on the computer, and renewed her inquiry on all the discussion boards: *I am looking for Guy Legacy.*

The answer she finally got was this: There had been a Guy Legacy in Wilmington, North Carolina, but he was not there now. The message came from someone named Parker Dean. She was not sure if this was a man or a woman. Veronica wrote back: How old was Guy? Was he a carpenter? Parker Dean ignored the question about Guy's age. Parker said only that the Guy Legacy in Wilmington hadn't been a carpenter. He'd been a stand-in for a TV show. Veronica couldn't imagine Guy working for a TV show. It struck her odd that there should be two men, both living in the South, with such an unusual name. She didn't write back.

Even if she found him, what would she do? Ask him to come to Maryland, to this house of death? Driving home after what she knew would be her last computer session, Veronica felt desolate the way she had only once before—the only time she'd ever been fired from a job. She'd been dismissed for stealing a sweater that had disappeared from a shelf and turned up, mysteriously, in her bag. To this day, she had no idea who had framed her, or why. No one believed her when she protested her innocence. She was mortified. She only wished she could do now what she'd done then—turn the car off this icy road in the familiar direction of the beach.

Back in that balmy southern autumn at sunset, along a shoreline deserted except for a few surf fishermen, she'd walked until her heartbeat calmed to match the ceaseless breath of the tide. Lapping at the sand in such immutable and unhurried rhythm, the ocean had finally dwarfed even her humiliation. And by the time she'd gotten home, the knot of pain had contracted into something she could easily hold in her heart.

If she had a beach to walk on now—even in this endless, frozen winter—if she had a beach to walk on now, this would be easier.

The next day, Ernie was so weak that she agreed to use the bedpan. Taking it out from under Ernie's bony bottom, emptying it into the toilet, Veronica knew there was a time when she could not have done this. Now, she would do it as long as she had to. But it was not a happy season. And it was hard.

CHAPTER 19

The thaw that finally came was brief and didn't arrive until the beginning of March. In the welcome, deceptive warmth, schoolchildren abandoned their jackets into piles of melting snow on the playground, and housewives asked at the hardware store for potted geraniums that would not be in stock for a month. Even Marshall, who was cutting fabric for a sofa he had promised by the weekend, was so seduced by the vivid brightness that, during what turned out to be the last hours of temperate weather, he took a break to go for a walk.

He felt exceptionally centered, heading out of the house into the daylight. The icicles hanging from the eaves above his porch had been melting steadily all morning. The thermometer on his windowsill read forty-two degrees. He meant to tramp through the cornfield behind Ernie's house and test how much snow had melted. He meant to be back in an hour.

Halfway down the hill, he spotted the brown Animal Control vehicle parked at the edge of the lane, almost hidden by a line of evergreen foliage. A few feet away, the unmistakable figure of Netta Brabham was making her way on foot toward Ernie's house. He could not understand why she was walking, unless she had a flat tire, which didn't appear to be the case, or because she wanted to be out in the open for a while, which seemed too human a motive to ascribe to her, or because she wanted to sneak around the property unnoticed, in hopes of discovering a few more illegal cats that had come out of hiding to enjoy the sunshine. When Marshall trod down the hill to confront her, she was so absorbed in her thoughts that by the time she noticed him, he was only two feet away.

"Can I help you?" he asked.

"I'm here to see Mrs. Truheart," she said, recoiling. She turned up the collar of her uniform jacket as if to protect her neck. It was a short, tan, leather jacket that stopped at her waist and made her look so thick and blocky that if he hadn't known better, he wouldn't have been sure if she was a man or a woman.

"Mrs. Truheart is sick," Marshall said.

"I'm sorry to hear it."

"You saw her in court. You saw what happened."

"I thought she'd be better by now." Her lips tightened into a thin line.

"She has emphysema. That's why she hauls around that oxygen tank."

"I see."

"Do you have business with her? I thought this was settled."

The stiff leather collar jabbed so hard into Netta Brabham's jawline that she was forced to pull it away. "Everybody knows those weren't your cats," she said slowly. "Mrs. Truheart said so herself. She probably has a dozen more."

"She's an old woman. She can't breathe and she's in pain. What difference does it make how many cats she has?"

Netta Brabham moved back a step. "I hear that all the time. The person is sick. The person has troubles." She frowned so deeply that a furrow formed between her brows. "If you're trying to play on my sympathies, don't. This is official business."

"I'm trying to appeal to your sense of decency," Marshall said.

"Decency!" Netta Brabham resumed her march toward Ernie's house with short, efficient steps. "You're the one who lied. Saying they were your cats. And her! Saying she wasn't here that day I gave you the citations."

Marshall fell in step with the animal officer and watched her struggle to get ahead of him. He made his stride longer, stronger, inescapable.

"You can't stand that you lost in court, can you? That you couldn't browbeat her into paying."

"Don't be silly."

"I heard you threaten her. Tell her she better have collars on all her cats. Is that why you aren't driving up to her house? Why you parked in the lane to sneak up on her?" He put his hand on her arm to make her face him. "If you're hoping no one will see you, forget it. I already did."

Netta Brabham yanked her arm out of Marshall's grasp. "It's not your concern," she said. "I could cite you."

Marshall laughed; a harsh, bitter sound that startled him. "Cite me? For what?"

Netta flared her nostrils, stared at him with glittery anger.

"I mean it," Marshall said. "Leave Mrs. Truheart alone."

She didn't acknowledge him, just whirled around and set off again, quickening her pace.

"I mean it," Marshall repeated. "Leave her alone."

Netta Brabham made a sound that might have been a grunt of dismissal. Marshall grabbed her arm again, wrenched it hard. When she turned to face him, her small eyes registered fear.

"Get off," she snarled.

"I'm warning you. She's dying."

"I don't care if she's dying!" Netta yelled, pulling away. "She owns illegal cats. She's going to pay for them. Then if she wants to die—good!"

Sometimes when a glass slips from a hand, beyond the control of reaching fingers, there is nothing left but to watch it fly through air, splinter onto the floor, splay shards in every direction. So it was with Marshall's mind after that: the beginning of a slow, unrecoverable dive. Already his body was the property of some other, cooler-headed man. Inside, he was again the boy of fifteen, watching Kevin Truheart's coffin being lowered into its grave.

"I killed him," he had said then.

And Ernie Truheart murmured back, "He killed himself," in such a low, assured voice that he had no doubt of her conviction. "He was wild. He would have gotten himself killed sooner or later anyway," she whispered. "You're lucky he didn't kill *you*."

Though Marshall's burden was too heavy just then to let him absorb this, later Ernie's easy forgiveness gave him permission for everything: to marry Rose, to rent the house Ernie offered him, to live his life in spite of what he'd done.

When he'd killed Kevin, everyone said it must have happened so fast that he didn't have time to think. They were wrong. The seconds after the car went out of control had elapsed with slow, unnatural clarity. Frozen terror and disbelief had registered on Kevin's face as the car began to lurch and career down the incline, and the boy's mean brown eyes sought Marshall's almost in supplication, as if he expected Marshall to save him. Marshall had been powerless to move.

There was nothing he could do. Kevin's mouth opened and stretched in a distorted, lopsided scream. And then there was a long grinding of metal against the ground.

Marshall woke up on the grass. The car was upside down. He had a clear view of the crumpled, open door through which he'd been flung to freedom and safety. His mind was very clear.

The sound of dying reached him then. It came from the other side of the car. He stood up and walked over. Kevin lay on his back on the ground, looking like a broken toy, blood seeping from his ears and his mouth. His eyes were open, but unseeing. The sound came from somewhere deep inside him, small but terrible to hear. The seconds ticked by very slowly. Marshall remembered the puppy after his uncle had broken its back. When a thing is suffering and there is no help for it, you have to kill it. He had time to contemplate everything.

His tire iron was usually in the back seat because the trunk did not open properly. But the car was overturned now and crushed. Everything from inside was now out on the grass. He circled the wreckage, and there was the tire iron, a little distance away. When a thing is dying and in pain, there is only one thing to do. Marshall hit Kevin once, and the sound of dying stopped.

He turned the body over, so it would bleed onto the ground. Then he walked. After a time—he did not know how long—he came to the lake. With all the force of his strong young arm, he cast the tire iron out into the water and watched it sink. His mind left him then. The next thing he knew, he was in Lou Burke's orchard, telling the farmhands what had happened. He had killed Kevin. He had.

Now, again, Marshall made a cool and studied choice.

When a thing is dying you must kill it. But if you can save it from pain and let it live, you must do that, too. He weighed Netta Brabham's need against Ernie's, and found the animal officer's case insubstantial. Now, as on that other day, time slowed. His hand was in the air. He saw what he was about to do. He felt none of the anguish of those other times. None of the horror or the guilt. Coolly, he watched the back of his open hand crash into Netta Brabham's cheek. He watched her mouth open, as Kevin's had in the car, into a skewed grimace of terror. Marshall made a fist and hit Netta again. He heard the crunching, popping bone of her nose, noted the large quantity of blood.

For an awkward woman, she went down gracefully. Didn't stagger, didn't weave, simply folded onto slush and gravel, her head clunking hard on the roadway. She landed facedown, blood gushing from her flattened nose as if from an artery.

There was no sound, no movement, save the drip of water coming off the iced-over trees.

Marshall might have taken her pulse; he considered this but didn't. He knew what he was looking at, knew very well. He'd carried death around inside him for thirty years. Blood colored the dirty, melting snow, red on gray, darkening to black. Then it was over. Marshall wasn't there anymore. He was off where his eyes took him, through the trees, through the cornfield, remembering what he'd set out to do when he left his house today. Take a walk.

Take a walk.

A cold front swept in from the west later that day. People said that so late in the season you'd expect a serious melt, but, by sunset, the temperature had dropped twenty degrees, and would drop fifteen more overnight. In the morning, Whisper Springs was buried under such a treacherous glaze of ice that police couldn't respond to all the accidents. Outside the post office, a customer slipped on the sidewalk and broke her wrist. The ski resort closed because of the condition of the slopes. Snow began to threaten at midmorning and started at noon, dropping a fresh six inches.

Except for the storm, Netta Brabham might have been reported missing sooner. In all the commotion, Animal Control thought she'd taken the SUV home and had been afraid to take a chance coming in to work the next day. Besides, the police were busy. In the end, it was the delivery clerk from the Whisper Springs Pharmacy who found her body as he inched up the farm lane to deliver Ernie Truheart's prescriptions.

Netta Brabham had fallen, apparently. Knocked herself out. Frozen to death.

By the time the news broke, Owen hadn't seen his father for a week. He and Simpson had been fighting—over nothing, but bitterly. Owen didn't want to risk seeing Simpson, or having her think he wanted to see her, by driving past Ernie's house. He called Marshall each evening instead and didn't worry until the deep freeze came and Marshall stopped answering the phone.

Owen found the house in its usual disheveled state. A bolt of fabric sat half-cut on the worktable. There were dishes in the sink. Marshall's truck sat in the driveway. Marshall had disappeared before, often enough. But never in this kind of cold. And since Owen couldn't conceive of his father falling or getting lost, even in unusual weather, the only scenario he could imagine was that Marshall had met up with the dead woman somehow—perhaps come across her bleeding, fallen body—

and been driven by the sight into taking one of his infamous walks.

He could be anywhere. Owen tramped down the lane toward the road, then back behind the barn and into the cornfield. His father often wandered there. Owen ran the whole periphery of the farm. When he reached the lake, the answer occurred to him. For a moment, the bitter air stuck in his throat and he thought he would vomit. He took deep, deliberate breaths. Then he ran back to his father's house and called the police.

From the upstairs window, Simpson saw Owen's car come down the hill and stop in the yard. The door opened and Owen bolted toward the porch so fast that she knew he'd come to make up with her. For an instant, she wasn't sure she could stand another reconciliation. She could hardly remember what the current argument was about, there had been so many lately. A week ago, when he'd stopped calling, she'd been almost relieved. But now, she was moved by the sight of him, his cheeks so red he might have been out in the freezing weather all morning, mustering the courage to face her. She couldn't help wanting to touch his face to make it warm.

She'd been out of work for two days. The polar temperatures had kept people home from the grocery, and the store didn't need her help. She caught up on her reading and watched dozens of old movies on TV. Except to feed the cats, she hadn't been outside, and except for a brief visit from the police when they'd found Netta Brabham's body, Simpson hadn't seen anyone, but Ernie and her mother. Even Lily was snowbound at her place, with sniffles she didn't want to pass along. Ernie, bedridden, had grown increasingly silent except for her coughing. Veronica prepared meals and handed out Ernie's medicine with bleak determination, wearing the same Wright Brothers Memorial sweatshirt she'd put on a week ago. Compared to all that, Owen was a ray of light.

Frigid air swirled in when Simpson opened the door for him, but he was such a vibrant patch of color against the dark sky that at first she didn't notice the cold. Then she took in his grim expression, the way he stood mute for longer than necessary, and the way he stared not so much at her as through her, with steely, sorrowful eyes. She motioned him to come in, but he stayed on the porch. She knew then that this was not about kissing and making up.

"What's wrong?" she asked.

"My father's missing."

Simpson's heart hammered fast for a few beats and then slowed because it occurred to her how unlikely it was for Marshall actually to be "missing."

"Usually he goes in decent weather," Owen explained. "Not when it's cold. And not when he's working. He never goes when he's working on a piece of furniture, and right now he's in the middle of cutting out a piece of fabric." In the open doorway, Owen's breath turned to steam and he clapped his gloves together to warm his hands.

"Owen, come inside. I'm freezing."

Mechanically, he stepped into the hallway. "I think he went down to the lake. There are no footprints. The snow covered everything."

"Well, sure," Simpson said. "He probably went to check the skating area. He always brushes it off after a snow."

"No. *Listen*. He went out before the snow. During the thaw. Maybe just before it got cold again. That's when he stopped answering his phone." Irritation roughened Owen's voice. He stood so close to the door that Simpson couldn't reach around him to push it shut. "He's been gone probably three days. I didn't think anything of it at first. He could have walked out on that ice and gone through."

"Oh, Owen, your father wouldn't do that. He knows enough—"

"Not when he wanders off." Owen was frowning now. "You've never seen how he gets. You don't know. If he went into the lake, it's impossible to tell where he broke through. It's frozen over, with new snow on top."

"Oh, Owen," Simpson whispered, and though it was a moment when she might have touched him, she did not.

"I want you to help me," he said.

"Well, sure. Whatever I can do."

"It's too cold to send divers down. But they could cut a hole if they knew where he was."

"How could they know that?"

"You can dowse for him. You can tell them."

Simpson realized then that the air in the hallway had frozen her fingers, maybe her heart. No words came to her lips.

"You could," he told her.

She had to swallow twice to make her throat work. "I don't believe a grown man would fall in and it would freeze over so you couldn't even see where—"

"It could. It's that cold. You grew up in the South, you don't know."

"Owen, you can't dowse on a lake."

He pulled off his glove and took her arm. His fingers were warmer than she expected, but his touch wasn't gentle and his eyes had darkened to the color of stone. "You found his car, didn't you?" he asked.

"That was different. I was drunk. Besides, you knew where it was. You probably helped me."

"That's ridiculous."

"You might have. Everyone knew where it was except me. There are small signals you can give." Her sense of logic was coming back now. "You can clue someone without even realizing it, when everybody's focused on a certain place."

"Yes, but I didn't. You found my mother's grave, too." A sorrowful haze seemed to drift across his eyes. "Simpson, help me." His voice was so thick and slurred that she might not have recognized it if he hadn't been standing there in front of her. "Help me. Please."

Then Ernie was shuffling down the hallway toward them, dragging her oxygen tank like a small, withered child lugging a toy. Her robe was pulled around her, her feet in thin socks. She had not been out of bed for a week.

"Ernie, what are you doing? You have to lie down!"

"Later."

For a moment the old woman looked almost strong, almost well. Time dropped away from them and they stood as they had in June when Ernie had marched across that field with an unlit cigarette hanging from her lips, looking like something from another century.

"If there's any chance," she told Simpson, "then you've got to help."

"You do," Owen echoed.

Simpson looked from one to the other, speechless, not because she didn't care, but because the horror of what they were asking kept her lips from forming words.

"If you don't want to," Ernie rasped, "then I will."

Every line in Ernie's face deepened. They all knew she

couldn't. She was drained just from leaving her bed. Simpson found herself whispering back—helplessly, not wanting to, not fully in control of her own words, "Of course I'll help him. Of course I will."

CHAPTER 20

Outside, the cold burned Simpson's lips, her throat; she had to put her gloved hand to her mouth to warm the air. Under the thick clouds, the light was so insubstantial she could hardly believe it was full day. Small shrubs poked from beneath the snow, frozen and immobile, as if nothing lived in all the landscape save Simpson and Owen walking toward the lake. Beneath their feet, the snow was topped by a thin crust of ice that made an ugly gloss as far as she could see. The encrusted trees, the dull sky, the long stretches of gray on white—the whole landscape looked as if its vitality had been bled from it forever. As if there were no possibility of spring coming in just a few weeks. Simpson remembered being a child unable to sleep in dank Southern rooms where heat clung to the sheets like a toxic gel. But this cold was worse.

She and Owen walked in step and their synchronicity unnerved her. The hollowness that had been between them since Christmas seemed mirrored in the bleak landscape. They had not spoken for a week. Owen's father was missing. Ernie was dying. There was nothing between them to make this easier.

On the hill, the remains of tall dried grasses crunched under their boots, and they heard the small pops of ice cracking, yielding to their feet. Simpson had always liked climbing this hill, anticipating the lake on the other side. But not now.

When they came to the crest, frozen and opaque water appeared below them, like a huge blind eye.

Parked at the shoreline was a sheriff's car. Seeing them arrive, two men got out.

One of the deputies presented Simpson with a forked branch when they reached the dock. "Use this," he said. There was no ice on the limb, so it must have been thawing for a while. The deputies must have known, even before Owen had come to ask for Simpson's help, what he had planned for her to do. Another time, she would have been angry.

She took off her gloves. In her hand, the branch was almost pliant. She held it out over the water and began to walk. Nothing happened. What did they expect? That other time, she had been drunk; Owen must have signaled her. She was not capable of the phenomenon everyone thought she was.

The surface of the lake was slippery. Before, when the water had frozen unevenly into ripples and chunks, it had been easy enough to walk across. Now, the top layer had melted and refrozen, flat and slick beneath the new snow. As Simpson edged out farther, over the deeper water, her boots began to slide and skid across the surface. It was all she could do to hold the branch in front of her without losing her balance. The wind began to pick up. Stinging shards of ice blew into her face. Her bare hands were growing numb. She didn't believe Marshall Banner was trapped beneath this ice. She was angry for being dragged into this bizarre and futile exercise. Continuing forward, too ashamed to turn back, she was not sure where she was going, or why. She slipped, caught herself, kept going.

"*Please,*" she whispered. A dark and angry request.

The calling began before the word had cleared her lips. It

came from just beyond a thin membrane she had not known existed, that separated the normal, accustomed world from the other, holier one above it, where everything was known. She did not have time even to be afraid.

The day she'd found the car, the calling had been like singing. It was more overpowering now. Not a sound at all. Silent, yet clear as a scream. If it had been music, it would have been heavy metal.

It drew her toward a place of no distinction, a third of the way across the lake. The branch in her hand was inconsequential, an impediment rather than a help. She threw it aside, let it skitter away. The slick skid of ice beneath her was of no importance. She would not have fallen. Her journey was different from walking. She was pulled like a magnet to metal. She was the divining rod itself.

Her heart beat erratically; her ears filled with mute sound. The call reached its black crescendo. She was dizzy now, the sky was swirling. When she came to herself again, she was on her hands and knees.

"You got something?" the sheriff yelled. "You got something?"

She must have tripped. Her bare hands were splayed on the ice, but they were not cold. The knowledge in her mind was deafening. She groped at the spot, clawed at the frozen lake. "Here!" she cried. "Here!"

The next thing she remembered, Owen was beside her. Reaching into Simpson's pocket, he pulled out her gloves, handed them to her. "Put these back on," he said.

The men slid pieces of equipment onto the ice, dug a hole. The body came up on the first try, on grappling hooks, smoking in the cold. The hair crystallized instantly. A moan escaped from Owen's throat. Simpson would have cried out, too, but her tears were chips of ice, foreign to her, and the body was so misshapen she didn't recognize it. She knew she could never tell Ernie.

Ernie didn't know how she'd had the energy to make it all the way down that cold hallway toward Simpson, but sure enough she had. And to walk back, too, when for weeks she'd gone nowhere but the bathroom in a wheelchair, and then only if she felt especially strong. She was so elated that, when she got back to the dining room, she didn't get into bed, but sat in one of the armchairs and read the articles Veronica had brought home about an experimental drug and new laser surgery for emphysema. She was almost finished when her energy left. Her fingers went to Jell-O, her heart became a staccato piano exercise, her limbs grew so cold that there was no blood in her hands or her feet. She must have been shivering ever since she'd stood in the frigid air that had swirled past Owen in the entryway.

What was wrong with her? How much did she think she could do? Cold as she was, the fluid in her chest was so hot and thick that it let only the barest trickle of oxygen into the swollen, frenzied branches of her lungs. She figured it was going to be some trick, moving herself over three feet into the bed.

She could have called out. In the living room, in plain sight, Veronica dozed over a magazine she'd been reading. Veronica had been doing laundry earlier and had missed the whole episode with Owen and Simpson; now her sleep looked too peaceful to interrupt. Ernie reached for the bed, pulled herself over, hoisted herself onto her mattress. There!

She willed air into her lungs and warmth back into her fingers. What had possessed her, that she'd wasted her last bit of vigor reading about medicine? She did not want to have surgery or take experimental drugs. She was not going to give up control of herself to doctors. Lord, no! Especially not now. She was going to rest the way Veronica was resting, effortlessly and without help.

The worst part was, she hadn't left herself enough strength to prop herself up on her pillows. A mistake to let herself get so weak. All she could do now was try to escape the sensation she was drowning. She closed her eyes and tried to take her mind somewhere else. Visualization; she'd practiced it for months. She imagined the snow gone, the springtime soil exposed, her fingers sinking deep into the bright clay. Then she saw her summer garden in full fruit, bearing such a glut of vegetables that she could be gracious even about the bugs eating their share of the crop.

These images didn't fool her. Her lungs were filling with fluid, and her tissues, too. Where her big toe pressed into her opposite ankle, she could feel the puffy fluid being displaced. In her chest, the rolling, intractable liquid might have been an inland sea. She'd been a woman who could spot water, a woman with a natural affinity for it, and here she was, drowning.

Then someone shifted her and the air hunger aborted a bit. She opened her eyes. Simpson, looking troubled, stood at her bedside.

"Find him?" she managed to ask.

"Yes, he was okay."

"Not at the lake?"

"No. Back home. He'd gone for a walk. By the time we found him, he was back at his house."

"Did you dowse the lake?" she gasped.

"Yes."

"Were you scared?"

"At first. Then not so much."

Ernie took a breath. "See? You did the scariest thing there was, and you survived it. It wasn't so bad."

"No," Simpson said. "I'm fine, and Marshall's fine. Everything's okay."

"Good," Ernie said. But it was winter, and the weight of all the cats in the barn had settled on her chest. And though she knew the other side of loss was freedom, when it hurt this much to move, when it hurt this much to draw air, there was no glory in it anymore.

She lost track of time then. Slept and woke, floating through darkness and light. Lily came in once, but Ernie couldn't understand what she said; then, silence. Was there no one in the house? It was so quiet she couldn't tell. She wished someone would come because she was cold again, damned cold. She was a warm-blooded woman, too, hadn't Knox always said so? She closed her eyes and tried to go to the garden, but her body was too heavy to let her leave right now. She was trapped inside, with her own hand picking at her chest, trying to pull herself out. She wished to hell someone would help her let go.

When a figure appeared in the doorway, it took her a while to focus her eyes. She expected Veronica. Maybe Lily. But this person was taller, a man. Even so, she was shocked to see Marshall. She thought he'd disappeared. Or—no, hadn't Simpson said they found him?

His hair was sopping wet; his clothes, too, even his jacket.

"What'd you do, go swimming?" she asked.

Marshall smiled. "A hell of a cold swim."

"I thought they found you. I thought you were back home. Or are you still missing?"

His smile widened, almost a grin. "I've always been missing," he said.

They both laughed. He came toward her, right up to the bed. This wasn't like him, reticent as he'd always been. When someone offered something so touching, so unaccustomed, you had to accept. He reached his hand out for her. She took it. And the minute she touched him, she wondered why she'd ever thought she couldn't breathe.

Marshall was buried in the garden beside his house, next to his wife. There was no church service, just a simple ceremony at graveside. Despite the bitter temperatures, the crowd was larger than expected. Many were Owen's friends, but not all. It was as if the community that had scorned Marshall in life had accepted him in death.

Veronica, shivering in a coat too thin for the weather, knew she'd scorned him herself. She was not proud of that. She stared at the gaping wound in the soil where the casket would soon be lowered, a slash of reddish clay beneath the frost line. She didn't raise her eyes to meet anyone else's, or linger afterward to talk. When she returned home, there was an extra car in the driveway. The nurse who'd come to sit with Ernie was waiting at the door for her, along with the doctor. They told her Ernie was dead.

All that day and the next, Veronica struggled not to give in to her desire to sleep. It was Lily who rallied to action, called the funeral home, made arrangements with the pastor of the church Ernie hadn't attended for years, placed the obituary in the *Whisper Springs Mountaineer*.

Donning a frilly apron and slinging a kitchen towel over her shoulder, Lily dealt with the cakes and casseroles that the neighbors brought. She brewed coffee for the visitors. She watched Veronica wander the rooms and told her to sit down. "You done what you could," she said. "Once you get used to no medicines or sponge baths to give, you'll be all right."

But until the day of the funeral, Veronica wasn't so sure about that. The pastor spoke longer than she thought was necessary, and she couldn't follow what he said. The line of people who came up to speak to her seemed endless. A woman she didn't recognize praised her effusively for caring for Ernie. Shrinking from her embrace, Veronica muttered, "I should have been there when she died."

"Nonsense," the woman said. "Once she died, she wasn't there anymore to care about it. She probably wasn't there much, during. What's important is what you did for her all those months while she was sick."

There seemed some sense in this. There had been a time a few weeks ago when, despite Ernie's refusal to see a specialist or go into the hospital, Veronica suddenly felt it was wrong to let the old woman languish in the house like this. But when she brought up the subject, Ernie steadfastly resisted.

"Listen, we've been over this a thousand times. Doctors, medicine, all this stuff you want me to do—you must be trying to make yourself feel better," Ernie rasped while Veronica was giving her a sponge bath. "Because if you think it's for me, don't bother. Or maybe you'd rather have me off your hands?"

"Don't be silly."

"Because you can go any time." Ernie drew a long, rattling breath. "I have Lily. The county will send a nurse if I need one." She paused just long enough to wheeze and cough.

"Don't go doing what's 'best' for me just so you can feel good about it."

"Ernie, that's not it at all," Veronica protested.

The idea that Ernie thought her so selfish filled her with shame. If nothing would cure the old woman, why buy her the kind of death she didn't want? It had been clear for some time that when an illness got this bad the only thing that helped— and not always then—was love. From that moment, Veronica stopped urging other treatments. From that moment, everything was settled. The hours were long and difficult. But they were the hours they'd agreed upon. In the end, perhaps the well-wishers were right. Veronica had done what she could.

She wept and smiled, wriggling her toes in shoes that hurt like fire, and reached out her hand to receive yet another stranger.

Back at the house after the trip to the cemetery, people sat around eating and chatting until well after nightfall. Simpson thought they would never leave. As the hours passed, she drank so many cups of coffee that her ears began to buzz, and she nibbled the various cakes until the cloying taste of sugar clung to every surface of her mouth.

"Buck up," Owen kept saying, an expression Simpson had never heard him utter before and didn't know why he'd adopted. The whole day, he'd never moved from Simpson's side. Every time she found herself about to tell him this wasn't necessary, the words caught in her throat. There was a certain warm, animal comfort in having him close to her. Earlier, as she'd watched Ernie's casket being lowered into the ground and had felt a wave of weakness, Owen had tightened his grip on her elbow before she'd had time to falter or sway. She wouldn't have wanted to endure this day alone, without his support. She just wished he'd stop telling her to buck up.

Simpson had never been to a funeral before. Now, in less than a week, she'd been to two. During Marshall's funeral a few days before, she hadn't been quite herself. Still stunned by what had happened at the lake, she'd functioned by rote and hoped her behavior was appropriate. She'd held Owen's hand and helped him tidy Marshall's house after the service. Later she'd gone with him back to his apartment in Hagerstown, where she'd rubbed the kinks out of his neck. They had made love in a mechanical, comforting way, and had nearly fallen asleep when the phone rang. It had been Veronica, calling with news of Ernie's death.

Now, in Ernie's kitchen, Simpson was so jittery from coffee that when Owen slid his arm around her shoulder and whispered, "Buck up. Eventually they'll all go home," she turned sharply to get out of his grip. "What's this new vocabulary? Buck *up?*"

"Maybe if we take the dirty coffee cups away," he said mildly, "people will get the message."

Simpson nodded and started clearing, but she was antsy, shaky, full of fire. She'd dowsed the lake for him not because she'd wanted to, but because she couldn't say no to Ernie. It had been far too much for Owen to ask of her.

Hadn't it?

She was too confused to be sure.

With the dishes cleared, the last of the mourners straggled out. "I'll call first thing tomorrow," Owen said, shrugging into his coat. "Try to get some sleep."

Simpson nodded. Couldn't he see she wasn't tired? The caffeine had kicked her system into passing gear. She closed the door behind him. After all his kindnesses, after all they'd been through this week, why was she so glad to see him go?

As soon as Owen left, Lily herded Simpson and Veronica into the kitchen to wash the dishes. "You won't want to look at these tomorrow," she said. "Won't want to be reminded." Lily seemed to have enormous stores of energy, after moping at Ernie's side these past few months—although unlike Simpson, Lily's energy seemed good-natured and focused.

When they were finished, Lily wiped her hands on her ever-present dish towel and removed her apron. "You know what she said to me a couple days ago?"

"Who?"

"Ernie, that's who. She said don't be a fool just because them dumb asses put down Rita. She said that—dumb asses. She said get me to the pound and get a puppy before they do him, too."

"Will you?"

Lily grinned, flashing her gold tooth. "Already did. I got me three."

"Three!"

"There's room at my place, Lord knows. Might as well save a few more." She winked, then let her expression grow sober. "Now that everything's done," she said, "we should read the will."

"The will?" Veronica looked as if she'd never heard of such a thing.

Lily retrieved her purse from the pantry and pulled out a folded sheet of legal paper. "She left me the van. Said you wouldn't mind, it ain't worth nothing."

"Of course we don't mind." Veronica had begun to twist her hair.

"She wants me to have it for hauling what don't load so easy into the truck." For the first time all day, Lily's eyes brimmed with tears. She took a tissue from her pocket and blew her nose. She unfolded the will.

Rather than read, she paraphrased the document item by item. Pearls and opal ring to Veronica. A silver bracelet for Simpson.

"I didn't know she had jewelry," Simpson said.

"Old jewelry," Lily explained. "I think some of it's from before she got married." She peered at the paper. "The house and what's left of the furniture, that's the big thing. She leaves it to the two of you equally."

The caffeine buzz in Simpson's ears grew louder. The house. Her mother talked about roots, but maybe what she meant was a permanent home. One she owned. A place nobody could take away. Maybe that's what Simpson wanted, herself. Maybe that's what she'd always wanted.

"On one condition," Lily said.

"One condition?"

"All of it has to be sold."

Simpson watched the look of puzzlement spread across her mother's face. "Sold? Why?"

Lily shrugged. "You'll still get the money. What difference does it make?"

Veronica lifted a hand and massaged the bridge of her nose. "None, I guess. Not really."

"Yes it does," said Simpson. A final jolt of caffeine shot through her, then fizzled out. In the space of a minute she'd been given a treasure and had it snatched away. "It means we have to move."

CHAPTER 21

Spring in Western Maryland comes in fits and starts, nothing like spring in the coastal Carolinas and Georgia, where the weather suddenly warms and a rush of dogwoods and azaleas and tulips bloom all at once.

In Whisper Springs, the beginning of April was still cold, with the trees just beginning to leaf out and only the crocuses and daffodils up. At least most of the snow had melted; at least the frosts came less often at night. And since most of the furniture had been sent to auction, there was enough money to get the house ready to put on the market.

Veronica had found a condo in Hagerstown she thought she would buy when the house sold. It had two large bedrooms and a tiny courtyard in back. After last summer, Veronica thought she'd never plant another seed. But just in case, there was room for a few flowers. She would take a nurse's aide course at the community college and work part-time. In the fall, Simpson would start school, too. Everything was planned.

So Veronica couldn't understand why sleep eluded her even when the moon was waning, just when she used to feel so lethargic that she thought she'd never fully wake up. She couldn't understand why restlessness made her spend her days in a frenzy of activity she thought would calm her, but didn't.

She scrubbed every inch of woodwork until her cracked, dry hands felt more like scales than skin. She paid Ernie's bills. She sorted Ernie's belongings into "Keep," "Questionable" and "Goodwill." She threw away old hairbrushes and toothbrushes and photos of relatives no one could identify. She invited Lily over to choose any mementos she might want, but Lily came only twice, and even then seemed anxious to get home to feed her pups and her chicks. Veronica was relegated to such enforced solitude that she had to turn the radio to its highest volume to avoid the jumble in her own head. Her hard work should have made her tired. Her plans should have made her feel settled. But her energy seemed to feed on itself, and all her thoughts were dark.

She had visions of Ernie during her most difficult days, trying to catch her breath. She had reruns of herself, walking into work seven or eight years ago, being summoned by her supervisor, accused of stealing, fired from her job. At night, she tossed in bed and looked at the clock hour after hour, and when she finally slept, she'd had frightening dreams. Ernie would be standing before her, smoking, and when Veronica yelled at her to stop, she would turn and walk away. Or Veronica would be in the motel room where she'd had her miscarriage, the cramps so real she imagined she could still feel them hours later. Once, during that dream, Guy burst into the door. "Why didn't you tell me?" he asked, with an expression so pained it hurt to look at him.

Blinking awake into the moonless dark of 3:00 a.m., with only the red numbers on her digital clock to look at, Veronica thought to herself, *Well, why didn't I?* And it suddenly occurred to her that she'd kept her second pregnancy a secret because she was afraid Guy would say it was all right, look what joy Simpson had given them, they would manage somehow. She'd kept it a secret because she knew "managing" would mean ending up in some inland town where the work was steady year-round and they'd be lucky to get to the beach for a summer vacation. She'd kept it a secret because she herself—not just Guy—hadn't wanted to stop moving.

Veronica got up and paced the floor. Here was the truth of it: For all her talk of wanting a permanent home, she had never been sorry for the way they lived. It was traveling that taught her the waters of the Croatan Sound were a completely different color—a browner, more sober, more northern color—than the bays in South Carolina. It was traveling that taught her the beach on any barrier island, no matter how substantial, felt more dangerous than a beach securely moored to land. Most people never thought of such things or cared. But for Veronica, they were the very substance of her life.

Tears streamed down her face and the taste of salt was thick on her tongue. After all this, she was as restless as ever. She dropped back into bed, not expecting to sleep.

But she did. Ernie was waiting for her there. Holding a lit cigarette in her yellowed fingers, looking remarkably healthy. "You can't live in the mountains," she said in the strong voice she'd had twenty years ago. "You're a daughter of the sea."

"A daughter of the sea," Veronica mocked. "You said we were all daughters of the sea, it didn't matter where we lived. All water flowed to the same place, and all that, all like knuckles on the same fist."

"Turns out there are some exceptions." Ernie blew a perfect smoke ring into the air.

"You can't smoke," Veronica told her. "It'll kill you."

"Already did." Ernie took another deep drag and winked in the most annoying way.

Veronica opened her eyes to the first light of morning and leaped up to ward off the possibility of more sleep or more dreams. She threw on jeans and a jacket and rushed outside, past the garden, past the cornfield, slogging through the mud left everywhere by melting snow. She didn't feel the dampness or the chill, and she didn't stop until she almost stumbled into a deep puddle at the edge of a field.

She found herself staring into the water at the reflection of tall pines in the rising spring light. They were so much like the pines on the coast, shimmering so gracefully in the breeze that rippled the water, that the back of her throat actually began to ache. *This is achingly beautiful*, she would have said if there'd been anybody around to talk to.

Now that she thought of it, everything looked better reflected in water—the trees, the sky, even her own form. All lives were more beautiful reflected in water, which was why she always had to stay close to it. Ernie was right.

Ernie had always meant for Veronica to move on; that's why she'd made the will she had, and left it in Lily's hands, so Veronica wouldn't know its contents. She hadn't meant Veronica to move to Hagerstown. If she had, she might at least have left Veronica some of her furniture. Suddenly the idea of owning a condo, of being tied to it for years and years, almost made Veronica sick. When Ernie had insisted the house and all its contents be sold, she'd known exactly what she was doing: giving Veronica no choice, really, but to return to the sea.

* * *

"Duck," her mother said to her when Simpson came into the house.

Simpson did. Nothing hit her or sailed past her head. She stood up, annoyed. "What's going on?"

"I mean the town of Duck," Veronica said. "Duck, North Carolina."

"What about it?" It was on the Outer Banks. Expensive, as Simpson remembered, north of Nags Head somewhere.

"That's where your father is."

Hearing the words *your father* made Simpson momentarily dizzy. She had not heard her mother utter those words since they'd arrived.

"How do you know?"

"Information," Veronica said.

"What?"

"I called information and they had him listed."

"What made you think of Duck?"

Veronica blushed, which was something she never did. "I called a lot of other towns first."

"Did you talk to him?"

"No. What if some woman answered?"

"I'll call him, then," Simpson said, and would have, immediately, if Veronica hadn't put out her hand to stop her.

"I thought I'd go see how he is," Veronica said. "Drive down there. I thought that might be better."

"You'd rather confront some other woman in person than talk to her on the phone?" Simpson crossed her arms in front of her chest. "Besides, I'm sure he isn't with some other woman."

"You want to come with me?" Veronica asked.

Simpson's heart stopped then, or at least she thought it did, a condition that left her unable to speak.

"We can go as soon as we get this house on the market," Veronica explained. "We can leave it with a Realtor."

This seemed so sensible and logical that Simpson could hardly believe her own mother was speaking.

"Well? Do you want to come?"

"I don't know." For a while after Ernie's death, Simpson had thought all she wanted was to stay where she was, feed the cats, be surrounded by familiar things. She didn't want the house to be sold, didn't want anything else to change. It wasn't until she looked at the rooms—really looked at them, after Ernie's bed was taken from the dining room and the other pieces rearranged—that she saw how stripped and empty the place already was, even before Veronica had begun her frantic cleaning-out and the items were tagged for auction. She saw then that what she'd wanted wasn't the house itself, but some quality it had once had—a comforting quality of stability. And from that moment, the house meant no more to her than the apartments they'd rented in the Carolinas and Georgia for the few months before her father got restless.

"What do you mean, you don't know if you'll come. Because of Owen?"

"No!"

"Then what?"

"I'm not sure."

"This doesn't sound like you. Are you sick?" Veronica approached Simpson with an outstretched hand as if to test her forehead for fever.

Simpson stepped back. "No. I just need to think."

"Well," said Veronica. "Make up your mind."

That night, Simpson told Owen about her mother's plan. His response would make her decision easier, she felt. But it didn't.

"We'll get married," he said at once.

"Get married?" she echoed.

"As in live together. Share the same apartment. The same bed. Cook meals together. Go skiing." He grinned at her and all she could register was the extraordinary whiteness of his teeth. "Okay, not skiing. Ice-skating."

Simpson was too stunned to speak.

"Are you saying no?" Owen asked after a time.

Was she? She felt so much for him—desire, gratitude, affection, resentment, warmth. Perhaps those were the emotions marriages were made of. Or perhaps not. For the first time, another emotion entered the equation: fear. She was afraid of making a decision at all.

She'd seen how every choice you made pushed you in a certain direction, cut others off, made your life narrower. She'd seen how her father couldn't work construction long enough to get promoted to foreman and travel every couple of months, too, no matter how hard he tried. If she wasn't careful she'd end up like her mother, as she'd been last summer, living in Ernie's house at the age of thirty-eight, unable to do anything but sleep; or like Marshall, burying his cars and his dead. She wasn't sure it was practical to get married right now, even if she stayed here and went to school. She wasn't sure of anything.

"I would have to get my mother settled first," she told him. "I can't let her go alone."

Owen's gray eyes grew opaque then, but not before they registered hurt. "You could," he told her. "She's a grown woman. She's not helpless. If you're saying no, say it."

"I'm not saying no," Simpson whispered. "I'm saying not yet." Because maybe she did love him. How could she know? She wouldn't dismiss the possibility the way she'd once dismissed dowsing. Nothing was that simple. Forces of nature were powerful enough to save you or destroy you, either one. You had to treat them with respect.

But, for once, she was grateful to her mother instead of embarrassed. Grateful Veronica had decided to leave, grateful for her timing. If Simpson didn't know better, she would have said Veronica had planned this deliberately, just to give her a reprieve.

By the time they actually got on the road in early May, Guy Legacy's phone in Duck had been disconnected. Veronica found out when, at the last minute, she decided to call after all, and the recorded message on the other end left her bereft of hope. There was no time to check through the phone book again. Guy might have gone north, now that summer was coming up. Or maybe not. In any case, Veronica and Simpson were on their way. Ernie's house was empty, turned over to a Realtor who thought she had a buyer. There was nothing left to do but go.

The night before they left, it rained. In the morning, the sun was shining and the light was reflected off all the puddles in the road, which Veronica took as a good sign. The little Ford Taurus was nothing compared to the Mercedes, but it would get them there, wherever "there" turned out to be.

"Let me drive," Simpson said almost as soon as they started.

"After a while."

But Veronica stopped at the first overlook, before they

even reached Hagerstown, and let Simpson take the wheel. She didn't want to think about watching the road. She wanted to concentrate on locating Guy. Settling into the passenger seat, she popped two Altoids into her mouth, hoping they'd light up her brain as well as her mouth.

At first, her thoughts were scattered. All she could think about was the possibility that Guy might be wherever he was with some other woman. After less than a year! Staring out the window on the interstate past Hagerstown, climbing the mountain that led into Frederick County, looking at the refreshing change of scenery, she was certain he'd be enjoying all kinds of entertainment with this new love interest. Entertainment that Veronica herself had been denied. The nerve! She said to Simpson, "Do you know I haven't seen a movie, except on TV, for almost six months?"

"Is that true, Mama?"

"It's true. It is. Six months!" Guy and his new woman were probably doing exactly the things Guy and Veronica used to do. When they weren't packing up for another move, they were out bowling or having a beer. They were sampling the seafood chowder in every town from Hilton Head to Virginia Beach. Guy was saying he couldn't understand why anyone would eat anything but cream-based soup and the new woman was probably making her case for tomato broth spiked with crabmeat and fish.

If he was eating seafood chowder with some other woman, she would strangle them both.

Assuming she could find him.

He could be anywhere, now that it was May. Not south of Charleston, probably. But anywhere else. Myrtle Beach. Oak Island. Emerald Isle. When she'd first come north, all those places had swum together in her mind until she could hardly distinguish one from another or remember which ones they'd lived in and which not. Now she recalled each town with perfect, stunning clarity, which seemed to do her not a bit of good.

She opened her tin of mints and put two more in her mouth. When her tongue began to tingle, she pictured the other woman in the same vivid detail with which she pictured the towns—a brunette, because Guy had never cared for blondes. Fuller breasts than Veronica's, tamer hair, younger. Veronica saw him picnicking on the beach with her, the way he'd once done with Veronica almost every weekend, saw him letting the woman sip his beer the way Veronica always had, saw the two of them climbing Jockey's Ridge.

Jockey's Ridge!

"What's wrong, Mama?" Simpson said.

Veronica had swallowed the Altoids whole.

"Mama, answer me."

"I swallowed a mint," she croaked.

"You sure you're all right?"

"Yes, fine."

"Well, you're breathing funny."

"Am I?" Well, of course she was. Jockey's Ridge! Lord!

"If I ever get lost, baby," he'd said one Thanksgiving, when they'd stood at the crest of the ridge watching the last light flame over the sound, "this is where you'll find me. Any night. Just about sunset."

"Even in the middle of winter?"

"Even then."

"Pull over, Simpson," Veronica instructed. "I've decided to drive."

* * *

They reached Nag's Head just after seven, at the end of a wicked rain shower that made it impossible to see even with the wipers turned on high. Except for that, the trip had been easy. Veronica had forgotten how pleasant it could be to drive far and fast, anticipating the look and feel of some new town. The old Taurus had cruised along so nattily that she might have been speeding down the highway in the Mercedes, doing eighty, ignored by the police.

So she didn't know why, when they were finally there, she almost lost her nerve.

"I don't know what the big rush was, Mama, but now that we've arrived let's eat and get a motel," Simpson said.

Suddenly Veronica was exhausted from having to drive through such hard rain. Even the clearing sunset sky didn't cheer her. All she'd had to eat that day were mints and a package of crackers. Sitting down in a restaurant sounded like a fine idea.

But in an hour, it would be dark.

"Not till we stop at Jockey's Ridge," she made herself say.

"Jockey's Ridge? *Now?*"

"Come up with me. You'll see." If he wasn't there, she'd make something up. If he wasn't there—

All day she'd been concentrating on Guy, holding her the way he used to, saying, "Oh, Veronica," over and over in her ear. It wouldn't matter that they were facing middle age, wouldn't matter at all. For a few months, they'd live off the money from Ernie's house, if and when it sold. They'd go out dancing and sleep until noon. Simpson would tease them about their sloth, but soon she'd be off to some four-year college—Veronica was sure of it—to get her degree. She and Guy would buy a little notebook computer and send her their new addresses by e-mail.

Or would they? As she pulled into the parking lot next to the Jockey's Ridge visitor center, such cheerful imaginings seemed childish and far-fetched.

"Come on up with me," she said again, needing company, just in case.

"No, Mama. I'll wait. The sand's all wet. It'll be dark soon. You sure you're okay?"

"Fine," she said, but wasn't.

She slipped off her shoes. Tackled the east side of the dune, shivered at the shadows and dampness, listened to her own blood buzzing in her ears.

The slope grew steeper; she dug in her toes. Soon the beach road behind her was a sliver; the ocean an immense swath fading to navy. Halfway up. In front of her, nothing but sand: gritty, monotonous, cold. She could not yet see the water on the other side. This was the place that had always made her shiver a little—scary, surreal, but thrilling, too, like walking on the surface of the moon.

She was not thrilled now.

Her feet stopped moving. If Guy was waiting for her, he'd be sitting on the other side of the ridge.

She didn't think she could go another step.

"*Please,*" she whispered.

She'd done this before. Doubled over with cramps, losing her baby, sure she was dying, she'd uttered the word and found that just beyond her pain, like another layer of a complicated cloth, was all the help she needed. A dimension separated by such a thin, invisible membrane that all it took was a moment of desperation to break through. Then the two worlds met, parallel and touching, with no time or space between them, so that her question was answered even before she asked. The bleeding had stopped; Guy and Simpson had been waiting for her at home; she had been given back her life.

She concentrated hard. *Please*. But her feet were stubborn and the grainy sand had buffed them raw, made them feel full of pins and needles. Her legs stayed put. *Don't be a fool*, she told herself. Think summit. Think pink-and-purple sunset, green lowlands, shimmering vista of sound. Nothing happened. Try again. Above all, don't look back. A commotion started behind her. Shouting, calling out. *Tourists*. Just when she was getting her mind in gear, too. She whirled around. Two figures waved their arms and scrambled up the dune toward her—Simpson and, wouldn't you know it, guess who? Her throat clamped shut; she couldn't swallow. Then the angle of sun shifted and she was better. Wasn't it just like him! To be coming as usual from the wrong direction, caught in the last slender ribbon of light.

*Turn the page for another exciting NEXT read
that will have all your friends talking.*

*Here's an exciting preview of the second book in
the Maggie Skerritt mystery miniseries by Charlotte Douglas,
available from Harlequin NEXT this December.*

The phone rang at 12:30 a.m., awakening me from a deep sleep.

"Give me a break, Darcy," I complained to the night dispatcher who'd called. "I'm still on vacation."

"Sorry, Maggie. According to the chief, you're back on the clock as of midnight."

George Shelton, Pelican Bay's chief of police, had been the bane of my existence for the past fifteen years, so his attitude didn't surprise me. I scribbled the address Darcy gave me and hurried to dress.

Ten minutes later, with a bad case of bedhead and my body screaming for caffeine, I drove east along Main Street, deserted except for the crowded parking lot at the Blue Jays Sports Bar.

Pelican Bay, a picture-postcard retirement town and tourist mecca on Florida's central West Coast, is populated primarily by retirees and snowbirds from the northern states and Canada, and few are night owls. Once the sun sets and television enters prime time, you might as well roll up the sidewalks, because almost no one ventured out—aside from a few of the younger folks and the occasional criminals.

The criminals are where I come in. I've been a cop for over twenty-two years and a detective with the Pelican Bay Department for the past fifteen, and being hauled out of bed after midnight was making early retirement seem more alluring by the minute.

The address Darcy had given me turned out to be a pizza place in a strip mall a few miles west of U.S. Highway 19, the main artery that bisected the county from Tazpon Springs at the north to the Sunshine Skyway Bridge at the mouth of Tampa Bay. All the strip stores were dark except for the center one, Mama Mia's Pizzeria. Lights blazed from the large plate-glass windows and illuminated a scattering of bistro tables and chairs in what was primarily a take-out joint.

I parked my twelve-year-old Volvo in a diagonal parking space between a PBPD cruiser and the sheriff's crime scene unit van, clipped my shield to the pocket of my blazer and climbed out.

A crescent moon hung high in the east and palm fronds rustled above the parking median's lush floral landscaping, but a chill wind, compliments of a late-November cold front, dispersed any semitropical illusions. I hurried into the pizzeria, as much to escape the cold as from any burning desire to fight crime.

Dave Adler, who'd been assigned as my partner at the beginning of my last case six weeks ago, met me at the door. Looking rested, bright-eyed and young enough to be my son, he greeted me with a grin. "How was your vacation, Detective Skerritt?"

At least I'd finally broken him of the habit of calling me "Ma'am."

"Terrific," I lied.

During the past two weeks I'd spent several pleasant hours on the beaches of Caladesi Island and the deck of the cabin cruiser owned by Bill Malcolm, my former partner when I first became a cop with the Tampa PD twenty-two years ago. But for the remainder of my vacation, I'd been bored out of my gourd. Accustomed to working 24/7 in our understaffed Criminal Investigation Department for a decade and a half, I'd forgotten how to relax and enjoy myself. Without new or cold cases to occupy my mind, I had wandered my waterfront condo, restless and unable to concentrate even on the popular novels I was so fond of.

"New hairdo?" Adler asked.

I resisted the urge to wipe the teasing grin off his too-young, too-handsome face. "What have we got?"

"Armed robbery."

"Anyone hurt?"

Adler shook his head. "The owner's shook up. She was the only one here."

"Mama Mia?"

He nodded, then jerked his head toward a door behind him. "She's back there."

"Okay, let's start a canvass. Maybe the neighbors saw something."

"Now?" Adler lifted his eyebrows in surprise. "It's almost 2:00 a.m."

"Most of these folks are in their seventies and eighties," I reminded him. "They won't remember squat by daybreak."

"That's cold, Maggie."

"We're in a cold business, Adler."

Starting over was never easy, but something's gotta give!

In eleven short months, Charlotte Wagner-Smith has lost her husband and her job, driven over 1500 miles with two cranky kids and moved in with her mother-in-law.

Tanya Michaels

D A T I N G
the Mrs. SMITHS

HN18
Available November 2005
TheNextNovel.com

Kate Austin makes
a captivating debut
in this luminous tale
of an unconventional
road trip…and one
woman's metamorphosis.

dragonflies AND dinosaurs

KATE AUSTIN

HN24

Available December 2005
TheNextNovel.com

The long walk home to what matters most is worth every step.

Three very different women learn to bridge the generation gap that separates them and end up becoming closer than ever.

A LONG WALK HOME

DIANE AMOS